IF ONLY HE'D TOLD HER

Katherine Markland

2QT Limited (Publishing)

First Edition
2QT Limited Publishing
Settle
United Kingdom

Cover design by Hilary Pitt
Images supplied by Fotosearch

Disclaimer
The events in this story are based on real events and described according to
the Author's recollections of the events and individuals mentioned, and are
in no way intended to mislead or offend. As such the Publisher does not hold
any responsibility for any inaccuracies or opinions expressed by the author.
Any enquiries should be directed to the author.

The Lion and the Dear - Jalaluddin Rumi, the author and publisher have
made all reasonable measures to source translater of this poem attributed to
Rumi without success. If information does come foward we will address this
in future prints.

Printed by IngramSpark UK Ltd
A CIP catalogue record for this book is available
from the British Library
ISBN 978-1-914083-19-8

Also available as an eBook
ISBN 978-1-914083-20-4

Acknowledgements

My grateful thanks are extended to Catherine Cousins and her team at 2QT Limited Publishing for their help, support and encouragement throughout the publishing process.

The Lion and The Deer

When you enter the garden of the heart,
you become fragrant like the rose.
When you fly toward Heaven,
you become graceful like the angel.
If you get burned like oil,
you become brilliant.
When you become thin like hair in yearning,
your joy leads the way.
You'll be the kingdom and the king.
You'll be paradise and the guardian angel.
You'll be infidelity, and you'll be faith.
You'll be the lion, and you'll be the deer.

~ RUMI ~

For Mark

OXFORD, OCTOBER 2004

1

She stirred the coffee round in her cup, one eye on the movement, one eye on her watch.

Ten past eleven. Five more minutes and she'd have to go. She willed the time to pass more slowly, yet at the same time she wished it was over, this strange act of duty, this strange request that only she had asked of herself. And she had to stick to time, to stick to the plan, otherwise she might never go. She hadn't been invited, she wasn't sure she would be welcome, she wasn't sure she should be there.

She put a spoonful of coffee into her mouth, raised her head and looked around the room. She was sitting at the side of the small café, her back to the wall, a single lady, aged around thirty, all dressed in black, except for her shoes. She was dressed well - her cardigan had an elegant shape that accentuated her slim waist, her trousers and jewellery were plain and expensive. Her shoes were scarlet. Mark would appreciate scarlet shoes. He would appreciate her whole outfit – stylish, sophisticated and understated, but the shoes, scarlet shoes, they were just for him.

The café was lively - the October sun glancing in through the window, the chink of cups, the whirr of machines, the buzz of chatter, a room full of noise, a room full of life. She looked at all the people around her. What were they doing? Why were they there? A normal Saturday, she thought, for most.

Her five minutes up, she finished her coffee, pulled on her

coat and continued. It took five minutes to find the road, but then only five more before she arrived. She parked her car and, unwilling to admit any hesitation, marched straight up to the building. People were standing outside, but they were all about to go in. She was glad she wasn't late, not this time at least.

'Emma.' Ahead of her stood an old work colleague. 'I knew you'd come.'

Emma smiled. 'You don't mind if I join you?' she asked looking round. 'I'm not sure who else I might know.'

They entered the building. Emma selected a row about a third of the way into the room and, as the first one there, moved right to the end to sit next to the wall. She lifted the order of service from her seat and glanced over it. She recognised the names but there was no-one that she actually knew, except, of course, the one on the front. Other people took their seats around her, mostly people she didn't know, the occasional person she had known once, people from her old place of work, people she thought she had left forever.

The service began, but she wasn't listening. She couldn't engage, she might start crying, and if she started she would never stop. Better instead to focus on other things – that man's lovely accent, his sandy blond hair, the sombre wood panelling, the lady in the front row, her tasselled scarf and small, black-gloved hands.

Emma did notice some aspects of the service. Virginia Lovett was reading a poem. That was puzzling – why was *she* there? What right had *she* to be on the stage? Even in death, she thought, Mark could still taunt her. She tried to be rational – she doubted Mark would have planned the event, but the jealousy inside her was increasing. She found other sights to distract her attention - the old-fashioned radiator on her left-hand side, the girlfriend's arm around her boyfriend's shoulders, the small slight watch of the man who was speaking.

Strange that horse racing was 'a favourite pastime'. She'd introduced Mark to horse racing only two years ago.

She wondered how well anyone really knew him. Not at all, she imagined, but Mark would have liked that. He liked to be unpredictable, to be complicated and contrary. It was fitting that no-one described him as brave, a word often used to describe those who die young. Mark wasn't brave.

The service was followed by the customary wait, a black-coated crowd caught in suspended animation. Emma held a few conversations, but none of it felt real. Returning to her car was a welcome relief. The hardest part over, she wouldn't stay long. She looked forward to being finished.

She took the long way to the pub, her knowledge of Oxford apparently not as good as she had thought, but, why would it be? Mark always drove - he liked to be in charge, to be in control, and they hadn't lived on this side of town.

Once on the right side of the city, she found the street easily and parked in the familiar row of cars. For a while she sat peacefully, looking up at the house that had been his, the house he had loved, the house that had been her home for a while, but was no longer part of her life. She wondered if the picture she'd painted for him still hung at the end of the landing.

Five minutes later, she took a deep breath, slid out of the car and stepped into the pub, the room full of people. She singled out one that she wanted to talk to - orator of the first speech, Mark's best friend from his school days, probably Mark's only friend from his school days, but someone who lived a long way away, so someone she had never met. She sidled up beside him at the bar, waited until he'd finished his conversation, then took her opportunity.

'A very kind portrait,' Emma remarked as he turned to face her.

He looked at her cautiously, then smiled slowly. 'Well, I

3

couldn't tell the truth, could I? Not with his family all sitting there. He was such a difficult git, wasn't he?'

She smiled in agreement and held out her hand. 'Emma.'

Duncan laughed. 'Well, you should know. Of all people, you should know.' He shook her hand warmly. 'You were supposed to come and see us, you know, near the start. He wanted to bring you, but ... I can't remember. Were you somewhere else?'

'Yes, Dorset.'

'Dorset, that's right. Thought he'd come and get you on his way up to see us, only it was in completely the wrong direction. Oxford to Scotland via Dorset! Even when he found out, he still wanted to come down and get you.'

'I'm sorry I didn't come, I would have enjoyed it. I like Scotland.'

'Oh, we didn't see much of Scotland.'

They continued for a further five minutes, tied by a strange mystic thread, an obvious connection through someone they knew, a connection that was now all but over. The conversation gradually broadened, included more people, and that allowed Emma to slip away. At the other end of the bar, she hesitantly approached her other target – Mark's closest sister, another person Emma had never met.

'Jill?'

'Emma.' Jill held out her hand. 'I recognise you from the photos.'

Emma smiled, and shook her hand.

'I was going through some of Mark's papers, and they were there, the ones from Jordan. It's easy to recognise you from them, you're in them all. There weren't many of him.'

Emma laughed. 'I think he might just have been selective in those that he kept. He seems to be in all the ones I have!'

'I was trying to find details he might have left ... you know, about the funeral, about a will. He said he'd made lists of people to call, things I should do, but I can't find anything.'

Emma wasn't surprised. He wasn't supposed to die that day. He wasn't supposed to die at all. He wouldn't have been ready. Being ready would have admitted his death might happen.

'If he'd made a list, I know you'd have been there,' Jill continued. 'I'm sorry I couldn't get hold of you. We tried your number but got some girl in Birmingham. I'm glad you're here though. Do you think he'd have liked it? He didn't leave any instructions, so we simply did what we thought he might like.'

Emma thought back to the most selfish thing she'd ever heard him say. As he'd left her once at the top of her road, in response to her request 'should anything happen', his reply had been simple: 'I don't want a funeral. I'll just disappear without anyone noticing.'

She smiled and turned her attention back to Jill. 'I'm sure he'd have liked it. You had to do something.'

'We put a small piece in the paper as well, but that was all. Do you think that's enough?'

'I'm sure that'll be fine, I don't think he'd have wanted a fuss.'

Emma paused. Jonathan Tenby, a colleague of Mark's, was loitering obviously at her elbow. She turned towards him, hoping he'd be quick, hoping she could again be left with Jill. There were so many things she still wanted to know. Had Mark really loved her? Had he really cared? Then, why had he pushed her away? Why had he not trusted her?

At least now she had answers about the funeral. For the whole of the previous week she'd been wondering when Jill would call or email her, then, why she didn't call or didn't email. Had she, Emma, not mattered at all? Had he not really cared? Should she not come?

'Jon,' she nodded expectantly.

'Hi,' he started. 'I didn't realise you were seeing Mark, not until recently. He never said.'

Emma smiled vaguely. 'No?'

'But then I hadn't seen him for ages. He stopped coming to work once he started the chemo', and then when he did come, I suppose we just dealt with other things.'

Emma wondered how stupid some men could be.

'We used to go sailing together you know,' Jon continued. 'I remember the first time that Mark ever came. He'd been saying he wanted to come for ages, so I took him one night, and… I remember he was quite concerned because of his leg. You know how he couldn't bend his right knee much, well…'

Emma lost concentration. So this was what people did at funerals - told stories, remembered good times. Emma wasn't quite up for that. She smiled periodically and engaged occasionally, but only on the outside. Inside, she still wasn't there. She couldn't deal with all this, not yet. She wasn't supposed to be here yet. Mark wasn't supposed to be here yet. Mark wasn't supposed to die.

A short while later she caught Jon looking at her expectantly. 'Sorry?'

'I was asking which one was his house. I assume this was his local pub, so I'm guessing he lived on this street?'

Emma smiled. So, all the times that Mark couldn't see her, for seeing Steve and Jonathan, he hadn't seen Steve and Jon either.

'It's down the street, with the blue front door and black pots outside.'

At least she'd seen him some of the time.

She extracted herself, and having lost Jill, she went to sit with the people she'd known, people who asked her how she was, what she was doing, where she was living. Through all their conversation, she wasn't listening. She answered politely but her heart wasn't in it. She was more concerned still with Mark and his sister. Did Jill really try and call her? Why would Mark have the wrong number? To have no number, she could understand - he could have deleted it when he was angry, but to have the wrong number, that made no sense. And even if the number was wrong, Jill could have emailed? She could have called Emma at work? Or left a message at Mark's work? Did Jill not realise Emma was important? Or maybe she wasn't? Had Mark not loved her, after all?

Most of these questions would never be answered. Mark couldn't tell her and Jill would lie, assuming Emma ever asked. And right now she couldn't face asking. She wasn't sure she could ever face asking. She was stuck with these questions forever. Forever unsure of how he saw her, forever unsure of how much he'd cared, forever unsure if he'd truly loved her.

The platitudes continued to go on around her, the false concern and superficial interest. For all their efforts, these old work colleagues, she couldn't engage. Their pretence amazed her, repulsed her, angered her. Did they feel nothing? Did they not realise where they were?

She wanted to leave. She saw herself putting down her glass, pushing back her chair, excusing herself with the phrase 'I can't do this'. And in her mind, she saw Mark do it too. She'd seen it before, quite often from him, an inability to tolerate the rudeness of others, their obtuseness and deficiencies.

Instead, she stayed. She smiled politely, she answered their questions, she looked every part the civilised person. She hated them still, but she didn't need to leave with her body, she had already left with her mind. With no sign of emotion, except maybe an unusual lack of it, she finished her drink at a well-mannered speed, gave her thanks to Jill and stepped out of that life forever.

2

For the rest of the weekend, Emma was due at her gran's house. Her mum was visiting, back from abroad, and she had easily persuaded her daughter to join her. Emma liked her mum, usually enjoyed visiting her gran and would be glad of the distraction that both could provide.

The journey from Oxford took nearly two hours, one hour to Gloucester, then one hour further. Both of the hours she'd covered often, the ride to Gloucester usually a passenger in Mark's soft-top Saab, with heated seats, his whispers in her ear, his hand on her thigh.

During the journey she noticed the scenery, the familiar landmarks, the places they'd stopped at to look at the view, the pubs that they'd stopped in for lunch or dinners. She smiled at the memories. Nothing specific, not certain times or set occasions, just general feelings – the feelings she'd had when she was with him, the love she'd felt, the sense of protection, the time she'd spent laughing. She could feel his strength, she could feel his passion, she could see the mischievous grin on his face. She could feel her apprehension also, her anticipation and longing. She still didn't cry. She still couldn't cry. If she started, she might never stop.

She arrived at her gran's in the late afternoon, and entered the house to find her mum sorting through clothes. 'Hello, petal. How are you?'

Emma shrugged. 'I'm not sure really. The funeral was weird. It was full of people talking, but I didn't know any of them, and they didn't seem to be talking about anyone I knew. There was one guy talking about horse racing as if it had been one of Mark's favourite sports, but he'd never even been until two years ago. I spent most of the time thinking how sad it is that you can live your whole life surrounded by people who don't even know you. It was odd.'

She paused, unable to describe the funeral in any more detail. 'Oxford was nice, I do like Oxford. I think some day I might move there…'

The sound of the kettle retrieved her again from a lapse in thought. 'Anyway,' she started, 'what are you doing?'

'Oh, you can help me,' her mother sighed. 'I'm trying to find some clothes for your gran, but I don't know which ones she wants. She said blouses, blue and pale green, but I can't find any that are those colours. You can go tomorrow, I was there all of today. I think you'll just have to take them all and see which ones she means when you get there.'

Emma smiled. It was nice that some things never changed.

For the rest of the evening she helped her mum tidy and sort out the house. It was her gran's house, but her gran was now confined to a care home with really no hope of returning, and her mother was slowly sorting things out so that when her gran died it would all be much quicker. Gran though, it turned out, was a real hoarder.

They stopped at seven for some dinner, though neither Emma nor her mum ate much. Emma wasn't hungry, despite her lunch of one gin and tonic, and her mum had been snacking all afternoon, so wasn't much of an example either.

***

The following day, Emma slept in late and woke to find her mum sorting again.

'Morning, sleepy head. How are you?'

'Alright,' Emma grinned. 'I must have been knackered.'

Her mum hugged her and smiled in return. 'Do you want to go and see Gran this morning? Then we can go to The

Plough for lunch and I can pop back there again this evening. Have you thought about when you want to leave?'

'No.' Emma shook her head vacantly. 'Just some time today. There's nothing much to do at home, but I do need to go back to work tomorrow.'

She arrived at the care home in time for elevenses. Safely settled in the bright, sunny lounge, her gran was lively and pleased to see her. She asked about work, Emma's previous week, what she'd been doing, and Emma answered her questions cheerfully, although not many of them with the truth. She didn't need to bother her gran with deaths and funerals, nor did she want to remind herself.

Elevenses over, they spent the next hour selecting blouses, chatting more and reading parts of *The Sunday Times*, mostly the horoscopes. Emma's interest in the horoscopes had always 'tickled' her gran. Many a Sunday when Emma had visited for the weekend, helping her gran after Grandad had died, they'd sat in the sun on the garden bench reading horoscopes with their morning coffee.

At lunchtime, Emma met her mum at The Plough for a Sunday roast and, after an afternoon of more sorting, tidying and organising, she arrived back in Bristol at eight o'clock.

***

Monday morning, she went back to work. She didn't feel like it, she hadn't slept well, but she couldn't just sit around at home. Last week she'd had some things to do, small household chores, tasks to keep her busy. This week, though, what would she do, if she didn't go back into work? Apart from sit and think about Mark? She thought it was better not to think. Besides, she had clients to see.

Emma was a research nutritionist. She saw clients – people who needed help with their diet or body weight, and she did research to try and understand why people needed help, and what the best ways to help them might be. She liked working with clients – the problem solving and advising, but she preferred the research – the reading, writing, studying, thinking. Most of all, she enjoyed the variety that both elements of the job gave her, lively conversations and the need for immediate solutions, coupled with reading, careful reflection and considered thought.

Today, she had clients to see. They forced her to focus, to concentrate, to deal with somebody else. Clients distracted her from herself. And it was working well until she took a break and turned on her email. There, right in front of her, was the sharpest reminder of the whole of the previous week.

Email: Sender: Adrian Hardcourt: Subject: Mark Alexander

She clicked it open, to be certain.

Hi Emma,

I'm sorry to have to tell you, but Mark died at his home yesterday. It seems he caught a cold from somewhere and then couldn't shake it. I thought you would like to know, but probably aren't on any official list. No details of the funeral yet, but I'll let you know when I hear anything. Adrian

Before she had even read to the end, the emptiness inside her began escaping, and tears began trickling down her face. She let them go for a second, but scared that she might never recover, she quickly looked up, focussed her mind on her next client and forced herself to remember her day. As she closed the email, the numbness required for daily life slowly returned, and as she went back downstairs, even a smile wasn't too much trouble.

After she'd finished her morning sessions, she passed through reception on her way back to her office.

'I'm going for lunch after this, if you fancy,' her friend Josh called out.

'You're alright,' she smiled. 'I'm going home soon.'

'Okay,' he paused. 'Although, you know, you'll be missing

out. I found a lovely new place at the weekend. Saul's parents were over for a few days, we came up here and there's a little place on the corner of Hope Street and Maudlin. Mexican, I think, but the coffees and chocolates in there are to die for.' He rolled his eyes dramatically and Emma laughed. She was glad that normal life was still out there.

'Some other time,' she responded cheerfully, '... definitely soon.'

'Your loss,' he chirped, grinning cheekily. 'Did you do anything nice at the weekend?'

Emma's face clouded. 'No,' she replied as she turned away, 'nothing special.'

A brief glimpse of normal life, but that was all.

By two-thirty, she was on her way home. She had no reason to be at home and nothing to do with herself when she got there, but she didn't want to be at work, and while she was being given some consideration, she was accepting it. She spent the afternoon lounging on the sofa, watching TV – *Murder She Wrote*, *Midsomer Murders*, a romantic film on Channel 5, television for the days when you were ill, television that didn't take any thought, but with enough story that she didn't slip into thinking either. She was putting off thinking as long as she could. She fed the cats, she fed herself, she bathed and changed, but the day really didn't feature very much.

The following two days were similar. She worked the mornings without event, she came home at lunch and then spent the rest of the day on the sofa, watching TV. She had no enthusiasm for anything else. On one of the days Mel searched her out to ask how she was, but quickly read Emma's evasive response and didn't probe. Emma appreciated the thought, both from her friend and from their boss who must have told Mel what had happened, but she wasn't ready for help, not yet.

By the fourth day, Emma's tolerance for afternoon TV was

starting to wane. She stayed longer at work, then stopped at Waterstone's on the way home for a book and a coffee, anxious for some everyday life. She perused the books on display, finally selecting the story of a girl whose husband had died early of a rare illness. She enjoyed her time in the upstairs café, surrounded by life, but only life that didn't touch her.

As she walked home, she was relaxed. Slowly, slowly, she might make it.

But then, with her guard down, without the slightest warning, she was suddenly reminded and everything changed. The lights of a Saab as she walked up the hill, a tiny flash, a fleeting glimpse, enough to make her start, enough to make her wonder if it was him, enough to remind her, a second later, that it couldn't be.

As she continued walking home, the feelings that she'd kept inside so well, would no longer stay. Tears streamed down her face, her thoughts started racing, her heart started pounding. She entered her flat, then had no choice but to sink to the floor. Within seconds, she was gasping for air, her tears choking, threatening to drown her. She felt so helpless, so utterly alone. She wanted Mark back, she couldn't lose him. Why should *he* leave? Why should *he* be the one who gets taken? Why Mark? Why her? Not just upset, she was angry too, and she was hurt. She felt betrayed, as well as abandoned. She wanted him back. That was all, she wanted Mark back. She remained on the floor, crying and sobbing, until exhausted.

The following day, she skipped off work. She had no clients so it was easy. She spent her day instead sleeping late, walking into town to run a few errands, and watching old films. Saturated now with daytime TV, she'd progressed onto watching old films, films she had wanted to see for a while, but had simply not had the time for.

Then, at the weekend, she suffered again.

She woke early to a bright and dry October morning, and

went for a walk in nearby Leigh Woods. She always liked walking in Leigh Woods. It was wonderfully green and lush and damp, and October was perfect for that - the heavy coolness of the misty air, the colours of the leaves as each tree turned, the swish and squelch of mud underfoot, the dank earthy smell of rotting leaves. And this morning, she wasn't disappointed. She swished and squelched and smelt and felt to her heart's content, and then to round off her visit, she stopped on her way home at Café Ricci's for a luxurious morning coffee.

She left the café refreshed and relaxed, but as she glanced up the road before crossing, she caught sight of a man with a walk just like Mark's. She could only see the back of the man, but the more she watched, the more it looked right. She ran towards him, slowed to catch her breath, then gently reached out to touch his shoulder.

As he turned though, the man in front of her wasn't Mark.

'Oh,' she started. 'I'm so sorry. I...' She faltered. 'I thought you were somebody else.'

'No problem,' he drawled, a long and slow American accent. 'Sorry to be a disappointment.'

Emma choked and turned away quickly. Distressed and confused, she waited and then she turned back. The walk was right, even the fit of the trousers was right, but this man couldn't be more wrong.

Almost stunned, she started walking back to her flat, but as she walked, the powerful feelings of loss, bewilderment, anger, confusion, again overtook her. Tears streamed down her face, heart-wrenching sobs choked her whole body, her heart restricted, her breathing raw. Once she'd entered, again she simply sank to the floor. Loss? Bewilderment? Abandonment? Emotions so strong and powerful.

She recovered slowly, but as she considered the rest of her day, she slipped into recollecting the previous weekend, then weekends before that, weekends in Oxford, weekends with

Mark.

She hadn't seen him for nearly six months, not since May, a bright and sunny weekend in May. She'd been to Oxford, arranged a visit for work to Oxford, but Mark had been open to seeing her, and while it had taken some time for him to warm up, there were parts of the weekend that she'd enjoyed - a fine Sunday lunch in his sunny garden, a relaxing morning helping and caring, a few pleasant drinks the evening before – reminders of a time when he was considerate and thoughtful, a time before he had become ill, before he became cross and nasty. For the first time, that weekend, she'd admitted he was going to die.

She'd texted and emailed, of course, since then, and she had also planned to visit, but he was never feeling well enough, or someone else was visiting instead. Only once had she made it - fed up with being put off, she hadn't warned him that she was coming, but when she'd arrived, the house was dark and the car absent. She hadn't even knocked. She'd posted the card through the blue front door and disappeared fast.

Maybe she hadn't really wanted to see him. He'd emailed about his deteriorating condition and she'd been positive in her replies, but she knew he'd see her feelings in her face, and she didn't want him to see that.

To distract herself, she spent the afternoon at Dyrham Park. A National Trust property slightly outside Bath, it was one of her favourite places, and somewhere that Mark would have avoided. Proud of his working-class background, he hated the snobbery of the upper classes and with it, he hated their country houses. In contrast, Emma simply loved them. She loved their elegance, their grandeur, their decadence, but most of all she loved their stories. All the events of these great houses, all of the lives that had lived there once, all of the lives that the houses had seen.

Dyrham Park also was perfect. A beautiful house, first

glimpsed from above, nestled at the base of a small hill, at the end of a long and sweeping drive. Emma stopped on the drive as she always did, to take in the first sight of the house, but she didn't continue towards it. She headed instead for the deer park and on up the hill. For almost two hours, she simply wandered. It was a bright day, she enjoyed the weak sunshine, and the deer and the cattle were entertaining.

By the end of the day, she felt better, she felt relaxed. She'd enjoyed the outdoors, she loved the house and the rural views, but she was wary and she was cautious. She needed to remember that Mark was gone, and that he wasn't coming back.

OXFORD, MAY 2004

3

The last time she'd seen him had been a disaster.

At 11.30am, one morning in May, Emma alighted from the train in Oxford and walked up the familiar streets to the University of Oxford Science Library. She needed some papers for work, and if she came to collect them, she could also visit Mark.

She hadn't seen him for a while, he hadn't let her. She knew he was suffering, that the cancer was progressing, that the depression was worsening. They had emailed, and although she'd been pleased with her supportive emails, Emma wanted to do more. She didn't want to be shut out and rendered useless, she wanted to do as much as she could.

She'd texted him a few days earlier and he'd agreed to let her see him. *'I'll arrive at about 2pm'* she'd replied, giving herself a relaxing start and some time for the work in the library, *'But, let me know if a different time would be better, E xxx'*

At 1pm, the library closed. After a successful morning, but in need of some time to prepare herself, she bought a sandwich in the covered market and ate her lunch in Christchurch Meadows. It was a beautiful day, one of those spring days that promise a superb summer to come. At half past one, relaxed, content and slightly less wary, she collected her things and set off for Mark's.

She walked up the street of terraced houses, selected the one she knew so well, blue front door, black pots outside, and arrived shortly before she'd said she would. It took him a while

17

to answer the door, but as soon as she saw him, it was clear that he simply couldn't move fast.

'Alright!' he snapped, with not a hint of a smile. 'Let's be patient, shall we?' Still dressed in pyjamas, he turned around and walked straight back into the house.

Emma stood on the doorstep. She hadn't meant to seem impatient, she didn't even think she had, and she was dismayed that he should be in a bad temper before she had even arrived.

'Are you coming in?' he shouted back at her.

'Yes ... thank you,' she responded brightly. She dropped her bag in the hall and followed him through to the kitchen. 'So, how are you?'

He looked up at her, still without smiling. 'I've been better,' he mumbled slowly, and then accusingly, 'I thought you'd be here before now.'

'No,' she replied, unsure of his tone. 'I said two o'clock. I had to go to the library first.' She was confused. 'Why?' she hesitated. 'Does it matter?'

'I was hoping you'd come early so we could go to the barber's.' An accusatory look now matched his tone. 'Should have guessed with you, I suppose.'

Emma ignored the attempt to goad her. 'Did you send me another text?' she queried. 'I'd have come earlier if I'd have known but I didn't receive one, and I didn't want to come too early in case you were sleeping.'

'No,' he sighed. 'I didn't text you.'

'Why not? I could have come earlier.'

'I couldn't be bothered,' he snapped back at her.

Emma felt exasperated. She'd come up to Oxford because she cared, and she'd wanted to let him know that, yet all he could do was snap and accuse, and with no reason. She fought the anger that was rising inside her and thought quickly, anxious to rescue the situation if possible.

'Well,' she said, 'we could go now. It's only about two,

they'll still be open.'

He sighed as if she should know better, ignored her suggestion, and pushed past her towards the rest of the house.

Emma's anger simmered and smouldered. She had come for herself – she'd wanted to see him, but she'd also made the effort for him. She'd offered to clean, to shop, to run errands, she was willing to do whatever he asked. She'd even checked about the time! She'd wanted to make things a little better, but she didn't deserve this - the snarling and rudeness, the hidden taunts, the snide implications. She felt confused, she felt upset, she felt angry. She'd been thinking of him, at least in part, yet in return he thought nothing of her.

Fighting back tears, she glanced at the shopping list on the kitchen counter and wondered carefully what she should do. She didn't want to leave, and not like this, but she also wasn't fighting. She decided quickly - she'd rise above him by doing the shopping, but then she would leave straight afterwards.

She followed him into the living room. 'Is this the shopping list for today? Is there anything else you want to add?'

'Sausages, please,' he replied plainly. 'Nice ones, though. Did you get the money and the key?'

'Yes,' she replied. 'I'll be back in a while.'

As she left the house, she was still seething. She made it to the end of the road, but by the time she had turned towards the town centre, tears were trickling down both her cheeks. She went over the scene repeatedly. What could she have done? What should she have said? Would it have been better if she hadn't come? Would he have preferred not to have seen her? She couldn't bear the thought that instead of making things better for him, she might only be making them worse.

She was upset though not only with him, she was also angry with herself. She was angry with herself for being upset. She was angry that his words could hurt her so much, that his lack of thought could still bring her to tears. She was angry for still caring so much.

Her anger and upset weren't easily quelled. She walked the long way into town, found all the shopping, and returned again via the same route, but even then, she still wasn't calm. She could choke back the tears in defiance, but she knew that her eyes were red from crying and at any moment tears might reappear.

She let herself back into his house and, without trusting herself to speak, went straight to the kitchen to unpack the bags. She heard him move from the front room. She tried to keep calm, to keep her mind clear.

'I'm sorry, Em.' He moved towards her. 'I'm sorry I'm such an ungracious host.'

Emma looked at him, wondering why he'd done it, wondering why he always did it. Unwilling to forgive him, she turned back to the groceries and continued emptying bags.

'You're such an angel. You never fight back, you always take it… It's easy taking things out on you.'

So the abuse was her fault too.

'It's alright,' she started. 'I think I just got something in my eye.'

He knew she was lying, that she'd been crying, she knew he knew, but she was no longer willing to expose herself. She continued unpacking, anxious to keep her eyes averted. He reached out to touch her but she moved away towards a cupboard.

'Please stay,' he offered. 'After you've done the shopping, the least I can do is cook you your dinner.'

She didn't want to leave, she wanted to stay. She could at least give him the chance. And to leave now would be almost as ungracious as he had been.

'Is it sausages, mushrooms and mashed potato?' she asked, as if that might make up her mind. He nodded. 'Okay,' she smiled, and her agreement made him smile too. For the first

20

time since she had arrived, she saw him smile.

'Let's go for a drink first though,' he stated, already on his way out of the room. 'Just let me get dressed. You keep yourself busy. This morning's paper is in the front room, you'll like some of the travel pieces.'

'You take your time,' Emma replied, feeling wanted and cared for and happy, reminded of times they had spent in the past, when everything he'd done had been for her. 'Just let me know when you're ready.'

It took him a long time to reappear. They left the house slowly, he with obvious difficulty, and as they reached the car he threw her the keys. 'You'll have to drive.'

He knew she'd be pleased. She loved Mark's car but had rarely been allowed to drive it. Only when it suited Mark's needs. She settled into the driver's seat, reminded herself of the controls, flicked the ignition and felt the engine purr beneath her. This was a Saab, a soft-top Saab with heated seats.

She turned towards him, ready to leave. 'Are you putting on your seatbelt?' she asked brightly.

'No,' he replied, 'it hurts my chest. And if you could avoid all the bumps and try not to brake, that would be great.'

'Okay,' she smiled, relishing the challenge he'd set before her.

They drove out to Wolvercote and The Trout Inn, a large village pub on the side of the Thames, one they had visited many times. Preferring the garden to the well-lit indoors, Mark passed slowly through the pub while Emma stopped and bought them their drinks.

The evening outside was beautiful. The light was starting to slip away, the air was still, and the river gently lapped at the edge of the lawn. They sat together at a wooden table, watching the moon slowly come into view, looking out for the first evening star.

For the first time since he'd seen her, Mark asked Emma

how she was. She told him of work, of the progress with her flat, her Easter in Dorset, a weekend in Dublin, stories she thought that might interest him. She was pleased to see him finally relax.

She missed out things that she thought might be sensitive – travel, activity, plans for the future, and, of course, things that she thought were dull. She played the role she had always enjoyed, one of caring and kindness, without fuss or overt concern, a role he hadn't let her play for a while. And at one point, she put her drink down not quite on the table, and reminded him that life with her was a little more amusing, and in return, his unsurprised smile and immediate offer of money for another, reminded her of his shelter and how much she enjoyed it.

They finished their drinks, and the evening still pleasant, they didn't go home, but headed instead for The White Hart. It was only a short drive but by the time they'd arrived the air had chilled, so they sat at the bar, and from there, they could see upstairs to the area for dining.

Mark noticed the candlelight flickering on the ceiling. 'Let's come back here tomorrow for lunch.'

Emma looked at him and considered.

'You are staying until tomorrow?'

'We could stay here for dinner this evening,' she offered lightly.

'No,' he was resolute. 'This evening's all sorted. We're having your favourite.'

Emma laughed. 'In that case, how can I object? Sunday lunch here will be lovely I'm sure.'

She followed his gaze to the ceiling above them, and was almost right back at the start. She still loved Mark, she always had. He so impressed her – his strong confidence, his quiet protection, also his sense of fun and mischief. She wished she could recover the time she'd had with him, that she could go back and do things differently, that he would do some things differently too.

They stayed for one drink, then returned to Mark's house. Emma read magazines and newspapers while he cooked dinner, but he was happy and, as a consequence, so was she. Unlike at other times, they ate their dinner in front of the TV. When Emma had mentioned laying the table, he'd responded enigmatically that a reminder of old times might be dangerous, that he was falling and he didn't want to. Emma didn't question him. She simply acquiesced and enjoyed her dinner under the bright lights of the front room.

She stayed in the spare room, as always woke early, and spent the morning alone while Mark continued sleeping. It was another beautiful day and Emma was disappointed to be trapped in the house, not sure when he might get up, but she busied herself with washing the car and weeding the garden, content to finally be helping.

At half past eleven, he slowly appeared and sat down in the lawn chair beside her.

'Morning,' she smiled. 'Did you sleep okay?'

'Like a dream,' he replied, and just for a second she saw the old smile.

'Tea? Coffee?' She rose from the flowerbed. 'I was just getting one for myself.' She looked back at him, stretched out, basking in the warm May sun.

'Tea, please,' he smiled.

He didn't move as she returned, but as she set his tea beside him he started speaking. 'Let's not go for lunch at The White Hart.' It was half a question, but there wasn't really a choice. 'I'll have to get dressed, and there's some pork in the freezer that we could have.'

Emma didn't care. She wondered briefly whether he might regret not going out, whether to push him, but decided against it. As long as he was happy, that was all that mattered.

For the rest of the morning, they stayed as they were - Emma weeding and tidying up, Mark in the chair basking in the sun. For lunch, he wouldn't accept any help, until it came to dishing up.

As she heard the clattering of saucepans, Emma went into the kitchen to wash her hands. 'I'll get the cutlery. I assume we're eating outside?'

'Can you get that dish up too?' he asked quietly. He lightly kicked a dish near the oven. 'I'll fall over if I bend down that far.' Matter of fact, but mumbling slightly, something he'd rather not have had to say. 'You'll have to take the dinners out too,' he continued. 'I'm not sure I can manage that either.'

Emma looked at him, but he refused to look back at her. She was amazed by the deterioration that she could see. He looked thinner and a lot older, although she realised the appearance of age was really tiredness and falling apart, but also he could hardly walk. Not through pain she thought, he didn't wince or compensate, but through fatigue and general weakness. For the first time since all this had started, she could see he was going to die.

'You've done all the cooking,' she smiled easily. 'The least I can do is carry out the plates.'

The lunch was as tasty as it would have been at The White Hart, and was possibly nicer because of the privacy of the garden. Conversation was intermittent, Emma having run out of things to ask without seeming fussy or overly concerned, but they were both relaxed and happy just to sit and eat together. There was no dessert, so they enjoyed their coffee on the lawn, then Emma quickly washed the plates and was ready to leave.

She stepped back into the garden to find Mark in his earlier position. 'Right then, I'm off.'

'What time's your train?' Nothing moved apart from his lips.

'Five past four,' Emma looked down at her watch, 'about

ten minutes. There's nothing else you need here is there?'

He looked up at her through one squinted eye. 'No, you've been great. Have a safe journey home.'

She bent down slightly and kissed him goodbye. He didn't move. He didn't kiss her, he didn't hug her, he didn't even attempt to get up. He simply gripped his chair more tightly.

As she closed the front door behind her, Emma was again already in tears. Tears for him out of love and pity, but tears also for herself. She felt so helpless, so inadequate. She'd done all she could, yet she'd made little difference, and the differences she had made weren't necessarily wanted. She still wasn't sure she had been welcome. She also felt so abandoned. She could see so clearly he was going to die, but it felt like she'd already lost him.

Confused and lost, she cried and kicked herself all the way home. At times she recovered enough to think about reading her book, but whenever she started, the turmoil inside her simply overtook her.

BRISTOL, NOVEMBER 2004

4

Five months later, Mark had died. For one month now, Emma had felt empty, numb and upset, alternating between these emotions, upset only if she tried anything other than empty.

The weeks in October had passed much the same; November though gradually she worked for longer and slowly, but surely, she did less crying. She suffered from no more overwhelming outbursts, but she still lapsed into tears when she read the email, when she was reminded in some other way, when she thought or wondered about him. For most of the time she simply kept busy. In the evenings, she could still manage little more than feeding the cats, feeding herself and watching TV. Occasionally, her friends asked her out, but she always found excuses.

Of all the times, weekends were the worst. She couldn't drown herself in work and there was nothing else to keep her busy. The weekend after she went to Dyrham, she started her Saturday making a list of things she could do, a list of things she should have done with Mark, but, for some reason, they never did. Things they'd said they'd do, then he'd been too ill or simply unwilling. If she did those things, maybe, maybe, that might help.

The first weekend she went to Bath. She'd asked Mark to meet her there some time ago, she'd thought of the places that they could go, and then he'd simply never replied. She wanted now to go to those places, to make the visit they would have made, to do the things he should have done.

She arrived by train at the end of the morning, ambled around for almost two hours, had lunch in a café behind the baths, sat in the square outside the cathedral, saw buskers and street entertainers, and finished with tea in Bewley's Café. She had a good day. She was disappointed Mark wasn't with her, but she hadn't been upset. Today, she hadn't been sad.

The weekend after, she went to Bream Down – a beautiful long and sandy beach, backed by dunes, contained at its end by a heathered headland. Another place Mark had never been, but somewhere else she thought he would have liked – the long, windswept sand, the gentle timelessness of the walk, the constant crashing of the waves, and then the ruggedness of the headland, the drama and starkness of the beauty, the wilderness.

The headland reminded Emma of Porth, and Mark had enjoyed Porth when they'd been there. So much, she remembered, that he'd been back the following day, skipping breakfast in order to do it. It reminded him, he'd said, of his home on the Northern Irish coast, its windswept beaches and untamed headlands.

She didn't stay for long at Bream Down, just long enough to remind herself, of good times, of love and laughter, of freedom and hope.

The following weekend, her friend Fay returned from a three-month working visit to the Netherlands. They met on Saturday for lunch and Fay recounted her time away – the things she'd done, the places she'd seen, the people she'd met, the things she'd learnt. And when she asked Emma in return, Emma told her of the things she'd done, the places she'd been, she was just selective. Only as they were walking into town did Fay specifically ask about Mark.

'He died,' Emma stated defiantly.

'When?' Fay replied. 'Oh Em, I'm sorry.'

She leant towards her friend to hug her, but Emma only pulled away. 'It's better,' she faltered as she blinked back her tears. 'It's finally over.'

Fay looked at her questioningly, giving her time to collect herself.

'The pain, the suffering.'

Fay continued to look towards her, a mixture of pity and support. 'Was he in much pain, in the end?'

Emma shook her head. 'I don't really know. I think he was suffering more from indignity. He was so proud. The last time I saw him, he was making lunch and dropped a dish, but couldn't bend down to pick it up. He asked me, and of course that was fine, but apparently the last time, the dish had simply stayed there until his sister could do it.'

She took a deep breath. 'He was so clearly deteriorating, even then, and he lived for a further five months after that. Everything was such an effort for him. He was weak, weary, slow at everything. I didn't see any signs of pain, but I imagine everything only got worse.'

They continued walking, Emma's mind clearly elsewhere, Fay with half an eye on her friend.

'It's not only that though, is it?' Fay said. 'The pain and suffering? It's not only that that's over, is it?'

Emma looked at her, trying to judge if she could trust her. Finally, she let out a sigh of relief. 'No, thank God… Now I can take back my life too. No more wondering how he's doing, no more wondering when I should call, if I should visit, no more anxiety, no more criticism, no more hatred.'

She lowered her eyes as she dragged out the words. 'Sometimes, Fay, he could be so cruel. He'd tell me off for the smallest thing, constantly criticise, laugh at me. The things he said, the looks he gave me. And the more I tried, the worse it would be. He'd snap or sulk or ignore me, and if I asked what was wrong or what would help, that would only make everything worse. He could be so unreasonable.'

She remembered back to the times that she spoke of - times of constant criticism, times he had snapped at her for no reason, times he had been deliberately spiteful. For all of those times, on all occasions, she'd always forgiven him. She'd reasoned it through, she'd understood.

Only once did she ever retaliate: the last time she'd seen him, her refusal to allow him in. She remembered it well, a Saturday afternoon in May, and mixed up with the memory were all the doubts of the past few weeks. With all that anger, with all that spite, did he really love her? Did he even care? Or had she simply been wasting her time? Again her eyes welled up with tears, but again she shook them back, refusing to let herself admit them.

Fay leant over, put her arm round her shoulder and squeezed Emma hard. 'He loved you really, you know he did.'

Emma smiled but wasn't convinced. 'Maybe at the start, but by the end I'm not so sure.' She paused and thought carefully. 'He was so lovely at the beginning. He made me feel cared for, so protected, little thoughts and careful gestures. He was so smart and so witty. He loved telling stories and they were always funny… He could make me laugh so hard. I loved him so much … but everything then simply fell apart. Of course there was the cancer and all the stress, depression, unfairness that goes with it. I can understand those. He could still be nice when he wanted to be, he was just so nasty in between.'

She lapsed into unhappy reminiscences. 'Do you know, towards the end, I think he was even wondering himself … why he bothered. I sent him emails almost weekly, chatty emails to try and make him feel better, remind him mostly that I still cared, and in reply he used to send the strangest responses: *"Why couldn't I write like everyone else? How could I see things so clearly? How could I know from so far away?"* As if,

29

even with his dying breath, he wanted to criticise or make fun of me. Why not just delete them? Why bother being nasty?'

Fay interrupted her. 'I'll tell you what,' she started, smiling. 'Just for a while, let's forget all about him. Let's go to the shops up at St Michael's. You can help me pick chairs for my flat and I'll treat you to a massive glass of wine.'

Emma smiled, more convincingly this time.

Fay leant over and squeezed her again. 'I love you too, you know... Oh, and I need a mirror as well as the chairs.'

5

The following weekend, Emma went to Lyme Regis. She was starting to feel better and she liked Lyme Regis. Her dad had once lived outside the town, and she and her family had spent many pleasant summers there. She liked most its old-fashioned nature – the ice-cream sellers, the rock and fudge makers, the deckchairs for hire along the front, the cinema with its different priced tickets and local advertisements.

Her mum phoned on the Friday beforehand.

'Oh, Lyme Regis will be lovely. It's supposed to be sunny and there won't be many tourists. Is there any particular reason?'

Emma shrugged. 'I want to be reminded of good times… I wanted to take Mark a while ago, but he wasn't keen or couldn't make it… I can't remember. He'd have liked it though - the sea, fresh air, the fresh fish for dinner. He grew up on the coast you know, north of Belfast, and he did like fish. If Lyme had had an expensive fish restaurant, he'd have been there, no problem at all.'

'Well, maybe you could have a nice piece of fish for him. You'll worry me if you're not eating properly.'

Emma smiled. Her mum was right, she wasn't eating properly, but she was also shaking her head. 'I'm going to buy a ring, something pretty, something I can wear always … to remind me of good times.'

For a long time, she'd stopped believing that Mark loved her. Not simply because of the funeral, the lack of invite, but from long before that – his hurtful comments, his dismissive emails, the number of times he couldn't see her, the number of times he wouldn't meet her. She'd told him once that she wasn't sure, that sometimes she didn't think he cared, but in reply he hadn't helped; he'd simply said that was how he felt too.

And after he'd died, this was what she needed. For all the time she'd spent with him, for all the things she'd done for him, she had no sign that it had been worth it. She wanted some jewellery, to remind her that he had loved her, that they had enjoyed some time together, that he had been worth it.

She set off early and as she left her car in the parking for the boat club, she was already glad she had made the effort - the smell of the sea, the crisp clear air, the fresh cool breeze. She walked round the boathouse and onto the Cobb. Such a touristy thing to do, she hadn't been on the Cobb for ages, and she walked the whole length of it, enjoying the wind dancing through her clothes, the sense of lightness, the sense of freedom.

As she stood at the end and looked out to sea, she thought of Mark. She wished he were with her, laughing and joking, pointing out things she would never have noticed, telling her stories, making up tales. But at the same time she thought of herself. The expanse of the sea reminded her of the rest of the world, of all the things she could do now, of all the things she could do now that Mark was no longer stopping her. She knew it was her who'd been stopping her, but she'd been bound to him, and now he was gone, at least she was free. He was free from the pain of the cancer, the indignity of disease, from the sympathy of others, she was free from the duty and obligation.

She left the Cobb and walked along the promenade to the main part of town, past shops and houses that reminded her of the happy summers she'd spent in Lyme. At the bottom of the main street she continued ahead to the Old Fossil Shop but, uninspired by what she saw, she headed back and up the main street. She climbed the hill slowly, stopping to look in shop windows, then at the cinema, she crossed the street, and walked back down towards the sea. Halfway down the hill, she went into Pennies.

Pennies was an antiques shop, full of trinkets from an era of elegance. Emma and her sister used to stand outside, their noses pressed against the window, marvelling at the tarnished treasures, the large costume jewels, the delicate furniture, the reams of voile draped across the ceiling. A glimpse of a world they could only imagine.

Emma entered the shop in search of her ring. She wanted a special ring, one with a history, unlike any she already owned, she wanted a ring that Mark might have given her. Before she went in, she bargained with fate: she would buy a ring from the ones in the shop, but without trying any of them first. If it fitted her ring finger, which she would rather, it was a ring she had bought for herself; if it fitted her middle finger, which Mark would much more likely have preferred, it was instead a present from him, to remind her that he had loved her.

She looked at the rings, and was disappointed; a wide silver band inset with green stones, a braided silver band with a single silver stone, and a ring of tiny pink flowers with silver stems and tarnished gold leaves. Emma didn't like any of them.

The shop assistant approached her quietly. 'Is it a piece of jewellery you're after?'

Emma turned. 'A ring specifically... Do you have any others?' She looked around but this was the only jewellery case.

'No, I'm sorry, that's all we have right now.'

Emma considered. Maybe she should come back some other time, or maybe try a different shop. But she wanted to keep her side of the bargain. She chose the ring she thought Mark would have been most likely to pick – the silver braiding with hematite stone.

Outside the shop, she slipped it on. On her ring finger, it

33

twizzled and turned, on her middle finger, it fitted perfectly. She vowed to wear it as often as she could, to remind her that Mark had loved her once.

She feared she would need frequent reminders. The emptiness and upset were increasingly replaced with anger and hatred, anger with Mark, not just for dying, not just for dying and leaving her, but hatred also for involving her, hatred for putting her through all this.

6

Three weeks after Fay's return and the support that this would bring, Emma was reminded of the support she could also gain from Christine. A sympathetic colleague, Emma found Christine easy to talk to, but she worked part time and Emma hadn't seen her since Mark's death. Two weeks before Christmas, Christine arranged an end-of-year coffee and Emma had gladly accepted.

'Coo-ee.' Christine rose and waved from the other side of the small café as Emma entered.

Emma quickly settled in beside her. 'Hello Christine. How are you?'

'Busy, busy,' Christine started. 'But it's always like that at this time of year – parties, choir concerts, school plays, and, of course, it was the twins' birthdays only last week.' She made a face that combined excitement, pleasure and relief. 'How are you though, lovely? I haven't seen you for ages.'

'No,' said Emma. 'I think I've been on the other shift.'

'Are you alright, though?' Christine looked at her with concern. 'You haven't been ill? You aren't looking great.'

Emma smiled. She'd forgotten that Christine somehow always knew what to say. 'Mark died,' she explained.

'Oh, you poor thing. No wonder I haven't seen you.' Christine put her hand gently on Emma's arm. 'When did that happen?'

Already the tears were pricking the backs of Emma's eyes. 'Two months ago,' she answered strongly. 'Early October. He died of a cold, because of the cancer.'

Christine slowly rubbed Emma's arm. 'Was he really sick?

Did he look really bad?'

Emma straightened as she shook back the tears. 'I don't know,' she answered crossly. 'I hadn't seen him since May. He wouldn't let me see him, would he?'

'You've been so good,' Christine sympathised. 'You've put up with so much. Anyone else would have left long ago.'

Emma half laughed in disbelief. 'How could I leave? You can't just leave a man who's dying.'

Christine looked at her almost mockingly. 'And didn't he know it? All the time and trouble you took, thinking about him, worrying about him, and in return he makes out he thinks nothing of you, always critical, always complaining.'

'He was sick, Christine,' Emma offered weakly.

'Oh come on, Emma. He didn't deserve you. He knew he should have treated you better.'

Emma, by this time, could not stop her tears – torn between missing Mark, wanting him back, and hating him for being nasty. She knew very well that Christine was right. She had one defence – that he was sick, but that didn't explain everything. She knew that he hadn't deserved her, that he should have treated her better, but she still wouldn't have left him. Emma squirmed, upset now, not only with him, but with herself too. She should have stood up for herself, she should have been stronger.

Christine could see her turmoil. 'Don't be hard on yourself,' she whispered gently.

Emma sniffed. 'You're right, Christine. He didn't deserve me. Maybe if he had survived it would have been worth it, but he didn't.' She gave in to another quiet rush of tears.

'All the time and effort you spent planning Christmas and New Year in Jordan, without any help, even after you asked,' Christine shook her head slowly. 'I thought you were a star.'

Emma didn't feel like a star. She felt like a fool, unappreciated, unrewarded. Abandonment and loss no longer featured, she realised now that Mark had abandoned her long before he'd died. She wasn't even angry with him any more for dying. She was angry with him now for picking her, angry for making her go through this, angry with him for wasting her time. He'd known from the start that he might die, but hadn't told her until it was too late, until she was already involved. And in return, what had he given her? She hated him for all the hurt.

'You think I should have left him when I had the chance?' Emma asked.

'I didn't know you'd had one,' Christine reeled. 'But God, yes! ... In fact, why didn't you?'

Emma smiled. 'I loved him so much in the beginning. If he'd survived...' She sipped her coffee. 'I couldn't throw all that away.'

'But, hang on,' Christine continued, 'you mean he'd asked you to leave him?'

'Yes.' Emma winced. 'Something I would rather forget.'

'Well,' said Christine. 'I don't know when that was, but you clearly survived. I know he didn't die before, but what happened last time?'

Emma smiled. 'It was roughly eighteen months ago ... around March. He'd mentioned wanting to go to the ballet, one more thing to do before he died, so I bought some tickets for Valentine's Day ... but it didn't work out well. I was miserable for months. I spent ages trying to work out what I'd done wrong. It took all day to write the apology for when I sent back his house key. I was so upset.'

She paused, and sipped some more coffee. 'But then, in time, I guess it passed. I started to think of the whole thing more as a holiday romance, a small interlude while staying in Oxford, never intended to last for long, never intended as anything more. Gradually normal life returned, ... and that was that really.'

'Well,' said Christine, 'maybe the same will happen now.'

'Maybe,' Emma replied, but categorically this was different. Mark wouldn't come back, he couldn't come back, and there was nothing that she could do. She couldn't apologise, she couldn't send notes. She had no control, she had no power. All she could do was accept this event, and only then would she start to recover. But acceptance was very hard.

'I'd like to do something to help.' Christine retrieved Emma from her thoughts. 'Will you meet me in January at Brandon Hill? I know Mark could be nasty, but I don't think he really meant to be, and I'd like to try and make you see that.'

Emma smiled. She appreciated Christine for trying, but she was unconvinced.

'Not yet… I can see you don't believe me at the moment,' Christine continued, 'but some time in January?'

'Sure,' Emma acquiesced, unwilling to bother making excuses. 'End of January, preferably a Friday?'

'Good girl,' Christine concluded firmly. 'Friday 27th, top of Brandon Place'.

She left Emma to relapse into sad memories of the time when Mark had asked her to leave him. A final weekend, a final visit to the Grand Café, as Mark had sat on the high stool beside her, advising her of her next career move, recommending places she really should visit, talking as if he wouldn't see her again. And of how she had simply let him, desperate for him not to leave her, glad just to be there, sitting beside him, mute and adoring.

OXFORD, MARCH 2003

7

A rmed with a choice of outfits that she knew he'd never seen, Emma pulled up her car outside Mark's house, took a deep breath and walked directly to the front door. It was a surprisingly warm day in March. She had left work early for the weekend, but the initial enthusiasm with which she'd left Bristol had gradually waned. By the time she was approaching Oxford, she was wishing she had never come.

Mark had been remote for a while. He hadn't phoned, he barely spoke when she phoned him and they hadn't met for over a month. Ever since the holiday in Jordan, things had slowly been falling apart and neither of them seemed willing to stop it.

The weekend after they'd returned, Emma was going to say something, but he'd tackled her about seeming nervous and she'd lost her courage. The following week he had then been nice, really nice, and Emma had convinced herself not to worry. Then, a week later, things were awkward again. He wouldn't answer when she called him, he kept saying that he couldn't see her, he hardly even sent any texts and the texts that he did send – in all, he was happy without her.

She'd done well on St Valentine's Day with ballet tickets for £70 each, and in return she'd received a drunken phone call at 2am, but since then things had continued downward. Emma worried less about him and gradually more about them, and now she was giving it one last try. The date of the ballet was this weekend, and when she'd phoned to remind him, he'd assumed she would be joining him.

They'd agreed to meet up at his house, but he looked surprised when he answered the door. 'Oh, you're very early,' he started. 'I wasn't expecting you until later.'

Emma smiled. 'I thought we could go for a late lunch.' That was her plan. She wanted to talk, to clear the air, to sort them out, then enjoy the evening regardless of outcome. She glanced at her watch. 'Unless, of course, you've eaten already?'

'No,' he said slowly. 'I'll get my coat.'

The walk into Oxford was friendly and civil, but then for the whole of lunch Mark read the newspaper. Emma kept waiting but after each story he turned the page and started another. Emma was unsurprised, but she was also disappointed - she wanted to know where she stood.

At five o'clock, they caught the train to London. As they found two seats in the busy compartment, Mark pulled a letter from his jacket pocket and handed it to her. She noticed his tension, saw the logo at the top of the page and skimmed through it as fast as she could. The general gist - he'd been promoted.

'Congratulations.' She turned towards him and watched him try to hide his pride. 'How long have you known?' She glanced again at the top of the letter. 'Why didn't you phone me?'

Mark shrugged remotely. 'I didn't think you'd be interested.'

Emma wondered why he was trying to taunt her. 'Of course I'd be interested,' she started. 'Why wouldn't I be?' She glanced down at the letter again and back at him, but he simply shrugged and turned away.

They arrived at Covent Garden an hour later. They started with drinks in a local bar but they hardly spoke, they didn't smile, they didn't laugh, it all seemed an effort. There was nothing personal, no intimacy.

At seven o'clock, they took their seats in the Opera House

stalls. The ballet was impressive as would be expected. Emma loved everything about ballet – the dancing, the music, the costumes, the stories, the beauty of it, the majesty. Mark was impressed with the whole package – the building, the seats, the occasion, and, as the evening went on, he gradually relaxed. By the second act, he was whispering to her, small comments, quick observations. By the second interval, they were laughing and joking. The improved Mark led also to an improved Emma.

At the end of the ballet they went for dinner, but by its end, the frost had returned. As they sat at the stop for the bus back to Oxford, they didn't sit close, despite her obvious signs of cold, despite his obvious want for comfort. The little things that they found annoying, they had resurfaced - his need to be in charge, her unwillingness to attract attention, his lack of thought for her feelings, her unwillingness to rise to his challenges. For the bus ride home, they slept lightly on separate seats. For the rest of the night, they also slept separately.

The following day, they both woke late, they stayed in bed for as long as they could, until eventually, they had to get up, they had to face what the day had in store. Emma was first. She showered and dressed and was halfway through a cup of tea when Mark came into the kitchen to join her. 'When are you leaving?' he asked her blankly.

'I'll just get some breakfast, if that's okay?'

'There isn't any breakfast,' he replied.

'No,' she stated, 'I'd spotted that.'

Mark paused. 'Let's go into town. I'll buy you breakfast and then you can go. We can't have you leaving on an empty stomach.'

They breakfasted at the Grand Café. It was brunch by the time they got there, and the only seats were at the counter, but it was Emma's favourite place, and Mark knew that, which was why they'd come. They ate their meal in polite civility, as had been the weekend's pattern.

'You know,' Mark said as he finished his coffee, 'you should be aiming for promotion too.'

Emma looked at him, surprised at his sudden interest.

'You've been a researcher for a while. You could move up.'

Emma smiled. 'Yeah, I know,' she answered slowly. 'I probably need to wait for a bit though. I've only been at Bristol for nine months.'

'Keep a look out,' he answered kindly. 'You're good enough, and the people at Bristol, they can replace you.'

Emma chewed the last of her bagel. 'Maybe,' she smiled, pleased with his compliments.

Mark pondered her carefully, then caught himself. 'Well,' he shrugged, 'it's up to you.'

Disappointed by the sudden change in his tone, Emma finished her coffee and prepared to leave. She considered his words as they walked home, not only the advice and the interest, the finality too of the conversation. He was advising her for the future, as if he wouldn't be there in her future.

When they reached the house, Mark was anxious not to delay her. Almost before she had put her belongings in the hall, he took them to her car and stood there waiting. She took one long last look around her, braced herself for a final showdown and followed him carefully.

As he loaded her bags into the car boot, he turned towards her. 'Thanks for coming. You did look pretty.'

'Thanks for inviting me, I enjoyed it.'

She shut the boot and took a deep breath. 'So,' she looked directly at him. 'Some time again soon? Or shall we not bother?'

Mark stepped back onto the pavement, his voice quickly becoming louder. 'I don't know,' he snapped.

'Well, shall we leave it?' She tried to sound reasonable,

thinking of him, not of herself.

He raised his shoulders angrily. 'If that's what you think.' He turned his blazing eyes towards her. 'It's not up to me.'

Emma looked at him dumbfounded, her emotions starting to bubble and boil, her words coming quickly. 'It's not what I want. It's not me who...'

'You know what,' he interrupted, almost shouting, 'I think you're right. I can't do this anymore.'

Emma looked at him speechless.

'Alright,' he shouted, 'I'm not doing this anymore.' He turned his back, marched into the house and slammed the front door.

Unsure of what had just happened, Emma opened her car door and sat in the driver's seat. So that was it - she and Mark were no longer together. He was not willing to think of her, consider her or care about her. After everything she had done for him.

She sat in her car seat, angry and upset, humiliated at the performance in public, but, determined not to let him see it, she started the engine and drove away.

Unsure then of what to do, she drove to Guildford. She didn't want to go back to Bristol, her flat in Guildford was empty, so she could sleep there, she could see Suzie and the drive would be long enough to calm her down.

As she reached the town though, she still wasn't calm. She took the road to her favourite place, parked the car and marched quickly up to the top of the hill. Thirty minutes later, breathing hard, she looked at the view, and felt better. She remembered the rest of the world from here, the smaller things, the bigger things, the natural things.

She stayed for a while, relishing the breeze that whipped through her hair, noticing things that she'd been missing, the chatter of birds, the turn of the fields, the signs of spring. With a sense of peace, a feeling that she would be alright, she retraced her path and returned to her car at the base of the hill.

Back in the car, she turned on her phone to call Suzie, to be greeted by two flashing texts. The first was from Karen: *Hello, sweetheart. Phone turned off, I guess all is going well. Love and hugs, K x*

No, Emma replied, *complete disaster, E x*

The second was from Mark: *I'm sorry Em, I just can't give what you seem to need. Take care, M.*

Emma looked hard, her anger resurfacing. To make matters worse, he was probably right. Honesty, openness, truth, trust – that was what she needed from him and that was what he couldn't seem to give.

Within two minutes, the telephone rang. 'Are you OK?' Karen's voice sounded.

Emma relaxed, appreciating the thoughtfulness of her friend. 'Well, I was,' she started, 'but now there's a bloody text as well. Apparently, he can't give me what I seem to need… He doesn't even know what I need.'

'So it didn't go too well at the ballet?'

'No.' Emma started strongly, but couldn't maintain it. 'It's all over, Karen.' She took a deep breath and steadied her voice. 'He doesn't love me anymore. It's been going downhill since we went to Jordan. I'm not sure why – maybe the cancer is getting worse, maybe it's all too much effort, maybe he's just changed his mind. It doesn't matter, there's no use pretending, he just doesn't love me anymore.' She stopped to choke back her welling tears.

'Of course he does,' Karen retaliated. 'He's having a hard time right now, that's all.'

Emma shook her head. 'You didn't see him. He was so angry… He's just so difficult. I try and be nice but I just make him cross. While we were in Jordan, most of the time, I seemed to make him angry, and since we've been back we've hardly spoken. I phone him and he doesn't answer. I try and text and he ignores me. I excuse him because maybe he's just feeling rough, but then he's off here and there with his friends, to follow the rugby, to do this and that… It's no use, Karen. The ballet was really my last try.' She stopped again to deal with more tears. 'Maybe it's all for the best.'

'Oh dear,' Karen sympathised. 'you *have* got it bad.' She paused but didn't receive a response. 'Why don't you come here? There's a spare bed in my room and I'm here all weekend with nothing else to do.'

'Karen, it's miles,' Emma laughed. 'I can't come up there, it'd take all day.'

'And what are you doing instead?' Karen waited. 'Look, if you're going to spend all day being miserable, you might as well be miserable on a train and then I can keep you busy all evening.'

Emma said nothing, undecided.

'Go on … it'll be fun … I'd like to see you, it'll be like old times.'

Emma wrestled with her thoughts, but allowed herself to be persuaded. 'I'll come up tomorrow. I'll send you a text with the time I'll arrive.' She took a deep breath, sniffed away her tears and prepared to drive back to Bristol. 'Thanks, Karen, I'll see you tomorrow.'

***

The train arrived in Glasgow at 5.45pm and, like the good friend she was, Karen was waiting at the end of the platform with kisses and a massive hug. She was staying in Glasgow for ten weeks for work. Not her home town, she knew no-one and having been in Glasgow now for four weeks, she was looking forward to some company.

'Right,' Karen started, all bossy and matter of fact. 'You and I are going to have a great night. We're not thinking about anyone else. We'll go to the hotel and drop off your things, get some dinner at Pizza Express, and then, on Wellington Street, I've found a superb little bar, full at the back, with endless rows of different vodkas – chocolate, apple, cinnamon, and so on. I thought we could go and try them all. It'll be ace.'

Emma laughed. She knew Karen from University, from days when drinking vodka was enough. Karen's enthusiasm was clear, and Emma knew that she could easily last far longer than her friend. 'Thanks Karen, sounds good to me!'

For the rest of the evening, they followed the plan. They talked mostly about Karen, of how she was, how her work was going, what she was doing with weekends in Glasgow, and once they'd exhausted that, the conversation deteriorated to life in general, plans for the future, all increasingly vodka tinted. Neither of them referred to Mark. Karen had been right the previous day – Emma had thought about Mark all day, and had been miserable all day too. Now she was happy to think, and feel, something different.

They had a good night. As vodka shots became vodka mixers, they moved instead on to other bars, then were out on the streets, still laughing and chatting, long past midnight.

Emma had also been correct - she could handle her alcohol far better than Karen, and when they woke the following day, it was definitely Karen who was suffering most. They skipped the breakfast at the hotel, and walked instead into central Glasgow. They found a small café, slightly off Queen's Square, took a table on the pavement, and sat soaking up the early sun with bacon butties and steaming hot coffee.

'You know,' said Emma, revived from the evening, 'he didn't deserve me anyway.'

'Too right,' Karen replied. 'And soon enough he'll realise that. Then you just watch him come crawling back.'

Emma smiled, but shook her head slightly. 'No,' she reasoned. 'You didn't see him. He was so angry, he won't be back.'

Karen looked at her quizzically. She leant over and touched her friend's hand. 'He will come back – they always do.'

Emma smiled. 'No, he won't.' She took a deep breath and smiled again. 'But, you know, it'll be okay.'

It helped to sound strong and optimistic, but deep inside she wasn't sure. She was cross with Mark, for treating her badly, for lying, pretending, for being a coward, but at the same time she knew she'd miss him, his kind comments, his shy little smile. She knew she would also miss the duty, she enjoyed thinking of him, remembering to call him. She had a sense of pride in their relationship, in dealing with his tempers, his strange dark moods, in being out with a man who was sick, feeling helpful and feeling needed. She wouldn't miss all the abuse, but even that maybe wasn't so bad. She'd been reminded by a colleague one time, that even to criticise, one had to notice.

Most of all, though, she felt humiliated. For him to leave her, that he had had the final word, when all she had been was thoughtful and patient. For him to decide that he no longer cared, that she was no longer good enough. All along, Emma had been most scared, not of Mark dying, but of him deciding he didn't love her, of this rejection, and now it had happened.

The following weekend, she sent back his house key. It took all day to write the letter, apologising for anything she might have done, what she might have said, what she might need, but then, with the key wrapped in cardboard to make it less obvious, she sadly posted it back to its owner.

There was no response. She wasn't surprised. She wondered if he even read it.

JORDAN, DECEMBER 2002

8

The holiday to Jordan started well.

Three days before Christmas and one day before they were due to fly, Emma arrived in Oxford, a mixture of tired and excited. She'd been busy recently - organising the holiday, finishing work, buying presents, seeing her family, all the activities that Christmas involved, and she was looking forward now to being away, to spending time with her lovely Mark, to being somewhere different, somewhere exciting.

Quickly and repeatedly she stepped from the train, each time with a different sized bag, until the pile on the platform stood at five items and the train was more than ready to leave. She looked around for someone to help, but not seeing him, she collected her luggage, struggled through the barrier and telephoned Mark.

'Hello?'

'Hello, I'm at the station. I was wondering if you'd mind coming to help. I've got quite a lot of bags, that's all.'

'Now?' he replied. 'Are you here now?'

'Yes, I'm in the station building. Are you busy?'

'No, I'll come now.'

Ten minutes later he finally appeared. Cold and tired, she'd spent the time wondering why he hadn't come of his own accord – she'd phoned earlier and he knew when she should be arriving, but as soon as she saw him, she stood up and stepped forward to kiss him. 'Sorry,' she started, 'I didn't mean to drag you out. I just couldn't face struggling home with all these.'

He looked at her. 'You shouldn't have brought so much, should you? I'm sure you didn't need to bring all this.' He bent down and started collecting.

'They're Christmas presents,' she retaliated. 'My family have made all sorts of efforts to get them to me so that I could bring them. I could hardly then leave them behind.'

He quickly stooped forward and kissed her cheek. 'Well, at least you didn't ask me to collect you from Gloucester. It takes hours to get to that station from here.'

They set off home, and with a little effort, Emma started to relax. It hadn't been easy for her family when she had changed her Christmas plans, and her mother had certainly not been pleased, but by the time she was safely installed in Mark's lounge, cup of tea in hand, feet in her slippers curled up underneath her, she was glad to be there. Days and days of endless nothingness stretched out before her, relaxing with this man of her dreams. Mark also seemed pleased to see her, but having already had days and days of endless nothingness, he was ready for more action.

'I'm so pleased you're here. I can't wait to go away - three weeks of sun in the middle of winter.' He walked in and out of the room, busying himself, preparing dinner. 'Can I ask you some questions?'

Emma smiled. Considering his lack of interest during the planning, she was pleased with his small-boy excitement. 'Of course. What would you like to know?'

He continued talking excitedly. 'The Aquamarina Resort first. How much is sorted? Is there anything else we need to do? And then for the rest of Jordan? Is there anything in particular that *I* need to do?'

She told him as much as she could, but she'd left most of it flexible in case Mark had specific ideas. Their flights were late on the twenty-third, arriving early on the twenty-fourth, the resort was booked until the twenty-ninth, but from then on, nothing was fixed. They'd hire a car, and she knew some options, but she'd left the details deliberately open. She'd had difficulty extracting opinions from Mark about anything, but she also knew there'd be no excuses if he wasn't happy.

She desperately hoped the trip would work well. She'd spent hours poring over guidebooks and brochures, considering his preferences, but also the cancer, looking for things that were fun and exciting, but not strenuous. She wanted simply to get it right, but didn't really know what right would be, except for expensive, which she couldn't manage. The only opinion that Mark had offered was a preference to not book a hotel for when they arrived, but to wait at the airport and drive to the resort from there instead. Emma wasn't sure this would make a good start, but after several attempts, she'd stopped trying to persuade him otherwise.

The following day had been left for packing and last-minute shopping. Mark had very little left to do, but he was happy to accompany Emma to town for a coffee. She, on the other hand, had plenty to do – she still had no presents for Mark, she needed some summer clothes, some sun cream, and she had a dress that she wanted to change. A quick coffee later, she despatched Mark to source the sun cream and set off in search of some Christmas presents.

She'd been thinking hard now for several weeks, but she still wasn't sure what to buy Mark. The only thing he'd mentioned was a watch costing £300, with no specifics other than price. She looked at the watches in a few windows but quickly decided against the idea. She wasn't sure Mark really wanted a watch, she didn't want to spend that much money, and the importance of price for Mark annoyed her, his need for reassurance through a figure decided upon by somebody else.

She wanted something special. She wanted something that showed that she'd thought, that she knew him, not simply a watch that anyone could buy. She also wanted more than one present. She'd brought a lot of presents with her, and opening them would be a lot less fun if she had to rush or feel bad because she had lots and Mark had only one. He'd already opened the presents from his family when he'd spent the weekend with them.

In the end, she bought him things he could use, and hopefully he would also enjoy: products to take care of his skin, at least one lip-salve for every coat pocket, and two massive candles, one square and cream to replace the stub on the mantelpiece, one more coloured. She was pleased with her choices, but also worried they wouldn't be enough.

She arrived back at the house at four o'clock. As she entered, she heard his footsteps coming across the room above and he appeared at the top of the stairs. 'Hello, you've been ages. You must have bought loads.'

'No, not really,' Emma started. 'Most of the time I was just looking. There are hardly any summer clothes, not even T-shirts, and you, I've found very difficult to buy for, but...' she paused, a smile on her face as she rummaged through shopping bags, 'look at this. This is gorgeous.' She pulled a dark-red satin bodice from one of the bags and held it up against her body. 'Isn't it lovely?'

Mark looked at the bodice and then at her. 'And when are you going to wear it?' he asked with a tone of disapproval.

Not quite the response she was hoping for, Emma shrugged. 'Oh, I don't know, but that doesn't matter. I could take it with us and wear it for dinner on Christmas day.'

Mark simply looked at her. He didn't quite sneer, but he might as well have.

9

They arrived in Jordan at 2.30am. For a few hours, they slept, sort of, on the Arrivals Hall floor, and then at 6am they hired a Nissan Micra and set off for the Red Sea. Once out of the airport, and clearly heading in the right direction, Mark stretched his hand over to his passenger, stroked her leg, and let his hand rest there. 'I'm so glad you're here.'

Emma turned towards him. 'Thanks,' she smiled. 'I'm glad you're here too.' She paused for a second. 'Goodness knows where we'd be if no-one was driving. But in fact you know, I'm glad *we're* here.'

He smiled in response and stroked her leg a little more. For the rest of the journey, they talked a little, mostly directions or practical concerns. Tired and content simply to observe the novel landscape, they travelled peacefully to arrive at the resort by mid-morning.

'I'm so tired,' Mark announced as they pulled into the car park. 'All I want now is a beer, a nice meal and to make love to you.' But within two minutes of entering their room, they were both on the bed, sound asleep.

Emma woke in the late afternoon. Slowly she drifted out onto their balcony to watch the sun glancing off the waters of the Red Sea. It wasn't hot, nor was there the hint that it had been hot, but it was warm - a gentle, calm, relaxing warm. She sat on the balcony watching the bay, enjoying the scenery, reading the guidebook, letting Mark sleep for as long as he needed. She was happy to simply be where she was.

He joined her later, happy to be where he was too, but by the time he'd appeared, Emma was in need of more activity.

In search of what the resort could offer, she left him reading, to return a little later with a bottle of wine and a lot of information.

Mark was on the balcony exactly where she'd left him. She handed him a glass of wine and inclined her head towards the guidebook, now abandoned for a novel. 'Anything you particularly fancy?'

'Lots of things, but let's not rush. Tell me what you've found that's closer.'

'Well,' she started, glad of the relaxed ambience. 'In the resort, there are two pools and two beaches, various things like tennis if you want to be more energetic, things like yoga if you want to do classes, or there's snorkel equipment we could borrow. I think my preference would be for beaches, and I'd like to snorkel or maybe go diving, but we can decide tomorrow. I'd like to make the most of being here and I've heard there are some great fish and corals in the Red Sea.' She paused briefly to smile at his nodding, and then continued. 'For this evening though, its dinner in the restaurant, or crisps and beers in the hotel bar – the bistro is closed.'

'Not dinner in the restaurant.' Mark offered. 'There's a seven-course meal there for Christmas tomorrow, and we can't eat in the same place two nights in a row. Are you sure there's nowhere else open?'

'Not that I could see. We can have a look later … but it might have to be crisps and beer.'

He shrugged lightly and returned to his reading. 'I'm not that hungry.'

She left him to it, re-entered the bedroom and settled herself for an evening of wine and present wrapping. She returned to the balcony every so often, mainly to replenish his glass, but she was happy amusing herself until he had read enough of his book, and was ready to venture back out.

They soon confirmed that the bistro was closed, but then

found the bar easily, took a booth and submitted themselves to whatever entertainment the bar had to offer – predominantly their own conversation, but there was an easy atmosphere and as satisfied diners spilled out from the restaurant, the place became lively, and conversation turned to singing and dancing.

They returned to their room close to midnight, and before going to bed arranged their presents on the chest of drawers. As Emma put her presents for Mark alongside those she had brought for herself, he picked each up eagerly, squeezed it, shook it and slowly returned it.

By the time she had finished cleaning her teeth, he only had one left in his hand, a long square present, hard to the touch, that didn't rattle. 'Can I open this one now?'

Emma was amazed. 'No, of course not! You can wait 'til tomorrow like everyone else.'

'But I want to know what this one is.' He stood in front of her, shaking it, holding it up to his ear.

'You'll only be disappointed tomorrow when I have a lot more presents than you.'

'If I can open it now, that'll more than make up for not having it tomorrow.'

'No,' she laughed. 'Put it back with the others.'

He didn't move but stood instead with a pleading look plastered over his face. 'I won't give you yours.'

Emma looked at him in disbelief. 'Well, that's hardly fair. I don't think you should open that one this evening, that's all.'

He still didn't move and didn't put it back.

She resigned herself to giving in. 'Oh, go on then, open it now.'

And he did as soon as she said it, quickly and urgently as if the contents might disappear. As he took the candle out from its wrapping, his eyes sparkled.

They slept well that evening, bathed in candlelight, happy to be there with each other.

10

On Christmas Day, they woke to bright sunshine and clear blue skies. As Mark threw open the window shutters, Emma scrambled out of bed, collected the presents, placed them on the bed in between them and started unwrapping. She was delighted with all her presents – several items of clothing and jewellery, and a book and some earrings from Mark.

Mark, of course, was disappointed. While Emma opened her many presents, his were all opened in less than half the time, and none were as good as last night's candle nor did they make up for the lack of a watch.

He cheered up over a large buffet breakfast, and soon they were on their way with towels and books and puzzles and pillows, for a day on the beach beside the Red Sea. The scenery was stunning - the clear blue skies, the sparkling water, the gentle lap of the tiny waves, and on the far side of the bay, they could see the desert hills of Egypt. Emma selected them two sun loungers, while Mark took a deep breath, turned around slowly and let out a long satisfied sigh. 'I love the Red Sea!'

They spent the day relaxing - sunbathing, reading, the occasional swim. They surrounded themselves with decadence – ice cream sundaes and cocktails, laughed easily at their fellow loungers, read extracts of novels and guidebooks to each other, and planned for three weeks of pleasure and interest.

Emma's enjoyment was only slightly marred by her concern for Mark. Yet again, she had no idea if he should be out doing so much, if he should be careful, what might happen if he did too much, or what she should do if something happened. She watched him carefully on occasion, but she was disappointed by his lack of trust, his lack of consideration.

'Are there any limits to what you should be doing?' she asked him at one point, to be returned by a blank look. 'I mean exertion … overheating … anything like that?'

'No, I don't think so,' he answered briefly, lying back against his sunbed. 'Anything for you?'

Emma was unsurprised. 'No,' she answered, unsatisfied, but not yet completely put off. 'You never know what might happen, do you?'

'Emma,' he responded, 'if I die here, stretched out under the Red Sea sun, I want you to know, I would die a happy man.'

Emma smiled, pleased with the compliment, but disappointed still by his lack of thought. It annoyed her that he didn't trust her, never spoke about his illness. The biggest thing probably in his life, and he wouldn't share it, he couldn't share it. 'Well, that's good … although I wasn't only thinking of you. I was also thinking of me, and I'd rather not have to make it all up on the spot if necessary.' She turned towards him, but he simply lay there, hands behind his head, eyes closed to the world.

Two minutes later he retaliated. 'Maybe we could find the local doctor, to know where he is if we need him.'

Emma could feel him smirking at her, showing not only a lack of thought, but a deliberate attempt to tease her. She offered no reply; she continued reading, refusing to rise to his taunts.

Finally, he thought of something to which she had to respond. 'Tomorrow I think we should stick to the pool.' She looked at him questioningly. 'I'm not sure the salt water is that good for me,' he continued.

'Do you really think so? It's much nicer here. We could be anywhere at the poolside.'

'I think I'd rather, I think it's safer.'

Emma would be disappointed to not make the most of where they were, to miss out, to not do it properly, and she thought he probably knew that. But she couldn't push him, she couldn't even ask him to try. How guilty would she feel if something happened and she had gone against his wishes? When it came to his health, he would always have the upper hand, and he knew it.

'Okay,' she smiled, resolved at least, to keeping him happy. 'If that's what you'd rather.' They left the beach late afternoon, the air no longer quite warm enough for sunbathing, and returned to their balcony. They read for a while, Emma telephoned her family to wish them all a Happy Christmas, then she and Mark enjoyed a quiet drink, and showered and changed ready for the evening.

When Emma returned from the bathroom, Mark was waiting. She detected an air of impatience and kissed him quickly as she passed, but as she pulled the red bodice out of her bag, she could hear his disapproval. 'Please don't wear that,' he almost pleaded.

She turned to face him, bodice held up to her chest. 'Why don't you like it?' she asked, interested. 'It's very Christmassy.'

He shook his head. 'It'll look awful ... particularly with that love bite there.'

Emma went back into the bathroom and inspected the love bite on the side of her neck. 'No-one will know,' she reasoned carefully. 'It could be a birthmark.'

'I'll know,' he stated. 'It's embarrassing.'

Emma reluctantly put the top back in her bag. She was disappointed. Not really though about the top, more that Mark thought he could choose her wardrobe, that he could tell her what she should wear. She wondered now if the love bite was nothing more than a means of preventing her from wearing the bodice.

She retrieved her frilly purple cardigan – pretty, but definitely understated, slipped on her heels and was ready. She recovered on the short walk to the restaurant, an easy walk full of Christmas lights and holiday thoughts, and when Mark wanted a quick drink before dinner, she was happy to agree, hoping he would recover too.

One drink later, they made their way to the restaurant, but instead of being seen, were left standing in the entrance for several minutes or, in Mark's case, pacing in front of the door. Finally someone came to show them to their table but, by the time they got to it, Mark was furious. He pulled out his seat, ripped off his tie and slammed it down on the table beside him. He was ranting to himself under his breath, '*bloody*' and '*treatment*' and '*tolerance*' and '*service*', Emma couldn't catch it.

She looked calmly at him from across the table. 'Don't be cross,' she started simply. 'They're just being rude.'

'Exactly,' he retorted.

'Just ignore them. Let's not let them spoil our evening.' She reached across the table to find his hand, but he snatched it away.

'It's too late now, it's already spoilt.'

Inwardly, Emma only sighed. She knew she would have to suffer this, keep her head down, try not to do or say anything wrong, and maybe things would pick up later.

Throughout the whole meal though, Mark was on bad form. Everything she mentioned was meaningless, trivial or stupid, and all the conversations he started were on topics on which they would disagree. She had the option of being criticised for her opinions, or being criticised for not defending them.

At least he was content with the food – fruit, pâté, seafood, duck, sorbet, dessert and then cheese, all small portions, but all unusual and very tasty. By the time for the cheese course, Emma was full. But, they weren't then simply offered one small cheese board. A whole trolley of cheeses appeared, from which they could choose as many as they wished. The waiter named them and patiently waited for madam's order. She looked at them carefully, admiring the choice, wishing she had some appetite.

'What will you have Emma?' Mark demanded.

She looked up at the waiter, smiled apologetically and put up her hand. 'None for me, thank you, I'm already full.'

Mark hissed at her from across the table. 'Don't be so rude. Which cheeses do you want?'

She turned towards him, ready to plead, but saw the anger flashing through his eyes. Confused and embarrassed, she smiled weakly at the waiter and chose quickly from the front of the trolley.

As soon as the waiter had left them, Mark continued, 'How could you be so rude?'

'I wasn't being rude,' Emma started defending herself, although she couldn't quite grasp the problem. 'I...'

But Mark wouldn't let her. 'You're so embarrassing. Don't you even know how to behave in a restaurant?'

'I didn't want any cheese, that was all.' She remained at a loss as to why he was angry. 'Any good restaurant would be glad I was full,' she continued indignantly.

He looked at her, exasperated. 'For God's sake!'

The rest of the meal and the walk to their room, they spent in silence. Emma tried to apologise, to take his arm, to soothe him, but he pulled away, preferring to walk very much on his own. In the room, he continued to ignore her with a hostile intensity, picked up his book and went back to reading. Emma, still confused, simply tried not to show how much he'd upset her.

***

The following day began again with beautiful weather and they both made an effort to forget the night before. They spent the day by the pool as they'd agreed, and the scenery wasn't to Emma's taste, the surroundings not quite as pleasant, but it was fine and Mark was happy. They read, sunbathed, and swam all day, distant compared to the day before, until in the late afternoon, the temperature again required something different.

'Tomorrow, I think we could be more active,' Emma started, as she entered the balcony, drinks poured for them both. 'Snorkelling, or even diving. Don't you want to see under the Red Sea too? … as well as on top of it?'

Mark looked up at her from his book. 'You can go snorkelling. I'd prefer another day of reading beside the pool.'

Emma was dismayed. 'Don't you spend enough time reading at home?'

'I like reading, I like it a lot.'

Emma kissed him lightly as she sat down beside him. 'Yes, I know, but you can read at home. Wouldn't it be nice to make the most of these lovely surroundings?'

Mark smiled at her. 'Tomorrow, I'm reading beside the pool. I'm making the most of those surroundings.'

'I'm getting lonely.' Emma pouted, as if that might persuade him. Christmas with her family was sociable - a big family who didn't live close, they used Christmas as a time to catch up, to play games, to do things together.

Mark however, was unmoved.

'Do you still want to go to the football, at least?' she asked quickly. There was a local match along the beach that evening, and not looking forward to another meal in a restaurant, Emma had been keen for the distraction that the football would bring. Christmas with her family was also fun. They laughed and joked and supported each other. They didn't hiss or criticise.

'Oh yes,' he smiled. 'I'd forgotten about that. Let's go to the football. Boxing Day is for sporting events.' He reflected for a moment. 'A day in the sun and then an evening watching sport – superb! That's exactly my kind of day!'

He pulled her towards him and kissed her warmly on the side of her neck, and as they watched the football, they nestled close, conversation interspersed with stories and small witticisms. Emma resolved to try harder, not to pick fights, or expect too much. Maybe tomorrow would be better.

Their last two days at the resort were calmer. They stayed by the poolside – reading, sunbathing and swimming, with a few forays for Emma to snorkel. Mark seemed finally to be relaxing, the days were pleasant, finished also with pleasant evenings. Despite the restaurant as a constant reminder, they laughed and giggled for entire evenings, memories of earlier times away, wishes and desires for the future. Mark could make Emma laugh so hard – his small observations, quiet witticisms, and he was smart, he had opinions, they had discussions, he made her think. When Mark was relaxed, when he was happy, it was easy to see why Emma loved him.

There were still criticisms, small comments, occasional looks or sighs or sneers, dark words for no apparent reason, but these had been increasing at home as well. Emma was becoming hardened to them, although possibly only on the outside. She wondered if the night flight and time in the airport had just been too much, the Christmas Day nastiness simply a result of fatigue.

***

The following day, they drove the short distance up the coast to stay in Aqaba. As they left the resort, Mark missed the turning for the main road, Emma distracted for a second while looking for something in her bag. 'I ... I thought we might like to try this road,' he said nonchalantly.

Emma laughed. She knew he was lying, covering up a silly mistake, and he knew she knew. 'Well,' she replied as she looked at the map, 'we'll need to keep a look out for the next turning for it. It'll be on the left.'

At the next crossroads, a small crossroads, Mark then turned left. As he did so, Emma laughed. 'And now where are you going?'

Mark looked around as the road he had taken turned into a narrow track serving only a farm and some outbuildings. 'I thought we might like to see this farm.' But as he said it, he swung the car round and quickly returned to the crossroads.

Emma laughed, pulled herself up out of her seat, leant over and kissed him. It was the first time she'd ever seen him laugh at himself.

Mark's detour resulted in a lot of driving, but they arrived in Aqaba in plenty of time to find a hotel and spend more time reading. Finally, by the end of the afternoon, Mark's book was finished. As he announced his triumph, Emma couldn't help feeling relieved. The resort holiday had not gone quite as she'd planned. She'd wanted companionship, fun and laughter, and she'd offered those things to Mark, and in return he'd given her a little, but it wasn't enough. She felt lonely. She attributed his manner to him being tired, but as he stated 'Another holiday ruined as a result of a book,' Emma couldn't have agreed more.

11

Resolved to now start a different holiday, Emma took Mark's finished book to the hotel's book exchange and returned to their room without a replacement. From now on, they were going to spend some time together.

Refreshed from the few days away from it all, they approached the evening eager for amusement, something exciting, something exotic. They ambled into the small town of Aqaba, a short stroll along the paved waterfront, perused the market and souvenir shops, and a few streets back from the water's edge, they selected a small rooftop restaurant. The evening air tinged with the smell of spices, the lively sounds of Arabian music, it was exciting, exotic, but it was also all slightly subdued, slightly faded, a hint of better times long ago. They dined on traditional fish dishes, smoked and steamed with spices and powders, a relaxing evening under the stars, a warm gentle breeze rolling in off the water.

The following morning, they returned to the fort and the museum; the fort – small, squat, made of dark stone that contrasted with its sandstone surroundings, the museum composed of small, musty rooms, crammed with scraps of pottery and metalwork, labels all hand-written in Arabic. It reminded Emma of an old school, with cases of specimens and once-marvellous exhibits, now shut up and gathering dust.

The afternoon was again spent on the beach, then to celebrate the New Year, they went to a floating restaurant on the Red Sea, small and intimate, once a boat, almost still a boat. There was a small cloud while they were dressing, but Emma recognised Mark's tone, and anxious to avoid any discomfort, knew better than to ask further. In a fancy restaurant he would be happy, and the setting on the Red Sea was exceptional - the gentle movement of the water beneath them, the lights of Israel and Egypt twinkling from across the bay, the stars in a velvet sky sparkling above them.

Relaxed and happy, they sat at the restaurant late into the evening, chatting and laughing, recounting stories of similar places, telling tales of similar scenes, imagining places and scenes to come. At 11.15pm, they left the restaurant and ambled back towards the hotel. The waterfront was now much busier, the section by the town centre almost crowded – packs of young men, groups of young girls, families with children, pairs of pensioners, all excited, all expectant. Mark and Emma found a space to sit and simply joined them, the excitement was contagious. Before long they were smiling and gesturing with their neighbours, part of the crowd, part of the party, yet they knew not the language nor the customs.

At a quarter to twelve, from the head of the bay, the fireworks started. Five minutes later, another display, from opposite where they were sitting. The New Year celebrations now begun, expectations grew, excitement expanded, but as twelve o'clock came, there was nothing more. People hugged and kissed each other, but there were no further fireworks, no count down, no bells and no gongs. Emma found it strangely refreshing.

As the crowds dissipated, she and Mark kissed a quick kiss, then hand-in-hand walked back to the hotel, stopped for a cocktail in the hotel bar, and laughing and giggling, tickling and wriggling, they returned to their room, anxious to be under the sheets.

Once there however, the bubble that had been, finally burst. Balancing on a knife edge since she wasn't sure when, Emma had been hoping things would improve of their own accord. Only they hadn't, and instead had been slowly getting worse. Mark's health was deteriorating and the strain on their relationship was increasing. There were still no physical signs of an illness, nothing but the lack of hair – the tell-tale sign of chemotherapy, but the unfairness, uncertainty, the possible loss of time to come, these were starting to cause pressure.

The moods had got worse, were more unpredictable, more inconsistent, the criticisms had been coming more often, were more hurtful and more unreasonable. A smile at the waiter and Emma was accused of desperation, an accidental flash of her skin while undressing and she was accused of exposing herself, embarrassing him, comments on her hair, complaints about her clothes. All of it, she put down to tiredness and illness. If he would just talk to her, then that might help, she might understand, but she was still waiting.

He'd talked to her once. It was one of the things that had first appealed '*I feel I'm not being honest with you*', but since then there had been nothing more. She was waiting. She was trying to understand, she was still supportive, she still loved him.

Halfway through lovemaking, Mark simply moved away from her. 'I can't do this anymore,' he announced.

Emma looked at him in horror. 'What do you mean?'

He didn't reply. He lay beside her, his body inert, his face turned away. She slipped out of bed, went into the bathroom, took a few moments, then calmly, gently, climbed back in, careful not to touch him, trying again to be patient, trying again to understand. 'What do you mean? What can't you do?' she asked softly.

She heard him sigh. 'I can't explain now. Let's not spoil a nice New Year's.'

Emma held her tongue.

As they sat down to breakfast, unable to think about anything else, Emma broached the topic again. 'So, what did you mean last night?'

'Not now, Emma. Why are you so intent on spoiling New Year's?'

Emma looked at him undeterred. 'New Year's was yesterday.'

'Oh, and New Year's Day doesn't count?'

They spent the rest of the day on the beach. There was no uneasiness, no atmosphere, but for the whole day, they hardly spoke. By the evening, things were slightly improved. With all day to think, Emma had decided she would wait, with all day to relax, Mark was simply in a better mood. They had an early meal in a small restaurant, then spent the evening comfortably in bed, watching TV, Mark's head resting on Emma's lap.

Emma knew they were falling apart. She didn't know why, she wished they weren't. She wished he would talk. She didn't know what else she should do, she couldn't think of what else to try, but she knew this wasn't all about her. She felt exhausted, resigned and saddened.

12

The following day they left Aqaba and moved northwards. They stopped first of all, at Wadi Rhum, for desert plants and noisy insects, surrounded by the sheer cliffs of the rock mountains. The sun was warm, the air was clear, their walk interesting, but conversation was lack-lustre. The lack of explanation still niggled Emma - she needed to talk, to understand, but she also didn't want a fight and she didn't want to upset Mark. She was becoming more frightened of his moods, the vicious comments, the unjust remarks.

By late afternoon, they reached Petra – one street reaching from a small rustic village to the ancient city, lined by large obtrusive hotels. They stopped at one, but the offered rooms not to Emma's liking, they continued on to a hotel that had been recommended. Again the offered rooms weren't as desired, and by the time Emma had returned unsatisfied and frustrated, Mark was waiting in the lobby. 'Well?' he asked impatiently.

'Well,' she sighed, 'we can have a room with no windows, or we can have a suite at twice the price with a view of the pool. You can't have views of desert it seems.' Having spent the whole day unsure and uncertain, she was tired and easily annoyed.

Mark left her and spoke to the receptionist. Within five minutes, he had everything arranged – they were staying in the suite for the cost of the room which also included their evening meals. Emma was impressed, but the whole business had left her cross. To make matters worse, Mark was pleased with himself for getting the deal, and didn't seem to understand she might be upset. She was tired. She was tired of trying to please everyone. She was tired of thinking of everyone else. As they entered the room, Mark tried to grab hold of her round her waist, but she simply pulled away.

To reinvigorate themselves, they left the hotel shortly afterwards, to find information on the ancient city. On arriving at the entrance gate, they quickly discovered that tickets for the following day could also include the last hour of today.

Emma hung back to allow Mark to buy two. 'What are you doing?' He looked at her strangely.

'I'm waiting for you,' she replied plainly. 'There's no point *me* trying, I'm sure the man won't deal with *me*.'

Mark looked straight at her, confused. 'Oh, I have to do everything, do I?'

'It's not my fault,' she retorted, all the annoyance from earlier returning – annoyance with the system, annoyance with the culture, annoyance with Mark for not understanding.

Mark stepped up and, along with the tickets, was handed a pen to complete their names. 'Do you want to be Mrs Alexander?' he queried.

'Why?' snapped Emma. 'Can you not spell Braunston?'

The tickets written, they made their way down the narrow wadi, a path long enough for Emma to relax, to think things through, and recover. The first of the sights, a breath-taking sight, was the Treasury. The carving, the stonework, so careful, so intricate, both of them were astounded. They stayed in the Treasury for the whole of their hour, then on their way back past the entrance gate, they booked two places for the evening performance of 'Petra by Candlelight'. Completely distracted by the beauty of the Treasury, and slightly ashamed of her earlier outburst, Emma easily acquiesced to Mark's request to see the performance, and later, as they walked through the candlelight, underneath the stars, Mark's arm linked through hers, she was pleased that she had.

The following day, they woke up early, eager to explore. As they were having breakfast though, Mark complained of not feeling well, and asked if he could have a lie down. Emma, of course, let him lie down and spent the time reading the guidebook, but after an hour, she began getting restless. She was keen to see Petra and didn't want to waste her time sitting in the hotel. 'Can I go in and meet you when you're ready?' she asked politely.

'Why, what's the matter?' he asked her from the bed.

'Nothing's the matter. I've read the guidebook and I'd like to go and see it… I'm excited, that's all.'

Mark smiled. 'Okay, but can you leave me the book?'

Emma looked at him in amazement. 'How will I know where I am, or what to see, if you have the book?'

'I thought you'd read it.'

'I haven't read the details. I'll read those when we get there. And there's a map. I'll need the map.'

'Well, maybe I want to read it too.'

She looked at him. She knew he didn't want to read it, he was being obstructive. She wondered again at his selfishness, but she wasn't giving in. 'There's no point you keeping the book, is there? You stay here until you feel better, then let me know and I'll come and meet you. I can start with the things that are furthest away, and I won't mind going back if you want to see things I've already seen.'

'Oh, for God's sake,' he sighed in return. 'Just wait five minutes and I'll come now.'

They stopped again at the Treasury, now busy with tour guides and their tourists, and from there they walked towards the main part of the ancient city, but before reaching it, Mark took them on a detour up high to their left, in search of tombs. Emma followed happily until they were walking further and further from the main site and she could see nothing ahead. She looked at the guidebook, unsure that Mark had read the section correctly, but he was adamant.

Eventually they agreed to turn back, and as they did, the heavens opened. On the tops of the mountains, wind and rain lashing around them, they ran back down as fast as they could, but they'd come further than they'd realised, and the path on the way back was not well marked. Anxious not to end up lost, Emma slowed them to a walk and carefully picked a route through the dark clouds. There were, of course, some jibes from Mark – what are you doing? he wasn't getting lost?, but this wild goose chase was his fault, that they had nowhere to hide as it poured with rain, the last thing Emma wanted was to stop and listen to his advice.

As they reached the main path, the rain began easing. Emma opened the guidebook to check their direction and found a sacrificial site nearby. Pleased with her route-finding so far, she pointed to the page.

'Look,' she started, 'while we're up here, further up this path, there should be a stone slab once used for sacrifices. It should be only around the corner.'

They continued ahead and as the path curved round, Mark took them on a short cut straight ahead. Before long they reached two ceremonial gates beyond which should have been the sacrificial stone. They searched around them, but couldn't see it. Slightly further, they still couldn't find it. Emma again consulted the book while Mark simply laughed. Cold and wet, she was again frustrated, and Mark laughing at her was not helping.

'Don't you want to see the sacrificial stone?' she asked him plainly.

He was still laughing as he replied, 'Clearly not as much as you do.'

'It says after the ceremonial gates.' She looked around in desperation, 'Well I can't see it.'

'Maybe it's back there? Maybe we missed it.' Mark

continued laughing.

Emma again consulted the guidebook. 'No, it can't be. There's a map and there are instructions.'

'Do you want to go back in case we've missed it?'

'No, I don't.' She snapped the book shut. 'I'm carrying on. You do what you like, I'll see you back in the valley bottom.' She was annoyed with Mark for making her wet, for taking short cuts that meant they got lost, for making her cross but, above all, for thinking it funny.

As she walked down the hill very much alone, looking occasionally into tombs and across at stunning views, Emma resigned herself to simply coming back some other time, when she could stop and see what she liked, when it would be pleasant, interesting and fun, when she wouldn't be constantly fighting. Cheered by these thoughts and the appearance of the sun, she reached the valley floor almost recovered.

Once Mark arrived, still cold and damp, Emma suggested a hot lunch, and soon they were both feeling much better. The warmth of the food, the shelter of the café, they recovered gradually, Emma particularly. The hot lunch had been her idea, and she liked it when Mark accepted her help.

They spent the afternoon in the further parts of Petra – the Monastery and some large houses, imagining themselves as monks, as merchants, and again they laughed, they made the most of the ancient city, they made the most of their time together. The mood continued into the evening, and Emma tried to keep it up, she tried to relax, tried to enjoy it.

***

The following day they were travelling again. From Petra, they continued to Shobak – a crusader fort on the top of a peak in a barren landscape, and then on to Dana. A nature reserve that ran from the village high in the mountains down a wide wadi almost to the sea, Dana was famous for the variety in its wildlife. They spent the afternoon walking the single track through interesting habitats, but there was little shade and Emma again began to worry. Mark didn't look good, she worried he might be doing too much. All afternoon she walked slower than him, inspecting plants, stopping for insects, and every so often she'd ask him to wait, and as she caught up she'd have a quick drink or she'd sit down, hoping that he would do the same.

He started well, but as they walked back up the hill to the village he became impatient. He strode on ahead of her, leaving her less chance to ask him to stop, but giving her also more reason to. Finally, at one bend, he chose to sit down.

When she reached him and sat down beside him, she took out the water, but he declined it.

'Do you want me to carry the pack?' he asked her.

'No,' she said plainly, 'it's okay.'

'Oh, it's okay,' he said mimicking her voice. 'What do you mean by "it's okay"?'

Emma looked blankly. 'I mean I'm quite happy carrying it.'

'Well, I'm glad *you're* happy,' he sneered in reply, then strode off again.

Emma sighed. Maybe the heat, maybe he was tired, but maybe it was her after all. She kept finding excuses, explanations for his nastiness, but maybe he was going off her. She remembered while she was in Norway, she'd wondered how long it would take before he would leave her. She trudged on after him up the hill, her enjoyment again marred by unnecessary comments.

He waited for her at the edge of the village. She knew he wouldn't apologise but she hoped at least he would have recovered.

'Have you got any sweets?' he asked, as she came towards him.

'Yes.' She turned slightly so that he could reach them. 'Right side pocket.'

'I thought you could give some to that boy.' He nodded towards a boy on a donkey.

'Why?' She looked at him confused. She was wrong when she thought he might have recovered.

'What do you mean "Why"?' he snapped back at her. 'Why not?'

'Well,' she reasoned, 'I wouldn't give sweets to a boy in the street at home. Why would I do it here?'

'Emma,' he said patronisingly, 'I don't think you'll corrupt him with a few sweets. I thought you might like to do something nice for a change.'

Emma said nothing. Mark would know she wouldn't want to give the boy sweets for no reason. She'd been to India, she'd seen the children with their hands out because they'd been rewarded for it before. It was part of what he called her 'ethical tourism' – 'leave nothing behind except footsteps – it's cultural and social as well, she would say, it's not just litter'.

As he stomped off through the village to the guest house, she was seething. Not about sweets – she could justify her actions there, but over his final comment – that she might like to do something nice. As if she hadn't been doing nice things, all day, all week, for all of the time since she'd met him. Again, a comment that was hurtful, vicious, and for no reason.

Back at the guest house, they had two hours before dinner, so, anxious for something to keep them busy, they set off to the viewpoint to watch the sunset. The view over the reserve in the fading orange light was spectacular, a wadi of scrubland playing to an orchestra of birds and insects, surrounded on two sides by shining red cliffs.

As they stood there, reflecting over the scene before them, the door to an adjacent hut opened and a very old man beckoned them in. It was a small single room, heated in the middle by a wood-burning stove, and from the belongings strewn about the floor, it was possibly the man's entire house, but it also doubled as a gallery for the reserve.

They sat as directed. Mark spoke one sentence of perfect Jordanian, but the rest of the time they spent pointing, gesturing, smiling and laughing. It was relaxing, the man seemed happy to let them look at his pictures, happy with their interest, their smiles and their small attempts to converse.

'Well, that was nice,' Emma started as they left.

'You could have put in some effort, Emma,' Mark retaliated crossly. 'You were just sitting there staring at pictures.'

Emma again, was confused. 'I wasn't just sitting there staring at pictures. I was enjoying the pictures and relaxing.' She continued, 'Not that it matters anyway. The man wasn't really interested in me.'

Having been so clearly reminded of the male domination in Arabic cultures by the hotel staff in Aqaba and Petra, she was happy now to accept it and enjoy it. Mark didn't respond.

A similar event occurred later. Dinner at the guest house was usually a communal affair, but because they were the only ones staying that evening, it was dinner instead with the local guide. He was interesting to talk to, interesting as long as Mark was listening. Emma tried to contribute, tried not to simply enjoy herself, but she felt almost invisible. Mark also did nothing to try and include her.

She knew she'd be criticised whatever she did. If she simply sat, she would be accused of not making an effort; if she tried to join in, she would be ignored, laughed at, criticised, or found to be failing in some other aspect. By the time they had escaped, she was exhausted. Not from the long day or tiring walk, she was tired instead from the constant pressure. She wouldn't be rude or discourteous – those were rules she could easily follow, but Mark's pressures and constant demands? That changed often? Those rules were harder.

As she lay in bed thinking over her day, she decided she shouldn't be feeling like this. This wasn't what relationships were. She'd bide her time, keep her head down for the rest of the holiday, but when they were home, when she got back, she would leave him.

BRISTOL, JANUARY 2005

13

Emma read the advertisement in the newspaper and absent-mindedly twizzled the ring from Pennies round her middle finger: *Senior Research Nutritionist, University of Bristol, Department of Health Sciences.*

Almost two years earlier, Mark had suggested she think about progressing her career. She'd agreed to stay in her current place until the end of a particular project, and she wanted to keep to her word, but the project would finish soon and she was keen to also take Mark's advice. His position was in research, he was, in fact, Head of a Research Institute, and she thought his advice should be valued. Before he'd died, he'd helped with her CV, her covering letter, advised her on the jobs to apply for, all she needed now was to turn his advice into action.

She telephoned for details on the advertised position and submitted her application one week later. She thought she had a good chance - she knew some of the people in the department, and she had worked with them before.

Everything else was quiet. Christmas had been uneventful - she'd enjoyed the comfort of the routine, glad to escape from her current life, to the safety of her family, to people who loved her, to people who cared. New Year had also been quiet, and now she felt somewhat refreshed.

Things at work were also easy. Her current clients kept her busy, and there were rarely new ones at this time of year. She was glad of the space to organise her paperwork, to tidy and sort, but she still needed to keep busy.

She had now accepted that Mark had gone, she no longer expected him to turn up, but the flat seemed somehow empty without him. It was ironic since he'd never even visited, but something was missing. Her evenings seemed empty, her life now felt empty, empty of worry and thought and distraction, but also of purpose and hope and excitement.

To fill her evenings, she stayed at work or, on occasion, she went out. All the things she used to do, they were still there, they still happened. She returned to the pub quiz on Tuesday evenings, she accepted invites to plays and films, she stayed on for drinks again after work. The distraction was good, but she never stayed long. Light and easy, but as soon as conversations became close, she'd excuse herself or change the topic or simply switch off.

She became intolerant of anything that seemed superficial – the latest TV talent show, the to-ing and fro-ing in the local election. She declined shopping trips, absented herself from small work decisions; in the interval of a play, as her friends picked apart the acting and lighting, she simply excused herself for some air. What did these things matter? The quality of acting? The next popstar? The one-up-man-ship of everyday life? Life and death - that was what mattered.

She was glad of Fay and regularly met her for coffee or lunch. She also resumed her trips to the gym and returned to swimming once a week with Mel. Fay and Mel, they were both safe. Caring friends, they knew the topics to avoid and they were happy to put in the effort.

Towards the end of January, exactly as arranged, Emma also met with Christine, Christine complete with candle and CD, Emma with simply a sense of intrigue.

'So, how are you doing?' Christine hugged Emma and kissed her cheek.

Emma hugged her back not quite as tightly. 'Oh, you

know,' she shrugged lightly, but realised that Christine would need more. 'Christmas was nice, but now I'm back here again … I miss him Christine, I miss him so much...'

Christine made a sympathetic face.

'… even though he was such a git.'

Christine laughed. 'You said all that the last time I saw you.'

'I don't see him any more, at least. I used to see him all the time – his eyes, his walk or hear his voice. I was almost expecting him to turn up at the front door on some days... That's stopped now, at least … that was awful.'

'Well, that's a start.' Christine smiled. 'And I know he wasn't really a git. I know *I* thought so, but why would you miss him if he was so horrid? Why did you love him if he was so nasty?'

Emma laughed. 'He wasn't horrid all of the time, of course, he wasn't. But that almost made it all worse. He was so up and down – I love you, I hate you, I love you, I hate you, except he never said that he loved me. The whole time in Jordan was terrible - he was so much fun when he was being nice, but then so awful when he wasn't. I decided several times that I should leave him, but then he'd be nice, and I never did. And at the start he was so kind, so attentive … and after that, well, it was too late, I already loved him.'

They walked through the gardens towards the tower, until at a secluded spot in the rockeries, they sat down together. Christine handed Emma the homemade CD.

'You recorded a song for me?' Emma asked in amazement.

Christine smiled. 'It's very fitting. I was singing it last summer for a concert and your story reminded me of it so much. I wanted you to have a copy.' She paused while Emma blinked away tears of gratitude. 'It's a song about a man who is banished from a city for defending his family, so he has to leave, but in leaving he also has to leave his one true love. She only loves him for defending his family but she's a princess or something, so she shouldn't love him and she can't leave. It's a story of a man who wants to stay but has to leave.' She paused to take hold of Emma's hands. 'I think that's Mark – he wanted to stay, but he had to leave. Every time he wouldn't talk, every time he wouldn't see you, I think he was trying to protect you.'

Emma was distracted. She knew Christine was trying to help, that she was trying to offer support, but she found Christine's words unconvincing. 'Trying to protect me?' Emma questioned. 'No, Christine, he didn't love me. He left me Christine, that didn't protect me. All that avoiding me, endless comments and complaints, they didn't protect me. He didn't love me, that was all there was to it.' She looked away.

'You know what annoys me most, Christine?' Emma turned back to face her colleague. 'Why bother being nasty? If he didn't love me – well, okay, but why not just leave? Why be nasty? All the times when he was so hurtful, why not simply ask me to leave him?'

'That's it, though,' Christine smiled. 'He didn't *want* to leave, nor did he want you to leave him. He knew he *had* to, but he didn't want to. He was cross about *that*, angry, upset, but he was also trying to protect you, I think. He didn't want to drag you down.' Christine paused. 'Trying to protect himself as well maybe, but I'm sure he was thinking of you.'

Christine lit her candle, asked about Mark, talked about him, but for everything she tried, Emma knew Christine had never met him. How could she know what he had been thinking?

Emma was grateful for her kindness, she knew Christine thought, she knew Christine cared, and she tried … but Christine's words just didn't make sense. If Mark had loved her, why would he leave? Why would he hurt her? Why would he hate her? And hate her he did, Emma was convinced.

She arrived back home cross and impatient, cross with Mark for wasting her time, impatient with herself for having let him. She put the CD on the top of the pile, abandoned until she might be more open.

JORDAN, JANUARY 2003

14

Enlivened by her future release, Emma resolved to enjoy the rest of her time in Jordan. They left Dana and stopped first at Wadi Hudeira, another impressive steep-sided gorge, the sides as tall as a three-storey house, the gulley so narrow they could reach both sides. They walked through it for half an hour but by then Mark had had enough, so they turned around and returned to the entrance. Emma again was disappointed – she liked to do things properly, but this time, she didn't show it. She acquiesced happily, and vowed to return some other time.

At Kerak, they stopped for the crusader fort, but finding it closed, they entered the busy small town instead, in search of lunch. Before long, they came across one of the few restaurants recommended in the guidebook, a local place with plastic tables and plastic chairs, busy waiters who didn't need notepads and food that came almost instantly.

They were offered two dishes – meatballs or kebab. Mark chose kebab but Emma, not wanting more meat again, asked if she could have falafel instead. Of course she could, and it took no longer than Mark's kebab. Emma was pleased, inspired by the normal life going on around them, and as they sat at the front of the busy restaurant, she was reminded how interesting travel could be, how kind people were and how fun and interesting life could be. When she got home, she would leave Mark.

For her new-found freedom, Mark seemed only to love her

more. He laughed and joked with her over lunch, and two hours later, when they arrived in Madaba, after another hot and dusty day, they were happy to simply shower and relax before going out to eat.

'You know,' Mark announced, as he returned from the bathroom, 'my hair's growing back.'

'I know.' Emma smiled. 'The shape of your face is coming back too.'

'Sometimes,' Mark smiled, 'I wonder why you're here ... but then you say something like that and I remember.' He smiled as he spoke, and she knew it was supposed to be a compliment, that she was supposed to be flattered, but she could only focus on the first part. As if she were only there for him.

The following day was again hard work. The lack of blankets and noise from the street had kept them awake, and by morning both of them were tired and miserable. They tried first to see the mosaics in the town, but told they would be closed until lunchtime, they set off instead for 'The Desert Loop' – a series of castles out in the desert, each a few hours' drive from the last.

The first desert castle was a large square caravanserai located in the middle of a large flat plain. A three-storey building surrounding a courtyard, the rooms looked more like boxes in a theatre than overnight accommodation.

As they started wandering round, they were joined quickly by a local guide. 'Hello there,' he called. 'Let me tell you the history.'

'Oh no,' sighed Emma. 'Please, can we be spared?'

'Of course,' Mark returned over her head. 'That would be great.'

Emma looked at him in disbelief. As the guide came up to them, she left Mark with him, and set off to look around by herself. She stuck to the ground floor, the upper floors possibly no longer safe, but slowly explored the rooms she could access, trying to imagine the long-lost tenants, their horses, their travels, their arduous adventures.

Finally, as she leant against a doorway, relieved to find a little shade, she felt a hand brush across her back and became aware of a man standing only inches from her. She jumped away quickly, startled and alarmed. She turned and recoiled as she recognised the willing guide.

With a vacant smile, he was already apologising. 'I'm sorry miss … I didn't mean to surprise you.' He reached out towards her, trying to console her, but Emma only recoiled further.

'It's fine,' she stammered, scanning the courtyard behind him for Mark, realising she was trapped and vulnerable. 'Please,' she begged him, 'please don't touch me.'

The guide now looked horrified, held up his hands and started to back away. 'I'm sorry miss. I didn't mean to upset anyone.'

Mark appeared from the adjoining room. 'Oh, don't take much notice,' he said casually. 'She's always getting upset.' He flashed a smile at the relieved guide and turned his attentions towards Emma. 'Can't take you anywhere, can I?' he queried. 'Stop bothering the locals and let's get on to the next castle, shall we? Have you finished here?'

Emma paused, pulled her clothes around her and smoothed herself down. 'Yes, thank you, I'm more than finished.' She was unsettled, she was still upset, but now she was also confused. Had she misunderstood? Had she felt threatened when there was no need?

As they walked away, Mark turned towards her. 'That was a nasty thing to do.'

'He touched my back,' Emma started to tell him. 'It was inappropriate…' but she could see he wasn't listening. 'I was only defending myself.'

Mark looked straight at her. 'From what, Emma?' his voice

angry, his eyes accusing. 'What did you think he was going to do?'

Emma turned away. As they reached the car, she continued to avoid him. She was upset, confused, but now she also felt betrayed – that he could think so little of her. After all the time they had spent together, after everything she had done for him, that he could think so little of her, that he could believe that she, for no reason, would be nasty.

As they drove on, he asked several times if she was okay, but his tone still sharp and accusatory, she could hear the sarcasm, the disbelief, she knew not to trust him.

The next of the castles was small and squat, lavishly painted on the inside, and with a separate small bathhouse. Emma was glad of the distraction from her thoughts, but Mark was still enjoying his. As she sat on the bath edge, imagining the hot and steaming water, the smell of eucalyptus, the luxury and comfort, he came over and sat down beside her.

'What must it be like to be you?' he asked.

Emma looked at him, open and genuine. 'Normally, I quite like it,' she started quietly. 'Sometimes though, things get out of hand.'

'You're not kidding,' he replied quickly, his voice still full of disapproval. 'Are you going to tell me what that was about?'

Not willing to expose herself further, Emma shook her head. 'I don't think you would understand.'

'Oh,' he laughed viciously. 'I don't want to understand. I'm mostly wondering what else I can throw at you.'

Emma gave no reply. Again, she decided she'd keep her head down and then once she got home, she would leave him.

'Don't be sulking either,' he continued, as they reached the car.

'I'm not sulking,' she replied calmly.

'Well, you could try talking more. This driving with you, it's like being with a mute.'

They left Qusayr 'Amra and continued on to the town of Azraq. An oasis in the middle of the desert, the town contained a ruined black fortress, but neither were impressive, and as the light faded and temperatures dropped, it had again been a long day.

While Emma warmed herself in a hot bath, the events of the morning again overtook her. She remained distressed over Mark's betrayal, his lack of thought, his deliberate misunderstanding, and on top of the background of constant comments and criticisms, she was angry still and disappointed – angry with him for treating her badly, disappointed with herself for letting him.

After not long, Mark came to find her. He asked again if she wanted to talk, but again she refused. How could she trust him? He hugged her as she stepped from the bath, but only for a moment. Within seconds, he'd moved away.

'What are you doing?' she asked, still fragile.

'The same as you,' he replied plainly.

15

The following day, a welcome new day, they set off early for the Shaumari Wildlife Reserve, supposedly home to ostrich, onyx and gazelle, but only the ostrich were penned in, so only the ostrich were close enough to see. They spent some time watching, speaking with the ranger, enjoying a quick coffee, then set off to finish the Desert Loop and continue to Jerash.

With Mark's comments still ringing in her ears, Emma chatted throughout the whole journey, pointing out things that might be of interest, commenting on things that she could see, even reading the guidebook in places. She felt better for having slept well, and thought she might as well do what she could to try and avoid yet more complaints. Mark was also responding well – he was contributing, suggesting an interest in what she was saying, answering questions, offering opinions. Even as they left Amman and Emma was unsure of the road, he remained calm.

'Well,' he asked, 'are we on the right road?'

'I'm not sure,' she replied honestly. 'There are two of them in this direction... I'm just not sure...' She trailed off, her head in the map.

'Look, there's a sign coming.'

She looked up, but the words were in Arabic and none of them matched any of those on the map in front of her.

'Well?' He turned towards her expectantly.

Emma shrugged. 'I don't know, Mark. I can read Arabic as well as you can. I suggest we keep going on here.'

Mark continued. He might not have agreed, but he also

hadn't disagreed.

They arrived in Jerash forty minutes later without a false turn. They found the entrance to the Roman city and, relaxed and happy, they lunched in the related café, bathed in sun and surrounded by souvenir stalls. They stayed there until the trail of departing coach trippers ceased, then entered the ancient city.

Both of them were impressed by the ruins – roads with cart ruts were still intact, shop fronts could be identified, basilicas stood amid grand courtyards, the city was still so easy to see. They skipped around it for the whole of the afternoon, lounging on pedestals, striding down streets, tying their horses, adjusting togas. In temples, they calmly contemplated. In the amphitheatre, they donned masks, then sat as the audience keenly watching. It was unclear why the mood was so light – a sunny day, an interesting place, a smooth journey, a good night's sleep, but Emma didn't waste her time reasoning, she was happy just to enjoy it. When Mark was happy she loved being with him.

At the end of the afternoon, they returned to the café at the entrance to the city, and debated their next move. 'Well,' Mark started, 'I don't think we should stay in Jerash.'

'No,' Emma agreed. 'According to the book, there's nowhere even really to stay.'

'So, the Dead Sea?' he replied excitedly.

Emma paused, and thought for a second. 'I think Madaba.'

Mark's face fell slightly. 'Not the Dead Sea? We might as well?'

Emma calmly turned towards him, dragging her eyes from the scene straight in front of her. 'I think Madaba would be better.'

Mark smiled, also relaxed. 'Okay then, explain your suggestion.'

Grateful for a reasoned opportunity, Emma explained. 'If

we go to the Dead Sea from here, now, firstly we'll have to drive in the dark, and then the night will be expensive. If we stay in Madaba, we'll get there, I reckon, just before dark, we can get a room for virtually nothing, we can see the mosaics in the morning, both in Madaba and at Mount Nebo, and we'll still arrive at the Dead Sea mid-morning, for the rest of the day, without having paid for the night before.'

Mark let Emma resume her viewing of souvenir sellers, and considered. 'For once,' he grinned at her, 'you might be right. Madaba it is.'

Emma smiled. 'Come on, then. Let's go!'

As Emma predicted, they arrived in Madaba just before dark and easily found their intended hotel. They spent the evening in a nearby restaurant, making plans for the following day, until shortly after 10pm, Mark playfully chased Emma up to bed. Things were maybe not so bad.

***

The following morning they rose early and before breakfast, headed out to Macherus. A small fort on top of its own hill, perched high above the surrounding hillocks, it was beautiful first thing in the morning, quiet and peaceful, and they had it all to themselves. Yesterday's mood though, was no longer present.

As they'd left the hotel, one of the porters had stood too close and Emma had visibly prickled. 'Careful with her,' Mark had offered. 'She needs a lot of personal space.'

Emma had refused to play. She still felt sore about the previous incident, and was reminded again of Mark's lack of thought. At her refusal, he initially sulked, then soon resorted to criticism – the clothes she was wearing, her general demeanour, her quiet conversation. When they arrived at Macherus, she let him explore on his own.

They returned to the hotel for breakfast, walked into

Madaba for the mosaics, and then left for the ones at Mount Nebo. These ones were more atmospheric, clinging to a hillside surrounded by walkways and old-fashioned fountains, but in both places the mosaics themselves were tired and worn.

Shortly before lunch they arrived on the shores of the Dead Sea. They drove to a large, purpose-built resort fronted by an imposing building and fancy car park, all carefully cleaned and manicured. As they entered, the sense of grandeur only increased. A large spacious room, almost empty, they walked up to the reception desk and the two men behind it, the only two men in the entire lobby, continued their animated conversation. Emma and Mark were appalled by their rudeness. Eventually, one of the men turned aside to explain that someone would be with them shortly. Emma's disbelief was quickly turning to awkwardness. Mark's disbelief was already anger.

Emma suggested that they sat down but, agitated now beyond sitting down, Mark went instead to visit the toilets. Fifteen minutes after they'd arrived, someone finally signalled for Emma to come up to the desk. She told him that they would like a room, and then went off to retrieve Mark.

She opened the door to the toilets a crack. 'Mark? … There's someone here now.'

'Really?' he replied. 'Good for them!'

She could hear the annoyance still in his voice but refused to be equally upset. 'I'll tell them you're coming.'

Two minutes later he reappeared, conceded to talk to the man, and was offered two options – a room on the ground floor with a veranda, or one on the first floor with balcony and view. Mark gave the choice to Emma. She preferred balconies and she liked views, but she simply picked the most expensive, a choice with which Mark immediately agreed. She wondered again why price was important, why the opinions of others should matter so much, why he was reluctant to think for himself. She'd seen it before – films where his comments matched those in the paper, plays he wouldn't see for bad reviews, restaurants he wouldn't visit for bad reports.

They went to inspect the offered room, then as they returned to the front desk, Emma wanted to change her mind. She knew she shouldn't, a voice in her head was begging her not to, but she wanted to see what would happen.

The look that Mark gave her though almost destroyed her. 'Why?' he hissed, eyes flashing with anger. 'What's wrong with you now?'

'I just thought the views might be nice,' she replied cautiously.

'Well, don't just think! We've decided. We're not changing now!'

Emma tried to acquiesce, to tell him that she didn't mind, that she was happy, but he wasn't listening, his back turned towards her, his face straight ahead, immune to attack, deafened by heat, rudeness and impatience. He paid for the room in tight-lipped agitation, then marched straight to it.

Emma retrieved their bags from the car and followed him slowly. She knew she should have kept her mouth shut.

On reaching the room, Mark relaxed considerably. He unpacked his bag, arranged his belongings, until he had recovered enough to step back again into the world. Emma arranged a few of her own things, changed into her swimming costume, then patiently read her book on the veranda until he was ready. She was becoming used to waiting.

They spent the afternoon in the Dead Sea – or rather on it. The Dead Sea had been the original reason for coming to Jordan, somewhere unique, somewhere neither of them had been, something neither of them had experienced. They floated on the surface of the salty water, marvelling at the assistance beneath them. Swimming was difficult, floating on your stomach nearly impossible, but reaching your feet was easier than anything. They stayed in the water until they were past wrinkled, then spent the afternoon alternating between the small stretch of beach and back in the water. By the end of the afternoon, they were both glad that they were there.

The restaurant was also good fun. A proper resort, the restaurant was full of regulars - couples who knew each other, couples who had their own tables, who knew the waiters, who were familiar with the set-up. Mark and Emma spent the whole evening simply watching everyone else, and by the end of their dinner, most of them had been given names: Foxy, Scarlet, the Harvey Wallbangers.

The following days were then almost the same - they alternated between the beach and the Dead Sea Spa Centre and gradually relaxed and enjoyed themselves. They read, they slept, they chatted and laughed, until on their last evening, they dined well at their familiar table, took a leisurely stroll around the grounds, through warm scented airs and sparkling stars, and then, at the end of an exhausting holiday, fell asleep in each other's arms.

BRISTOL, FEBRUARY 2005

16

Almost three weeks after sending her application, Emma was invited for interview, and two days later, she was told she had been unsuccessful. She quickly consoled herself - she wasn't sure she'd have fitted either, and one interview over, she was happy to continue looking for others.

The next advertisement was particularly appealing: *Senior Researcher (Methodology speciality), The Queen's University of Belfast.*

She had always wanted to visit Belfast, but as a guest, not as a tourist. Mark had promised to take her several times, then he'd been busy or not up to it. If she applied and was asked for interview, she would be visiting as a guest.

She was also growing tired of Bristol. Her main project was nearly finished, her work was dull and repetitive, her days were dull and repetitive, and the constant rain and dark nights and mornings weren't helping. Her flat was cold, she arrived home most days cross and unhappy, she worked so hard she felt constantly tired, and she seemed to have almost no friends. Fay was away and abroad again, and Mel was too busy to spend her time chatting or, when she was free, she had others to chat to.

Emma submitted her application, and in response, some weeks later, received an invitation to Belfast. With short notice and pre-booked clients she couldn't stay for as long as she'd hoped, but she enjoyed her day, she was pleased with her interview, and the following day, she was offered the job. She accepted the next day.

She was due to start on the 1st of September. As soon as Easter was over, Emma started planning for her future life. She put her flat on the market at a price that would sell it and within a week she had a buyer. She visited Belfast to meet her new colleagues and, one month after she'd sold her flat, she found the house in Belfast she wanted to buy – a small terraced house in a beautiful street, with a long garden, all in need of some work.

Between finishing in Bristol and moving to Belfast, she arranged to stay at her gran's house in Hereford. Slowly over the intervening months, she emptied her flat, and as she packed up her lounge, she found and played Christine's CD. *'A long song,'* Christine had described it, *'a bit warbly, but beautiful if it was sung well.'* Emma listened. She could hear the beauty, but she still wasn't convinced. It mattered less, but she still felt sore, used and abused, when she was reminded of Mark.

The last three weeks in her Bristol job, Emma then took as holiday. She spent her time mostly in Hereford, lounging in the garden, visiting her gran, on day trips out to local houses, on visits to some rather grand gardens.

In August she also went to Edinburgh for the Fringe Festival. Emma loved the festival, not so much for the culture or the entertainments, for the atmosphere, for the markets and fairgrounds, the buskers and street entertainers. She stayed with friends, Janet and Michael. Janet was a friend from Emma's school days, who'd been to University in Edinburgh, been relieved from the angst of husband hunting when she met Michael, and had then simply stayed ever since.

Janet was working on the Friday, so Emma spent the afternoon happily wandering the streets and gardens, letting everything soak in. She loved being surrounded by so much life. Hereford was peaceful and pleasant and easy, but Edinburgh was lively and fun.

At ten past four she made her way to Tess's Teashop. A cosy place, full of student adverts and tatty posters, Emma ordered 'an endless pot of tea', settled on the sofa in the window, and within five minutes, Janet had arrived. She ordered a second cup for the tea and plonked herself down by Emma's side.

'I'm so tired,' she started slowly, her head resting on Emma's shoulder. 'And I know you... You'll be all lively and ready to go.'

Emma smiled. 'Absolutely! Look at it all – performance this, discussion that – how can anyone not be excited?'

Janet sighed. 'Maybe Michael will go out with you. He's here this evening but then he's away at his mother's for the rest of the weekend.' She sat up and poured out a huge mug of tea. 'He had to go some time, and this seemed like a good excuse for us to have a girls' weekend too. We could go to a show if there's any you fancy?'

Emma adjusted herself to her friend. 'That would be lovely. And if we're out tomorrow, there's no need to be out tonight as well. You're obviously tired, and it'll be nice to catch up with Michael. We can get a programme on the way home and look for something for tomorrow.'

The weekend planned, they then quickly lapsed into talk of the day, of the month, of the year, a general catch up of all that had happened since they'd last met, but only pleasant things, only good things.

By the time they'd returned to Janet's house, Michael had made most of the dinner, and for the rest of the evening, they enjoyed their meal and the company. By the evenings' end, Emma had caught up thoroughly since her last visit - stories of the new house, stories of their new life, and she'd enjoyed viewing their wedding album almost as much as they'd enjoyed showing it.

The following morning they all woke up early, Michael out of necessity, Janet and Emma partly from noise and activity, but partly from excitement for the potential day. The morning, they'd decided, they would spend shopping. Emma was keen to spend more time at the Festival stalls and Janet was hoping to make the most of a willing shopper to help her through the indecision and procrastination that clothes' selection usually entailed. Emma was only too happy to help – shopping with somebody else's money was one of her favourite pastimes.

They finished the afternoon at the travelling fairground that occupied most of Princes Street Gardens. It was a bright and clear afternoon, most of the fun came from street entertainers, comedy artists, magicians, jugglers, musicians and bands, and it was the perfect weather for sitting and watching, absorbing, but after a while, Emma grew restless.

'Come on, Jan.' She put her camera back into her bag, slipped the shoulder strap over her head and jumped up from the bench where they were sitting. 'Let's have a go on the merry-go-round.'

'What?' Janet looked at her in amazement. 'You're far too old.'

'Oh, come on.' Emma tugged at her arm. 'It looks so pretty.' She looked longingly at the fairground ride. 'They're made of fairy tales, don't you know – unicorns and flying horses. All your dreams will come true if you take a ride. You'll only miss out if you don't.'

Janet still wasn't persuaded. 'Look, okay, my dreams have come true – I married Michael. But if you like, I'll come and watch you. You can go.'

'Excellent.' Emma grinned unperturbed – a solo flight on a golden horse. She walked over, selected her steed, hopped up on its back and before long was flying round and round and up and down. Her dreams were of a new life in Belfast, a beautiful life, a beautiful house, a gorgeous garden, a lovely new man. For three solid minutes, she really was flying.

She returned to her friend, alive and enraptured. 'You

know,' she started, 'I think Belfast will be alright.'

Janet smiled. 'Good for you! … And now,' she continued, 'would you like a ride on the big wheel too?'

Emma shrugged. 'Sure, okay, if that's what you fancy.'

Janet smiled weakly. 'To be honest, I can't think of anything worse … but if you're feeling invincible … well, I can at least try.' She followed the cars as they circled from the ground to the sky. 'I've never been on a big wheel. I'm so scared of heights, but I've always thought it should be done. Every time the wheel comes, I wonder what it must be like, to see the city from that great height.'

Emma hooked her arm through her friend's. 'Well,' she smiled, 'come on, let's find out.'

For the first revolution, Janet saw nothing. As soon as she entered the car, she closed her eyes and practised her breathing. As they then rose, Emma commented on the changing sights, suggested that Janet open her eyes, but she didn't push, she guessed the process would be gradual. For the second revolution, Janet held her hand in front of her face and opened her eyes behind it. She resolutely kept looking straight ahead, at pale blue sky and then leafy green trees. By the third revolution, she was encouraged to look around more. She was impressed by Arthur's Seat rising from behind the palace, but by the time they reached the end of the ride, she couldn't wait to be back on the ground.

Emma was flattered by the trust that Janet had placed in her. Proud of her friend, she told her as much, and took her for ice creams to celebrate. It was maybe only one small step, but it was certainly one step forward.

For their evening at the festival, they went to a performance of *Shakespeare's Hamlet* in black and white mime – an interesting show, full of atmospheric music and exaggerated performances, definitely different, and to Emma it felt like true festival fare.

The following morning, they woke early to a beautiful bright and sunny day. Anxious to leave the noise of the city, they breakfasted over maps of The Trossachs and were soon on their way for a day in the hills. Two hours later, they started on the path to the top of Beinn Chabhair. The mountain top looked far away, but from the map they could see a lot of uphill walking to start, then a long stroll along the ridge to the summit. They arrived at the ridge after around two hours, and stopped for a break and a look at the view.

Emma looked at Janet sideways. 'So you're alright looking at the view from here?'

Janet laughed. 'It's hardly the same, I can't fall off here!'

Emma laughed.

'But where I *can* fall off,' Janet nodded towards the summit, 'I might not be looking at the view from there.'

'Okay,' Emma smiled. 'We'll see how we go!'

They reached the edge in under an hour, and not wanting Janet to stop and think, Emma simply continued ahead, picking their route across the widest places. Only after a while, did she turn round to check on Janet. 'Okay?'

Janet looked at her, nervously. 'Just don't ask.'

Emma continued to watch for a minute, but satisfied that Janet was at no risk, she turned to face the summit again and continued selecting the best route she could. Janet resolutely took one step at a time, following the confident blue boots ahead of her, and slowly but surely they progressed on upwards. After ten careful minutes they crossed the edge, and ten minutes later they reached the trig point, recognised themselves as at the top, and sat down at the base of the monument. Between them, they captured the world beneath them, skilfully matching the hills and villages with those on the map in front of them.

'I haven't been hiking,' Janet started thoughtfully, 'for over three years.'

'Doesn't Michael like hiking?'

'Oh, he does,' replied Janet. 'We just don't seem to find the time. First there was the wedding, and that took forever, and since then we've spent all of our time simply doing up the house. I think the last time we went hiking was just after the wedding.'

'Has it been three years since you two got married?' asked Emma, surprised.

'Three years, and it's going so well. I can't remember what life was like before I met Michael. It's so nice being so happy and settled, none of that anguish, none of that worry.'

Emma smiled, anguish and worry not her remit either.

'And things with Mark?' Janet asked timidly.

Emma turned towards her. She'd known this was coming, she knew she hadn't told Janet her news and she couldn't have simply found out. 'He died last October.'

Janet looked sympathetic. 'I thought he might have. You haven't mentioned him for ages, no trips to Oxford, no mention of Guildford, and then the move to Belfast soon. Was it very distressing?'

Emma paused and thought for a minute. 'No, not really, and to be honest, it was a relief. It sounds like such an awful thing to say, but it was obvious for ages that he wasn't going to get better, and at least he died while he was still at home, before he had to be looked after, before he lost his dignity.'

'And what about you?'

'A relief for me too.' Emma smiled. 'At least now I can somehow move on, put it all behind me.' She paused carefully. 'I couldn't even start trying before. It was such a difficult relationship, at least for me. It was so one-sided. He was always in control. He chose what we did, he chose where we went, who we saw, and so on, and so on. You can understand it - he liked to be in control, and of course, he couldn't control the cancer, so he was just trying to keep a rein on everything else.'

'But you don't like to be controlled. I can see why that might have been hard.'

Emma nodded. 'Do you know, in Jordan, we had Mark days and Emma days, in an attempt of his to keep the peace. But even then, on Mark days we did want Mark wanted, on Emma days, we did what Mark thought Emma wanted.' She smiled at the memory, an observation that hadn't escaped her at the time either.

'It must have been hard for him,' Janet suggested. 'Hard for you both.'

Emma nodded. 'It *was* hard, you know. It's taken me ages to realise that - it was hard for me too. No wonder we fell apart when we did – both of us looking after Mark, nobody looking after me.'

Janet hugged her friend, shaking her head with sympathy.

'But,' continued Emma, 'at least I came out the other side.'

'You were very good to stay for so long,' Janet continued after considering.

Emma smiled. 'You can't leave someone who's dying… Even while he was pushing me away, I wouldn't let him!'

BRISTOL, JANUARY 2003

17

Five hours after they'd left Jordan, they arrived at Heathrow, and Emma, at least, felt slightly rested. Following Mark's words from the previous flight, she had laid her head on his shoulder, put her arm around him, snuggled up and slept comfortably. Mark, by comparison, had not slept at all. Trapped in his seat by a sleeping Emma, he'd simply been unable to settle. The inflight entertainment also wasn't working, the food that was offered hadn't looked appealing, and the large Jordanians who surrounded him had clearly been up all day without a shower. For five long hours he read bits of the magazine provided by the airline, a few short chapters of his book, but for most of the time he simply wished he could go to sleep and resented those who were clearly more able.

Emma woke as they landed, stiff and wrinkled, but satisfied and slightly refreshed. She detected Mark's lack of sleep as soon as she heard his tone. She did what she could to try and appease him, kissed him good morning, straightened his hair and pressed down his shirt, collected their bags from the overhead locker, but he wasn't happy, and as they waited for their hold luggage, his mood worsened.

After a long wait, longer than she thought it should be, Emma decided to go to the office. Mark hissed and snarled for impatience, but by the time she had reached the front of the queue, he had been persuaded to join her. She looked at him enquiringly.

'The bags aren't coming,' he stated blankly. 'The word's got round.'

As they were called forward, Mark immediately began the talking, demanding to know where their luggage was, criticising and complaining. The man from the airline explained the situation, took their details and promised to send bags as they arrived. His calmness and carefulness didn't please Mark, his offers and promises weren't well received. Mark continued ranting and snarling.

Emma simply sat and watched him. She could have handled this herself. She would have handled this better. She knew there was no point in getting angry, the bags wouldn't appear for getting angry. Anger only made everything worse. Mark, though, simply couldn't be stopped, and she now knew better than to try.

As they made their way to the bus station, Emma tried to point out the positives – they had no bags to bother them, but Mark wasn't listening. He bought a newspaper, took the only empty seat in the bus shelter, and shut out the world.

Resolved not to be downhearted, Emma left him to it and sat in the next bus shelter along. At 10.55, she noticed the Oxford bus on its stand, with Mark standing beside the open door. She quickly gathered up her belongings and went to join him.

'Where the hell were you?' he snapped angrily. 'Think I'm enjoying standing here, looking like a lemon?' He turned his back and got on the bus.

Emma again was flabbergasted. She hadn't been sitting that far from him, and if he was going to get upset by losing her, he should have taken more care to start with. She quietly got on the bus behind him and sat on the double seat across the aisle. She tried to rise above it, tried to understand, the angry taunts, the petty snarls, the lack of thought. She sat calmly but she was upset.

The missing hold luggage also meant she couldn't make a

clean break. With all her belongings, she could have talked to Mark today or tomorrow, and then she could have simply left. Now her luggage, when it arrived, was going to Oxford - she'd either have to wait or come back at some other time, which would be awkward.

She returned to Bristol the following day. Without her hold luggage, she felt naked, and to make matters worse, she'd included in it, her mobile phone, so now she couldn't phone or text Mark. She emailed on Tuesday and again on Thursday. On Friday night he called from Bristol airport, on his way back to Belfast. He had her bag but he had been late, so hadn't had time to drop it off.

The following weekend, they met at The Highwayman, an inn between Bristol and Oxford. They'd arranged to meet at 6pm, and while Mark was early, Emma was half an hour late. Having underestimated her travelling time, she arrived flustered and apologetic.

'I'm so sorry,' she started, 'I thought it was closer to Bristol than this. Can I get you another drink?'

Mark shook his head. 'It was closer to Oxford than I thought as well, I've been here a while.'

'I'm so sorry,' she stated again and left for the bar. This wasn't how it was supposed to be. After no contact for the previous week, added to the holiday, Emma was ready to leave Mark, but now he had the upper hand, she wasn't sure how she should proceed. She returned from the bar, sat down at the table and wondered exactly where she should start. Mark continued reading the newspaper.

'Are you nervous for some reason?' Mark started as he looked up calmly. 'You've got that funny red blotch on your neck.'

Emma smiled and handed him the painting she'd brought with her. 'This is for you. It's for Christmas really, but you obviously couldn't have it on the day.' She left for the toilets, anxious not to need a good reaction if he didn't have one.

He unwrapped the tissue paper and saw beneath it a painting of Aqaba - the Red Sea, the waterfront, the small town – the view from their balcony, the style the same as the birthday card that had stood on his mantelpiece for so long. She'd painted it for him since they'd returned – her thoughtful present, her heartfelt present to show that she cared.

With a moment to herself, Emma wondered what she should do, how she should start, disappointed she hadn't already thought. She wanted to tell him that she wasn't happy, she wasn't coping, that somebody needed to look after her. But, she didn't want to whinge, she didn't want to fight. Anything negative wouldn't work, and she wanted to rescue their relationship if possible. She wished she'd been early, had time to relax, had time to think, to figure this out.

She left the toilets, resolved to speak to him some other time. She wasn't sure when.

As she returned to the table, Mark folded his paper, smiled up at her, and asked for her news. She left her troubled thoughts for polite pleasantries, until they had finished their drinks and it was acceptable to leave.

Out in the car park, she retrieved her luggage from the boot of Mark's car. 'Shall I see you next weekend?' she asked politely.

'I'm not sure. I think Jill is coming,' he answered plainly.

***

The following weekend, she didn't see him. She arranged instead to visit Helen. Helen was a friend from University, reassuringly always slightly later, slightly less organised, slightly less prepared than Emma. They'd spent many evenings, just the two of them, laughing and joking, sometimes over others, but mostly about themselves. Emma had been meaning to see Helen for a while, but she had always been visiting Mark.

Now that she wasn't, she was taking the opportunity.

On Wednesday evening, she telephoned Mark. In case it might not be too pleasant, assuming he even answered, she waited until she was on her way out and couldn't linger.

To her surprise, he answered quickly. 'Hi there, Em. What are you doing?'

'…Hi, I just thought I'd call and say hello.'

'It sounds very noisy. Are you outside?'

'I'm waiting for Mel. We're going to see the new film *Chicago*.'

'Oh no, rather you than me … although it has got some good write-ups.'

Emma smiled. 'Well, that's why I'm going with Mel. I didn't think it was your sort of thing!'

They chatted for a few minutes, other films they fancied seeing, other films that didn't appeal, other films with good reviews.

'Maybe you could persuade Jill?' Emma suggested.

'Jill's not coming… Maybe you could come instead?'

Emma exhaled, a mixture of disappointment and self-righteousness. 'Sorry, no. I'm going to Helen's. I might be able to call in on the way? I think my train goes through Didcot, but I do already have my tickets.'

She tried to remember her ticket times, wondering if she could squeeze in a visit. She wasn't keen, she'd made her plans, but she wished he'd mentioned the uncertainty of Jill's visit when she'd asked him before. She would have preferred to have seen him, but she wasn't messing her friend around, and a side trip to Oxford might not be easy. 'Listen though, I have to go. I'll call you if I think I can come.'

When she got home, she looked at her tickets, and after she'd thought, she was glad she hadn't agreed to visit - it would add a lot of travelling time, and some other time would be better. Maybe as well, he would learn from this and tell her his plans more clearly when she asked.

On Friday night, as she wouldn't see him, she telephoned.

'Hi there, Em. Are you on your way?'

'No.' Emma laughed, slightly confused. 'I'm not coming.' She heard the silence from the other end. 'Please don't tell me you thought I was coming? I said I'd call if I was going to, but it didn't really work, with the trains, that was all. I'd have loved to be seeing you but I'd already made the arrangements with Helen.'

'I thought you were going to stop on your way.' He sounded despondent.

Emma felt awful, but she also felt manipulated. Last weekend she'd wanted to see him but he had been awkward so she hadn't pushed. Now she could see him, if only she wasn't doing something else. And next weekend, when she was free, no doubt, he'd be busy. She reasoned she shouldn't feel bad, that he had simply made a mistake, but it didn't help, she couldn't help feeling that she'd been played.

On Saturday morning, she caught her train, to reach Peterborough at 11.40am. She was soon at Helen's, and they didn't do much for the rest of the day. They went shopping, looked around the town, and in the evening, they went to the pub with Helen's friends. It was relaxing and very pleasant. Emma loved Helen. They'd known each other for what felt like forever, didn't see each other often, but when they did, they didn't even seem to catch up, they just slotted in, back where they were.

The following day was equally relaxed. They spent the morning in front of the TV, as was Helen's habit, and then went out for Sunday lunch. Emma's train was at 3.15pm, so the pub they went to was in the town, did a wonderful roast with all the trimmings, and had a great selection of puddings.

When Emma reached Paddington, she still felt uneasy about Friday. She checked the departures board for trains to Oxford, and seeing one leaving in twenty minutes, she telephoned Mark. 'Hi,' she started as soon as he answered. 'I was wondering if you were busy this evening?'

He didn't answer.

'I'm at Paddington, I could come and see you. I feel bad about missing you on Friday… But only if you're not busy?'

'I'm not really busy, but don't worry. Maybe you could come next weekend? Call me in the week some time.'

She called in the week, but she didn't go. By the time she had called, Jill was visiting. The following weekend he was also busy, this time with Steve and Jonathan. She busied herself with things she enjoyed, and every few days she called or texted, but gradually he replied less and less, or when he did, he seemed to be busy or happy without her. She was always pleasant, hoping he was doing well, glad he was enjoying himself, but she missed him. She worried also. She wondered if he was really seeing people, or if he was hiding, or drinking too much, and getting depressed. She would know better if she could see him, but he wouldn't thank her for worrying. She wanted to see him, but she also knew that that wasn't enough, she needed him to want her too.

After a while he seemed only to text to tell her he was happy – he was going racing, walking, to the rugby, and no, she couldn't come with them as well. He texted from the airport to tell her he was going to Rome, wives and girlfriends were included, but he hadn't wanted to ask her. He was busy and he couldn't see her. He had helpers, he didn't need her. St Valentine's Day, she sent him two tickets for the ballet – something he'd said he would like to do, and in return, she'd received a drunken telephone call, but things didn't improve. Gradually everything just fell apart.

BELFAST, SEPTEMBER 2005

18

One week after visiting Janet, Emma and her cats arrived in Belfast. With her belongings packed into a transit van, her brother beside her to help with unloading, the two cats sitting next to him, they journeyed from Hereford to Belfast in one long day.

By the time they'd arrived, it was already dark. They were tired and hungry and the house was cold, but Emma was happy. Her new home was perfect - a tall Victorian terraced house in need of work and redecoration, with a long garden also in need of attention. Within years it would be beautiful. 'You know,' Emma started, a relaxed smile across her face, 'I think it's going to be okay.'

Phil nodded, left the room and returned with two cans of lager.

'I only need to stay for three years. I think I might manage.'

Phil opened his can, and held it towards her. 'To a new life in Belfast. Best of luck!'

They returned the van the following day, Emma made the trip back again in her own car, then for the next ten days she settled in. She wanted to make some changes to the house and was keen to start before she got comfortable. She spent her ten days contacting workmen, finding fittings, while also discovering her new surroundings, her neighbourhood, her new home town. Not far from the house, there were two shop-filled roads, one full of grocers and small supermarkets, the other full of craft shops and delicatessens. Emma was impressed with the choice. Her access to Belfast was also good – her closest bus stop was serviced often, or she could drive or walk in easily. Belfast too has a small city centre, populated with all the usual shops, plus a number of less common options. Interspersed with architecture, cafés and attractions, Emma liked the city. She was satisfied with her new location.

After ten days, she started work – a pleasant stroll across the park, along the river and then up through the Botanic Gardens. Her only instruction for her first day was to call on her boss at 10.30am. A calm, friendly man, he was pleased to see her, glad that she'd joined them, and within five minutes Emma felt the same. Shortly after she was introduced to the general office, taken round the corridor to her new office and introduced again to her line manager.

Jim was exactly as Emma remembered – a considerate, thoughtful, gentle man, with the same coloured soft blue eyes as Mark. Emma was left in his capable hands, so he shut up his office and took her off to morning coffee, a daily event for the whole department. The rest of the staff were also friendly, and for the rest of the week she timed her days around morning coffee. She met different people on different days depending on duties and workloads, but she was getting to know them. By the end of the week, she'd arranged her office, her computer and all her accounts were working, and she'd been invited to Wendy's house for evening drinks.

Wendy was another new colleague, a friend of Jim's who lived only five minutes from Emma.

'So,' started Jim, as Emma sat down, 'how was your first week?'

'Oh,' smiled Emma, 'I think I'll survive. Everyone's really friendly, it'll be nice to get to know them better.'

Jim smiled. 'Well, let's hope you still think that as you do!' He laughed, clearly thinking of some of his colleagues. 'But for now though, let's hear more about you.'

'There's not much to tell. I've just come from Bristol, but I come initially from Dorset.'

'And it's only you?'

'Yes, only me. Well, and two cats.'

'And what do you like doing?' He paused, expectant. 'Apart from hiking? I told you, you must meet Ann, didn't I? She's away at the moment but she does a lot of hiking, she and her fiancé William. Ann works with us, in the general office, and she and William, they go away a lot, hiking here and travelling there. They love the outdoors, and they're very nice, I think you'll like them.'

Emma was looking forward to meeting Ann. She continued talking about herself, but as soon as she could, she encouraged Jim to talk about himself instead, his life, his pastimes, his work, his town.

The following week, she felt more settled. One week down, this week, she started work proper. She still prioritised coffee and colleagues, but projects would begin shortly and she wanted to prepare for things to come, to maintain ongoing work with Bristol, and to start some new projects too.

The Friday evening, she was invited to dinner by Theresa – a friendly neighbour, a nosey neighbour, or perhaps simply an under-occupied neighbour, but Emma recognised the value of local friendship and support, and enjoyed a very pleasant evening. Theresa was a font of local knowledge.

On Sunday, she visited The Giant's Causeway. She'd visited before while house hunting, but now the place had more meaning. Stuck to her computer at work, in her line of sight on a daily basis, was a postcard from Mark of The Giant's Causeway. The message on the back: '*Way nicer than a badger, hope you get here sometime, M x*', and although he'd always promised to take her, he never had.

Mark had always liked The Giant's Causeway. It was once his special place, and now it would be her special place too. She could see Mark here, imagine his peace, imagine his pleasure, and while she was there she felt closer to him.

Sunday as well was a perfect day – bright and clear but cold with a wind, it was a true autumnal day and consequently it wasn't too busy. She walked the short path from the road to the Causeway, climbed up onto it, picked her way among the steps, and after a while she sat herself down, calmly focussed on the waves, and spoke to Mark. She could feel him here, she could hear his responses to her small worries, hear his laughter at her indiscretions. She missed him so much, she wished that she could have him back, but she felt comforted here, his ongoing presence, his ongoing care.

One month later, she missed him so much she took the day off. Exactly one year ago, he had died.

She rose and set off for work as usual, but as she crossed the park, thinking of him, wishing he was still with her, she changed her mind about going to work, and veered instead to the cafés on the main road. As she ambled up the familiar street, tears began trickling down her face, the ring on her finger twisting and turning. She missed him so much. She wished that she could have him back, just for a while, just for a single conversation.

She recovered enough to order a coffee – no, a hot chocolate, with whipped cream, marshmallows and a flake, but not enough to stem the tears that ran for the time it took her to drink it. Sometimes she still couldn't believe he was gone. She didn't still see him, not anymore, but if he'd walked in, she wouldn't have been surprised. She missed him most when she felt alone – cold and wet waiting for the bus, tired and walking home in the dark, weekends her family were having without her. She still wondered what he would do when she got stuck, what he would say, what he would offer. She comforted herself by feeling him near her, watching her, by revisiting the times they had had together, the things he did to make her smile, the things he had said to make her laugh.

By the time she had drained her chocolate cup, she felt better. Calm and relaxed, she ambled slowly round the shops near the café, the boutiques and craft shops of the Ormeau Road. Mark had always liked nice things. One burgundy scarf and a sequined purse later, she headed back home, the danger over one more time.

BRISTOL, NOVEMBER 2002

19

They decided on Jordan one weekend in Bristol.

Mark had come to visit her. 'It's unfair for you to always be travelling,' he'd said when she'd called, 'and I'd like more of a look round Bristol… Anyway, I want to talk to you about your email.'

Emma had agreed readily, trying to remember the contents of her email. As she hung up, she realised with a smile - the suggestion of a holiday at Christmas. She'd been thinking about it for a while because of the way Christmas would fall, so last week she'd agreed it with her boss, then sent the email. She hadn't really thought Mark would be able, with treatment and other commitments, but it would still be a nice thought.

She continued with her evening out, but as she neared the pub for the Tuesday night quiz, she sent him a text: *So? Where do you want to go?*

For the rest of the evening, her phone was turned off. She checked for messages on her way home, then several times the following day. Eventually, while she was walking home, a message arrived: *New Zealand.*

After all the hope, the anticipation, she was suddenly brought back down to earth: New Zealand, the current home of Virginia Lovett. Emma knew the way Mark talked about her, she'd seen the messages he'd received, he'd even shown her his replies - all so admiring, so complimentary, all so lustful.

Emma despised Virginia Lovett. She was pretty, younger, and she worked in Mark's Institute so she had every excuse to see him, every opportunity to dazzle him. Emma was jealous, so jealous of Virginia Lovett, and she knew Mark knew. From the very first time that he'd talked about her, he'd seen the green spark in Emma's eyes, and from then on she had never been sure how much was real, or how much was just to taunt her. A genuine desire? Or was it a game to keep him amused? She tried not to react, but her face usually gave her away. Either way, she was not trekking halfway around the world to spend her Christmas side-lined by Virginia Lovett. She didn't text back.

The following day, she still hadn't replied.

'Christine,' she started, as she heard her colleague preparing to leave, 'if your boyfriend was about to die, would you let him spend his last Christmas with his favourite woman instead of you? Actually, no, as well as you? Would you trek halfway round the world with him, just to spend your Christmas with her?'

'Certainly not!' Christine cried in horror. 'No, not at all. It's a cheek of him to even ask.'

'But if it were his last Christmas? If that was the one thing you could do?'

'He shouldn't have asked,' she replied promptly. 'He shouldn't be messing around with you.'

Emma still wasn't too sure, but grateful for Christine's conviction, she texted Mark that afternoon: *It's an awful long way for only 3 weeks.*

Four hours later, she received a reply: *And your choice would be?*

Emma smiled. *Russia? Morocco? Mehiho?*

***

Emma was ready when Mark arrived. In her enthusiasm to see him, she'd rushed through her last pieces of work and by the time his car purred down the road, she was sitting on the wall outside her building, patiently waiting. He stopped briefly to let her get in, then continued on to the Black Boy Inn. Undeterred, she knelt comfortably on the seat beside him, put her arm round his neck, kissed him heavily on the cheek and whispered that she was glad to see him. He made no reply but she could see the smile on his face.

They parked alongside the Black Boy Inn, spent three hours watching the rugby, then looked around for somewhere to eat. Fishworks was opposite, but it wasn't a Fishworks kind of night, they had already had too much to drink. Instead, Emma suggested the curry house at the end of her road, so they left the car and set off walking. All the way there they talked of dinner, of what they might have, what they most hoped for, until they were a short distance away and Mark complained of being starving.

'Come on then,' Emma started, a cheeky grin across her face. 'I'll race you there.' She took off up the steps ahead, and he followed her closely until his lack of fitness caught up with him. But instead of letting her win fairly, he reached out, caught her, and dragged her to a stop.

'You cheat,' she screamed, amid fits of giggles. 'I don't believe it! one little race!'

They reached the Aga Khan, still giggling. Decorated in gold and red, with plenty of pictures of Indian gods, it was dimly lit, but resonated loudly with the sounds and smells of an Indian restaurant. They ordered in the waiting area, twittering and fidgeting, and then were shown to a secluded booth.

'I feel like I'm on a first date,' Mark whispered, as they took their seats.

Emma giggled in agreement. 'So,' she started once she'd recovered, 'you don't fancy Russia, Morocco or Mehiho?'

'Oh, *Mexico*,' Mark laughed out loud. 'I recognise it now that you say it. I was looking at your text with no idea where

Mehiho was. They don't say it like that, surely?'

'They do,' Emma grinned, pleased to know something that he didn't.

He shook his head. 'Not Russia – it'll be far too cold and I want relaxing. Not Morocco either ... better, but I went there not that long ago. It's nice, you'd like it, you should go, but not with me ... at least, not now. Mexico...' He put his head on one side and slowly helped himself to more rice. 'Maybe ... I've never really thought about it. Is there much to do apart from beaches?'

Emma laughed. 'I thought you said you wanted relaxing!'

'Yeah, but not boring.' He could see she was about to interject. 'And I don't want you getting bored, either. That'd be even worse!'

Emma laughed. 'Absolutely!' She helped herself to more of the banquet. 'Anyway, I've been thinking. I assumed Mexico would be no good, otherwise I thought you might have replied, and we need to go somewhere interesting and somewhere neither of us have been before. My brainwave,' she paused for dramatic effect, 'is the Dead Sea.'

Mark looked at her, the idea slowly sinking in.

She continued. 'It's not too far, it should be warm, it'll be relaxing but there will be things to do, neither of us have been before and it'll be different. Haven't you ever wanted to give it a go?'

'Are you thinking for all of the time that we have? From Christmas and on past New Year?'

Emma stopped and thought a little. 'I don't know... I don't know what they do for Christmas, but we could easily find out. So long as we have accommodation, we should be okay.'

Mark continued eating slowly. 'The Dead Sea would be excellent, good idea, but not for Christmas. An all-inclusive resort for Christmas? Somewhere on the Red Sea? There must be some.'

Emma inhaled sharply. 'I could go diving.' She looked up, excited. 'Red Sea diving is amazing … and you could snorkel or just sunbathe if you don't want to come diving too. It would be relaxing. Oh yes, let's go there.'

Mark leant across the table, slowly stroked his hand under her eager face and smiled gently. 'Why not, my love? And then the Dead Sea for New Year!'

BRISTOL, JULY 2002

20

Emma had moved to Bristol several months earlier, at the beginning of July.

She arrived in Bristol on a Wednesday morning at 10.34am, with no more of her life's possessions than a rucksack of clothes and some toiletries. Before she had even stepped off the train, she received a text from him: *You didn't say good bye!*

Emma replied as soon as she saw it: *I wasn't leaving. I'll be back before you know it!* She could almost feel the smile on his face as he read the message.

This weekend?

Next weekend. This weekend Cornwall to collect the car. Is next weekend OK?

Any time is fine, you have your own key.

The rest of her day passed very well. The first day of a new job, she felt confident and enthusiastic. She'd wanted to work at the University of Bristol for a long time, she'd been looking forward to moving there, and her new job was exactly what she wanted – Research Nutritionist in the Medical Sciences. She would spend her time between seeing clients and conducting research, helping with problems and making discoveries.

'First days' she also always enjoyed – the intrigue of meeting new people, the excitement and trepidation of the unknown, a pressure only to be nice, no pressure to be anything more. She had a meeting with her new boss, someone she already knew, met the rest of the team, rearranged her office, met her new office mate. Late afternoon, she was about to go home to investigate her new living place too, when Mel came up from the office downstairs. 'A quick introduction to the local bar?'

Five minutes later they were in The Blue Room - a basement bar with funky blue lighting and cool décor, at that hour, almost empty. They ordered two glasses of red wine, and within thirty minutes, they'd finished those, and Mel had returned to the bar for a bottle. Emma liked Mel. She was chatty, fun and very keen on drinking wine.

At the end of the same week, exactly as planned, Emma went to Cornwall to collect her car and the associated freedom. The following week then passed quickly. She started getting busier with work, but she was also keen to make the most of her time in Bristol. She had lunches with colleagues, tried new cafés for morning coffee, on Tuesday she went with Mel to the pub quiz, she went to the library, she joined the gym, she took an interest in lunchtime classes.

Every evening she texted Mark. Little messages, that was all, to show that she cared, to show that she was thinking of him.

Every so often she also called. She loved his voice, his soft and gentle Northern Irish voice, and she preferred talking than sending texts, but he rarely answered her calls. She didn't even really expect it.

At the end of her second week she returned to Oxford. Having not seen Mark for the past ten days, she was excited. She arranged to finish work at 4pm, to then be in Oxford by 6pm, but midway through the morning she decided she'd rather wear a short skirt than jeans, to impress Mark with her beautiful legs. She returned home at lunchtime, but despite spending as little time as she could, she was then back at work late by twenty minutes. She finally arrived at Bristol train station just in time for the train at 5.30pm, to discover it late, the platform crowded and impatient. As she stood with the rest of them, fidgeting eagerly, her telephone rang and Mark's name flashed up.

'Hello,' she started brightly, the pleasure of his call obvious in her voice. 'How are you?'

'I'm alright,' he responded. 'I'm just wondering where you are? Are you nearly here?'

'No, I'm sorry, I'm still in Bristol. The train is delayed. It should be here shortly, and then I'll be with you in almost an hour. Go have a pint – I'll be there before you know it.'

'I've already had one. Just make sure you get here soon.'

An hour later, she stepped off the train, glided down Mill Street, and as soon as she knocked, Mark opened his front door. She stepped into the hall and reached up to kiss him. 'Hi,' she smiled. 'I'm sorry I'm late.'

He bent down to kiss her gently, encircling her waist with his strong arms. 'Well, you're here now.' He smiled as his eyes moved from her smile to her shoes. 'And with you looking so good, I think we should go straight back out again.' He reached for his coat and held out his bent arm. 'Madam,' he nodded to his arm with a slight bow. 'Anywhere in particular for dining?'

'Hmmm,' she replied and smiled thoughtfully, 'I'd just like to dine where you're dining.'

They set off together into Oxford, a familiar route, a familiar pattern and went again to eat at the Captain's Rose. They spent the evening very much as they had before, talking, laughing, joking, storytelling. Emma told Mark of her new job in Bristol, her new colleagues, and her new home. Mark was interested in the pubs she had been to, the cafés she'd visited, but in only two weeks and without a weekend, she didn't have very much to report. She asked him instead of the pubs he had been to, the cafés he'd visited, and he, by comparison had been to hundreds, none of them unfamiliar to her, but she was glad he was getting out. He told her too, of his walks along the river, round Wytham Woods, of the new friend he'd made

119

while playing golf - someone else who was playing alone, but who seemed to be playing remarkably slowly in order that Mark should catch him up. Emma laughed. She loved his stories, his small observations, and she loved the way he liked telling her, fuelled by her interest, her disbelief and outspoken objections, her untamed laughter.

When they got home they separated only for Emma to pour them two glasses of port, while Mark took her weekend bag upstairs and placed it neatly inside his room.

The rest of the weekend was then much the same as those they'd enjoyed before Emma had moved, with only a few small exceptions. Saturday morning, Emma was still up before Mark, she still did the washing up while making the tea, but then she took her cup along with his, back to his room and carefully climbed back into bed. They still walked into Oxford for brunch, via the river and Christchurch Meadows, but this time all the way they were jostling, giggling, and laughing. They still chose the same scrambled eggs and mushrooms, still read the newspapers, enjoyed extra coffee, but once they had finished, they didn't float lazily round the bookshops, not quite sure of what to do, they went back home full of plans for the day and the whole weekend.

That afternoon, they went to the cinema. As part of her taking care of Mark, Emma wanted to introduce him to afternoon cinema and the option of going by himself. When Emma had told him she was leaving Oxford, one of the downsides he'd expressed was that he'd miss going to the cinema. Emma was astounded when he'd first said it. 'Why can't you go to the cinema?'

'I can't go by myself, can I? I'd look like a right twat, sat by myself with no-one to talk to.'

Emma laughed, 'You're not supposed to be talking!' She stopped laughing and added seriously, 'Of course you can go by yourself, loads of people do. You just have to go at the right time or to the right films.' She paused and continued softly, 'I used to go by myself all the time, in Guildford, at around 6pm. After an afternoon shopping, and loaded with bags, why on earth would I be with anyone else? It was great too – I could see what I wanted, have it last in my head for as long as I liked, and when I got home, I still had the whole evening ahead of me and didn't have to be out in the cold.'

Mark looked at her blankly. 'Some people prefer being out in the evening.'

But she wasn't about to be deterred. 'We'll try it some time, a weekday afternoon or early on a Saturday. It's great, you'll see.'

Dirty Pretty Things was the perfect film for it - slightly arty, slightly off beat, shown in the arty, off-beat cinema in Jericho. The audience was small, but at least a third of them were by themselves.

'I'm sure you could go to other films too. The more mainstream ones just take a little more bravado.' She smiled as she said it and turned her head away, a cunning smile, the comment a challenge more than a suggestion.

The following day, the skies were clearer, so Mark took Emma to the Uffington White Horse, a large chalk horse drawn in the hillside not far from Oxford. A bright day, but windy, it was cool as they picked over the chalk figure and walked the circle of the hill fort above it, Emma skipping over the tops of the ridges, Mark walking around the bottom beneath her. As they'd done in Paris when they'd stood looking at Foucault's exhibition, they spent their time wondering how life would have been, how they would have lived, what they would have done, none of it based on actual knowledge, instead from snippets from magazines, assisted by two imaginations.

On their way home, they stopped in the Bear and Ragged Staff, for a large Sunday lunch of roast beef and gravy. There was then just time for a quick cup of tea before Emma's train took her back to Bristol.

'Will you come again next weekend?' Mark asked.

Emma turned to look at him with a slow smile. 'Would you like that?'

'Yes, I would.' His hand trailed down her side as she collected her bag from the bottom of the stairs. 'I really enjoyed this weekend.'

Emma smiled. 'Me too.' She turned her head up to the sky as if she were thinking. 'I'll tell you what, I'll come next weekend, provided we can go to Newbury races.'

'You mean to the horses?' a hint of surprise sounded in his voice.

'It'll be fun,' she answered him. 'I haven't been for ages.'

Mark looked at her, unable now to conceal his surprise. 'Can't say I've ever been, but I guess I could give it a go. I suppose it will be something new.'

'Excellent. They're on Saturday afternoon, and it'll be easy to go from here. I'll see you next Friday night.' She reached up and kissed him quickly on the cheek. 'Hopefully at around the same time.'

21

The week in Bristol passed much the same as the previous one and before she knew it Emma was back on the train to Oxford. This time she didn't specify the train and instead texted Mark once she was seated to let him know her arrival time.

Within three minutes, she received a reply: *In Rosie's. Abrupt. 5 letters?*

Pleased to have something to do on the train, she thought for a while: *hasty? rapid?*

No, h second

She thought again but soon gave up: *don't know, something else please*

Insatiable, 8 letters

Again she thought and again she gave suggestions, but again none of them were suitable. They continued then until Emma arrived. As the train pulled into the station, she sent one final text: *Still in Rosie's?*

He replied straight away: *Right hand door.*

Rosie O'Grady's was a traditional Irish pub, and a regular haunt of Mark's. He liked a pint, just one before dinner, and Rosie's sold the best Irish bitter and best Irish banter in Oxford he said.

A five-minute walk from the station, Emma entered through the right-hand door and sidled up to the group of three men at the end of the bar. 'Finished it then?'

'No.' He handed her the newspaper, lifted his pint and nodded to a full one beside him. 'Cheers! Good to see you.'

Emma nodded and lifted her pint glass. 'Cheers. And look,'

she pointed to the top of her pint, 'no shamrock – I must be a local, if the shamrocks are for tourists.'

Mark smiled. 'No, I bought it, and I'm a local!'

They drank their pints sitting at the bar, then slowly walked back to Mark's house. By the time they got there, he had dinner all planned and was happy then to busy himself, while Emma sat on the kitchen stool chatting away about her week, asking him also about his. He spent his time focussed on the cooking – cutting, chopping, warming, softening, but she didn't mind, she just carried on, and she could tell that neither did he. After half an hour, she went to lay the dining table, and they spent the evening, bathed in candlelight, dining on salmon, coffees and whisky, surrounded by a full orchestra.

The following morning, Emma was up early and soon collecting the newspaper. As they sat at the breakfast bar, each flicked through the sections most interesting - Mark the news and then the sport, Emma the horse-racing, then the crossword. By the time Mark had surfaced from the sports pages, Emma had looked through the horses, abandoned the last of the crossword clues and was ready for a quick walk for some groceries.

'How long is it to Newbury racecourse from here?' she asked as she put on her jacket.

'40 mins,' he replied distractedly.

'So if the first race is at 12.50 we need to leave at around 12.10, plus some time to find somewhere to park, and for a bit of a look in advance. Half past eleven? 11.45?'

'Half past eleven. You'll be fine, you have almost an hour.'

Their journey to Newbury was quicker than expected, but the traffic when they got there was far worse, and for thirty minutes they scarcely moved, Emma fidgeting, easily anxious, Mark enjoying the radio. He tried to calm her, but to no avail, and at 12.45 they were still sitting in a queue of cars.

They finally arrived at around one o'clock. They'd listened

to the first race in the car and Emma was grateful of the money she had unwittingly saved, but they were quick to place bets for the second race. Emma was keen not to miss out on any more of the fun, and was perfectly confident one could pick a winner based purely on a name – *No. 4. Lady Lolita.* She scanned the trackside bookmakers, settled on odds of 8–1, then returned to the place where she had left Mark. 'What did you go for?'

'Albacazham, 5–1, good write up as far as I can see.'

'No, Lady Lolita, a much better option. Never pick a horse where you can't pronounce its name.'

Mark laughed. 'What kind of a rule is that? And anyway, I can pronounce the name, Albacazham.'

Emma smiled at him knowingly. 'Well, we'll see … and while we're waiting, let's go find the paddock. There's not really time for a drink before the race, and I love the paddock. It is better to choose your horses based on looks really … rather than names.'

Mark looked at her with a smile. 'Oh, is that right?!… Come on then, let's go find the paddock.'

They reached the paddock just in time to see the horses leaving, then quickly moved to the top of the grandstand. It was busy but not crowded, and they easily found somewhere with a good view of the whole course. Within five minutes, the race had started.

The horses exited the starting gates on the far side. Glancing between the track and the big screen, Mark and Emma tried to glimpse the horses that they had backed. As they came around the corner and flashed past the grandstand, the two out in front were easy to distinguish, but all of the others were a short blur. Both of the horses that they had backed were somewhere mid-blur. As the horses travelled on, they listened intently for snatches of names. The trailing body gradually closed on the two front runners, and they continued together as they rounded the far side of the course. Only as they started returning, did they start to separate. At the final approach, two of the horses were clearly ahead. The crowd willed them on, until they fought it out as they came to the grandstand. The winner by a short head was Albacazham – the horse backed by Mark. Emma's horse came in a miserable fourth.

Emma's disappointment was easily overridden by the excitement of the finish and her happiness for Mark. She stood on tiptoe and quickly kissed his cheek. 'Congratulations. How much did you win?'

He beamed contentedly. 'Fifty quid. Not bad for starters.'

'Not bad at all,' she smiled in return. 'A drink, I think, to celebrate. I'm assuming you're buying!'

They visited the bar, then returned to the stand for the next two races, Emma occasionally running down to the bookmakers. In both these two races, she backed favourites, based on the name, and the favourite won. Mark lost on favoured outsiders. He wasn't quite as gracious as she'd been on losing, but congratulated her none-the-less and sent her off to collect her winnings.

Following two losses, made even worse by Emma's two wins, Mark sloped off for a further pint, consoled by the fact that she'd only backed favourites so hadn't won much. Emma instead went to the paddock to view the horses for the next race. She picked her horse, a fine looking brown, placed bets for them both, and returned to the bar to find Mark seated, and aiming to stay and watch on the TV. Not to go far, she watched the race, this time, from the rail, enthralled by the proximity of the horses, the speed with which they travelled past her.

Neither Emma nor Mark backed the winner that time, and as she turned her back on the course and the horses, Emma saw Mark quickly coming toward her. 'No luck that time. Were you watching inside?'

'Yeah, started heading out as everyone else started heading in.'

Emma laughed at his dispirited face, and took hold of his hand. 'Come on, there's still one more race to go.'

He looked straight at her, his eyes shining, with love, gratitude, peace, fatigue, she wasn't sure. Slowly he hooked his arm inside hers. 'Alright then, let's go to the paddock. You've got one last chance to show me your system.'

'A long-legged skinny one, that's what we need for a long race like this one, one that looks like a marathon runner.'

Mark laughed quietly, and looked at her sideways. 'I can see I might need some convincing!'

They waited at the paddock as the horses filed in and circled in front of them. Emma admired them greatly - their speed and power, their grace and perfection. Mark was more interested in reviews and cast them only a glance as he emerged from the programme. After five minutes, their horses chosen, they set off again for the bookmakers and the top of the grandstand – 'Seadart' for Emma, 'Devil's Soldier' for Mark.

They stood to watch in their earlier position – a long race, almost twice round the course, but all the action in the closing stages. They gazed after the horses as they sped away, ran along the long stretch on the far side, and then gradually started returning. They flew past the grandstand on their first circuit, all closely packed. They continued the same for the next half lap, but then as they rounded the far bend, an order clearly began to emerge. Mark's horse was also now looking good. Sat back in sixth for the journey so far, he was still going strong, riding on now in a comfortable third. Emma's horse was still back in eighth. As they started coming closer, the distances between them also became clear. As they rounded the final bend, two horses were in front – 'Aztec Blue' and 'Cardinal's Bay', with Mark's horse only slightly behind. They pounded on towards the grandstand, then all of a sudden, as if from nowhere, the third horse came through between the others. For a flash of a second all three horses were running together, then before anyone was aware it was happening, Devil's Soldier was clear of the others, galloping as if he had just started. As they came to the finish line, Devil's Soldier was a clear winner, Cardinal's Bay a courageous second, losing by only half a length, and fourteen lengths ahead of Aztec Blue.

Quietly confident for the whole race, Mark was overjoyed. He tried not to show it, but Emma could tell. He accepted her congratulations without remembering she had a horse too, boasted about his system, which was still a mystery, and swaggered off to collect his winnings. Emma was pleased, and not only for him - had he not won, or worse if she had won instead, he would have been sulking all night. He was still grinning when he returned.

'Well then, how much did you get?'

'£80. Better, I think, than £15 and ... £20, was it? Was that what you won?'

Emma laughed. 'It's not about the money though, is it?'

'Of course it's about the money... What else is it about?'

Emma stopped and looked at him carefully, not sure he could really be asking. 'It's about the game. It's about winning, it's about being right... It would be just as much fun without the betting, the betting just makes it more important.'

Mark looked at her as if her words might be worth considering, but not right now. 'Well you celebrate winning if you like, don't think you'll be spending my money!'

They stopped on the way home for a quick drink, a need more for warmth than for alcohol, and decided to celebrate the following day with a walk in the morning and big Sunday lunch. The evening they spent as they had before, dining by candlelight, surrounded by music.

For Emma, it had been a perfect day. She loved Mark more than she could imagine. It wasn't just that he was fun to be with. He made her feel special. He looked out for her, he protected her, but he didn't smother, he didn't need her. She could be herself, except with him, she was more than herself, she sparkled and shone with brilliance and love.

The following day they did exactly as planned. They were out of the house by 10.30am, and walked along the river, across the meadows and on up into Wytham Woods. It was a beautiful summer's day, warm and breezy, with a few clouds, but only a few. Two hours later, they arrived at The White Hart in perfect time for Sunday lunch. They took a table in the dappled shade, ordered roasts and settled to read while they were waiting. Before long they were feasting on pork and summer puddings, animated by memories of the day before, coupled with reviews and tales from the newspapers.

Satisfied, some hours later, they returned to their route, took the track through the fields and finished their circuit at the bridge outside Oxford from where they'd started.

Back at the house, with half an hour until the train to Bristol, Emma went upstairs to pack her belongings. Mark came up behind her, put two cups of tea on the top of the bookcase, sat behind her on the bed, and leant back to sprawl his upper body over the duvet. She twisted round, stroked the side of his face and bent down to kiss him lightly. As she straightened, he looked at her calmly. 'We never talk, you and me.'

Emma looked at him, questioningly. 'Yes, we do. What do you mean?'

'Not about important things... We never talk properly.'

Emma looked at him, still not really sure what he was asking. 'OK, well, what would you like to talk about?'

'Children? Contraception?'

'I didn't think we'd need to,' she said carefully, 'with the chemotherapy.' She was trying to be sensitive, trying to be tactful.

'Well, no-one's said anything to me.'

'Okay,' she replied. 'But we can't really talk about these things now, I have to catch a train in ten minutes.' She noticed the disappointment on his face. 'Do you really want to talk about these now?' she asked softly. She could catch a later train if she had to.

He smiled up at her, still half lying across the bed, his hand stroking the bottom of her arm. 'No, you catch your train.'

'We'll talk properly next weekend.' She stood up and quickly kissed him on the cheek. 'I'll call you in the week.'

22

She called on Tuesday night as she'd promised, and as was becoming more frequent too, Mark answered quickly. 'Hello, only me... I thought I'd phone to talk about contraception.'

She heard his sigh at the other end. 'Oh no, not now. Let's not talk about dull things. Tell me something interesting.'

Emma smiled at his contradiction, but she knew she would be accused again. She didn't have anything interesting to say, but made something up to play the game. At the end of her story, she didn't forget. 'We'll talk properly, at the weekend, when I can see you.'

'Are you coming here?'

'I thought I might. Are you doing something else?'

'I thought I might go to Bristol. The London Irish are playing in Gloucester, a charity match or something like that, to keep them busy over the summer. I could come down on Friday, you can show me Bristol, then we can go to the game from there.'

Emma shrugged, happy to be given her plans for the weekend, happy to feel he was making an effort. 'OK,' she smiled.

On Thursday lunchtime, though, she received a text: *Please call re weekend, poss change of plan, M.*

With slight trepidation, she rang him later. 'Hi,' she started as soon as he picked up, 'is everything okay?'

'Hi, yes, fine. I was wondering if you'd mind not meeting this weekend, after all?' He sounded concerned. 'I'm really sorry. I'd half arranged for Steve to come over, and first he couldn't make it, but now he can. I'd rather see you, but he's arranged it all with his partner, and he thinks he's coming.'

Emma relaxed. 'Of course I don't mind. I can spend some time in Bristol myself. I'll find some good places for when you do come.'

'Are you sure? It's only because he's already agreed things with his partner.'

Emma laughed softly. 'Honestly, I don't mind. You have a good weekend with Steve. I'll just see you next weekend instead.'

She walked home slowly, planning her weekend in Bristol alone.

Not for long though. Within thirty minutes, she received another text: *Change of plan again. Steve not coming. Coming to Bristol. See you tomorrow. M.*

Confused but pleased, she replied quickly: *OK, excellent, see you tomorrow, E x.'*

The following afternoon she received a text at about 4 o'clock for directions and then another, nearly two hours later, announcing his arrival: *Here now, looking for mischief.*

Emma smiled as soon as she saw it, and called him immediately. 'Hello, here where?'

'In Bristol, of course,' came the reply.

'No, whereabouts? Are you at the Uni'?'

'I've parked on your road, and I'm just going for a quick explore.'

'Okay, I'll be about half an hour. Can you be back then?'

Thirty minutes later the buzzer sounded, and as she opened the door, Mark stood beaming down at her. She reached up to kiss him, honoured that he had taken the time to drive down to see her. 'Thanks for coming.'

That evening they went to eat at Fishworks. Decorated blue and white, with an open and airy atmosphere, the front of the restaurant was lively and noisy, but they were quickly taken to the back of the room where the atmosphere was quiet and romantic. The menu was crowded with mouth-watering dishes, the wine list full of expensive tastes. They both loved it. Mark loved the luxury, the expense, the grandeur. Emma loved the elegance, the simplicity, and the simple fact that she was with Mark. She loved him, and in a place like this he would be happy.

As they sat opposite each other awaiting their drinks, she looked at him carefully, and as she did, he reached across the table to take her hand, his eyes full of love and kindness. She smiled in response and entwined her fingers with his. 'I'm glad you could come.'

The following morning, they also ate out. A frequent fan of brunch in a café, a new city full of new cafés was an invitation for Mark. They drove into the city and Mark selected Le Chat Noir, a small stylish café looking perfect for brunch. They ate as was their custom in Oxford, then sauntered down the hill, turned their steps to the right and perused the shops and pubs on the quayside.

Purely by chance, they arrived just in time for the next harbour cruise. Interested in boats, Mark suggested they cruise, and always happy to try new things, Emma agreed. It was windy and the cruise was cold, but they huddled together, a witty commentary their constant companion, and both of them enjoyed it.

From the quayside, they left for Gloucester. As they drove the short distance up the motorway, Mark explained the rules of rugby, told her tales of the games he'd attended, large internationals where scores really mattered, and taught her one of the Irish songs. Emma, as ever, enjoyed his stories, laughed along where she was supposed to, asked him questions where they might help her. She had trouble grasping the song but he enjoyed repeating it, and she was happily making him laugh.

They found the ground easily, and as Emma climbed out of

the car, Mark went round and opened the boot. 'I've brought you a present.'

'Excellent,' Emma grinned, playing along.

'Now don't get too excited. Would you rather the green or instead, the white?'

She tried to see over his shoulder, but the boot was dark and he wouldn't let her. 'Green, I think please.'

He pulled a green Irish rugby shirt from his bag and held it towards her. 'Well, you've got to look the part.'

'Thanks,' she replied, glad she hadn't been expecting a real present. 'I'll put it on over my cardigan.'

Mark watched her struggle to pull the shirt on top of her other clothes. 'You don't have to wear it… Only if you want to… You do look a bit silly and you might get into trouble.'

'No, it's fine, I won't get into trouble. It'll keep me warm if the skies cloud over, and you're right, I've got to look the part.'

'I don't think I'll wear mine,' he hesitated.

'Well, I'm not taking this off now!' Slightly wary in case she did attract trouble, she jammed her cap back on her head and stood waiting. He leant over, quickly kissed the side of her face, then locked the car and was ready.

They strode in with the other supporters, purchased their pints, and chose a position near the middle of the pitch, a few rails back. In the minutes before kick-off, Mark pointed out the London Irish team, told her who to watch and what to look for.

The action started as the whistle blew. Within seconds, the Gloucester team had taken possession of the ball and were charging towards the far end of the pitch. The London Irish defended well and were quickly also part of the game. Mark explained scrums, conversions, line outs, Emma shouted when she saw fit. By the half-time whistle, the score was 13–5 to Gloucester. The Gloucester side were clearly better but the London Irish were fighting hard.

As the game wore on, the action reduced. Tired players kicked the ball back and forward, up and down, the game dominated by line-outs and throw-ins. Despite her extra rugby shirt, Emma was also getting cold. The stand had been shady all afternoon, and the air temperature was cooler than she'd expected. Standing behind Mark, she put her arms around him, gently stroking the tops of his thighs, resting her chin on his shoulder. The final score was 18–10 to Gloucester.

They returned to Oxford for the evening. As they came to a stop outside the house, Mark leant over. 'Thanks for coming, I enjoyed this afternoon.' He gently stroked the side of her face and moved closer.

Emma watched him as she undid her seatbelt, and he became suddenly trapped in by his. She laughed promptly and kissed him on the end of his nose. 'No problem, gorgeous. I enjoyed it. Thanks for taking me.'

They spent the evening enjoying Mark's cooking, then slipped upstairs for an early night. The following morning they woke up early, made love again and again and again, and then slept in until late morning. It was 11.30am when Emma crept out of bed, keen to let Mark continue sleeping, but by the time she was back with her cup of tea, he had woken. She climbed back in next to his warm body, and he lay there calmly, his head on her stomach, his hand gently stroking her thigh.

At the end of her drink, they showered together. Hard and fast, the heat of the water pounded their bodies. As they stood together, screeching and giggling, Mark washed Emma's hair, his hands immersed in the thick curly mass, glued together with shampoo. 'Do you mind?'

'No, of course not. And if you kiss me here at the same time' – she pointed to the side of her neck, 'I'll let you do it every day.'

In return, he wouldn't let her wash him. Still embarrassed

135

by his lack of body hair, he was happier looking after her.

The rest of the day they spent in the city, sitting in cafés or standing in bookshops, until, at 4pm, Emma collected her bag, kissed her lover goodbye and caught her train back to Bristol.

BELFAST, SEPTEMBER 2006

23

One week in Belfast, one month in Belfast, quickly turned into one year. Work was going well. For the most part, Emma enjoyed her job, and the parts she wasn't sure of, she treated as a challenge. Her house and garden were also progressing - she'd fixed the roof and leaking drainpipes, installed fireplaces, re-plastered rooms, she'd ripped all the plastic out of the garden, planted fruit bushes, her favourite flowers, and slowly, but surely, the place was beginning to feel like hers. She knew her local shops well now too, she knew the town centre, she enjoyed the theatre, the evening entertainments, all of the options for Sunday visits.

She'd been back to Bristol twice since she'd left it, once to see Simon, Professor Stein, and once to see Fay for a weekend away. The visit to Simon was quick, mid-week, purely for work, but one side of work she was happy to do. Like the trips she'd made before she'd worked there, she'd enjoyed the inspiring walk up Park Road, the welcome greetings and smiles of Simon – a respected professional, so much busier than she was, but always happy to take her to lunch, and she loved the old college canteen, the high ceilings, the tall windows, the gentle palms reaching far above them. It reminded her of the Grand Café.

The visit to Fay, she made twelve months later, when she was more open to clear reminders. She arrived on a Friday at lunchtime, and while Fay still had to finish work, Emma spent the afternoon visiting the road on which she used to live. The middle of the day, she was in no danger of meeting anyone, so she calmly stood, looking down the Georgian terrace, tired and worn, the uneven pavement, the jammed-in old cars. The things that used to make it charming, that used to make it feel like home, now tired and shabby and simply unloved. She crossed the street to extend her view, and towards number seven, she noticed the sign in about the right place. Her curiosity piqued, she set off down the street, and the sign 'FOR SALE' applied, it stated, to 'Apartment 4'. Emma smiled at the word 'apartment', and wondered how much they were asking for it, how much had changed since she had left, and how much had stayed the same.

She slowly turned, left her thoughts with her memories, quietly pleased that she'd sold her flat and left when she had.

Café Ricci's was quiet when she arrived, so she settled in easily for the afternoon. After a while, Fay bustled in, reeling from hours of busy meetings and missed appointments. 'Hey, Emma.' She stooped down to kiss her. 'How are you doing? You look like you've been here all day.'

Emma smiled at the sections of newspaper scattered around her. 'I didn't get here until around three, but I have been here since then. How are you? Busy day?'

'Uhhh!' Fay took a seat with a thump and launched into a tirade of annoyances and complaints appropriate to her afternoon. By the time her coffee had arrived, she had released. 'Anyway,' she continued, calmer and happier, 'how are you? And how is Belfast? How long have you been there now? Almost a year?'

Emma nodded. 'Yeah … I like it,' she admitted, almost surprised by the thought herself. 'It's small, but lively. There's plenty to do, theatres, concerts, films, and so on, and the people are nice. My house is gorgeous and getting better, I have a beautiful garden, and there are plenty of places for afternoon visits, plenty of things for me to see.'

Fay simply smiled.

'Every weekend I can go somewhere new, and you should see my house. You should come over, I've plenty of space.'

'I will,' replied Fay, 'that would be lovely. I'm sorry I haven't been already. I meant to come sooner, back when you left, but I've been so busy, I haven't even got round to thinking about it.'

Emma smiled, unsurprised by her friend's words, but reassured by her intentions. 'Spring is supposed to be nicest anyway.'

'Well in that case,' Fay smiled, 'I'll come in spring.' She drained her coffee cup. 'But for now, what would you like to do this weekend? We're going to the Comedy Club with Brad's friends this evening, but for tomorrow, what do you fancy?'

Emma responded quickly, the question one she had already considered. 'Would you mind if we go to Bath? I forget how pretty Bristol and Bath are when I'm not here, but all of today I've been reminded. Clifton is lovely, but I've done that now. Bath would be great, if you don't mind?'

'Not at all,' Fay smiled. 'We'll go on the bikes, you can use Brad's. It's supposed to be sunny, and then on Sunday, we can simply recover. I was thinking of asking Jenny and boyfriend to dinner tomorrow evening, and that will work fine as well.'

Emma's face showed surprise and interest.

'He's new,' Fay continued, 'I've never met him, but I'm intrigued.'

'Dinner, then, a definite must. I haven't seen Jenny since I left here either.'

The evening passed well – an evening full of humour and laughter, and then as planned, on Saturday, they cycled to Bath. The day was pleasant, the route was pretty and the incline never too steep up or down. They lunched in a small friendly basement café where Emma had been before with Mel, then looked round the shops for a quick half hour, but not feeling right in their cycling clothes, they returned to Bristol via the train. Both were happy with their day out. Fay had greatly enjoyed the cycle and Emma had always loved Bath. It made her think of luxury, of splendour, of opulence. It was a shame that Mark had never been, he would have liked it, but she'd invited him more than once.

They heard from Jenny while on the train and returned to find Brad happy to cook. Their guests arrived around 7.30pm, and while they were all pleased to see Jenny, they were more intrigued by her new friend. By consequence though, the conversation was rather stilted, Jenny and Stuart, all nervous and worried, Fay, Brad and Emma, all questions and queries. Jenny and Stuart were also not skilled at evading questions. By the end of the evening, neither Fay, Brad nor Emma were very impressed. Jenny and Stuart excused themselves early, eager by appearances to be spending all their time together, and Fay, Brad and Emma enjoyed themselves more after they had left, finishing the wine and discussing their victims.

The following morning, tidying and cleaning was easily rewarded with a leisurely Sunday brunch.

'You know,' started Fay, 'you're doing so well. You must miss Mark, but you seem okay. You're not moping around and all withdrawn, you weren't jealous last night of Jenny and Stuart. You didn't wish that was you?'

Emma laughed. 'Having noticed and highlighted all his deficiencies?'

'No,' Fay laughed. 'Not Stuart. I don't think I'd wish a Stuart on anyone! But one of your own. Someone to look at you like that? To hold your hand under the table?'

Emma laughed again. 'I'm not really the holding hands type!' She stopped but could see she needed to say more. 'I don't think Stuart would compare.'

'So you do still miss Mark?'

Emma smiled. 'All the time. I couldn't imagine another

man… But I still have Mark, I still talk to him when I need advice. I still think of him when I need support. I don't think I'll ever need anyone else.'

She twisted the ring round her middle finger.

BRISTOL, AUGUST 2002

24

The Tuesday after they'd been to Gloucester, Emma received a pleasant reminder: *Hi,* the text started. *I wish you were here, it's much better watching sport with a partner, love M.*

Emma smiled as soon as she read it, first she's his partner, and next he loves her. She could see her patience was paying off.

Wednesday night, she gave him a call. By the time he phoned back she was in the bath, but she still answered, she'd been looking forward to talking with him.

'Hi,' she started luxuriously, 'and how are you?'

'Alright. How are you?'

'I'm good thanks, I'm in the bath. It's gorgeous. It's so warm, and I'm so tired, I think I overdid it at the gym... What are you up to?'

'Oh, you know, I'm just back from Rosie's, wondering what to have for my dinner.'

She asked him for details, keen to hear him talk, pleased he had called her. She worried about him, all by himself, with only his thoughts and his troubles. He gave her tales of the last three days, then came to a natural pause.

'Anyway,' he recollected, 'I was thinking about this coming weekend.'

'Oh?' she started, surprised he might have made plans again.

'I was wondering if you'd mind going to the garden centre

on Saturday?' He paused. 'I was going to go tomorrow but the hospital have called and asked me to go, and the car's away at the garage on Friday. I want some new pots for the front path.'

Every so often, she forgot he had cancer. She started with what she thought was more important. 'Why did the hospital call? Has anything changed?'

'It's the date for the screening thing, that's all. The appointment was supposed to be next week, but they've got a cancellation and asked if I could go. I've got to go sometime.'

'I suppose so… Do you want me to come with you?'

'Thanks, but no. It's not very nice.'

Emma winced as she thought of his pain. 'I wouldn't mind, not if it made it better for you.'

'No, it wouldn't.' He ended the line of conversation abruptly, but his voice relaxed as he continued with the previous one. 'About the garden centre though? Would you mind?'

Emma paused. It annoyed her, his unwillingness to let her help, to let her in, to tell her what was upsetting him, his need to protect her, to keep her apart.

'Hello? Are you still there?'

'Sorry,' she returned, the tenderness still in her voice. 'If you're sure you don't want me to come to the hospital, I was wondering, in fact, if you'd mind if I didn't come to Oxford this weekend at all? I have to go to Guildford soon to sort out my flat and this weekend would be good for me. I want to put it up for sale this autumn, and I need to go and get things moving.'

'Oh I see.' She could hear him smiling as he spoke. 'You're doing the fortnight thing.'

'What?'

'The fortnight thing. I saw you last weekend and I'll see you next weekend, so this weekend you want to yourself.'

Emma smiled, pleased he wasn't trying to make her feel

bad. 'You don't mind, do you? You can go to the garden centre on Saturday for as long as you like, buy all the pots you want.'

'Yeah, thanks.'

'Or you could come to Guildford? I only need to see some estate agents, it shouldn't take long.'

'No, you're grand. I'm going to the garden centre.'

She phoned again the following day, but he didn't answer. She left her message, tenderly and cheerfully as always, hoping he was okay and hoping to hear from him soon. She was unsurprised by his lack of response, but couldn't help her agitation as she wondered what had happened at the hospital, ready to change her plans if she was needed.

His responding text arrived two hours later: *All well.*

Emma stared down at her phone. She was glad to have received the message, glad that everything was 'well', but disappointed not to have received more. Did he really mean 'all's well' as in 'I'm getting better', or was he again shutting her out?

She thought carefully then sought an answer as tactfully as she could: *And at the hospital?*

Won't get results until next week.

Take care, E x.

***

Saturday morning, she visited her flat in Guildford. At two o'clock, she started meeting estate agents, and by four o'clock she'd selected one, and all the paperwork was signed. At six o'clock, she arrived at Suzie's after a long relaxing walk.

Once in the door, Emma was met coyly by one small girl and quickly swept up by two others to play princesses. The girls were in need of a queen, and Emma was very happy helping them out. Playing a queen involved tiaras, necklaces and quite a lot of sitting on the sofa, but before they could exhaust her completely, they were collected up and taken for a bath.

Emma occupied herself stirring the dinner. As she did, her phone bleeped her a text: *Vodafone certainly know what they're doing, giving their free calls to you.*

Emma smiled as soon as she saw it. 'Rob,' she leant out of the kitchen, 'I'm popping out to get you some wine. I meant to get some earlier then completely forgot. Would you rather white or red?'

Rob shrugged as he took over the stirring. 'Red probably. Suze prefers red.'

'I'll be five minutes.'

As soon as she was out of sight of the house, Emma dialled Mark's number. He answered almost immediately. 'Hello.'

'Hello,' she replied lusciously. 'Apparently I don't call enough.'

'I never said that.'

'No,' Emma laughed, 'but that was what you meant. And you're probably right. Maybe I don't call enough... Anyway, I'm calling you now. What are you doing?'

'Oh, not much... I'm missing you... I bought my pots.'

'Excellent, what are they like?'

'Black, tall, they're nice, you'll like them... And how about you? How is the flat?'

'Well, I saw all the estate agents, I've signed up with one and the flat will go on the market as soon as they're ready. It's all sorted. And since then I've been playing princesses. Apparently, I make a very good queen. Such a good queen in fact, that I'm now Lily's best friend.'

'Lily's best friend huh?' There was a pause. 'Now I'm certainly wishing you were here. I've suddenly come over all possessive.'

'Really?' Emma was pleased. 'I don't mind you feeling possessive.'

By the time Emma had arrived back at her friends, Suzie had returned from the upstairs, the girls were settled and sleeping for the moment, and dinner was almost ready. They spent a lovely evening – dining, drinking, catching up. Suzie was another old friend from school who by chance had lived round the corner from Emma while she had also lived in Guildford. Good friends for a long time, with her move to Bristol, Emma missed Suzie – her careful questions, her sensible comments. Kind and caring, she was very grounded, unassuming. Emma would never forget when Mark had confirmed that he was ill. It was Suzie she came to, Suzie who helped, it was Suzie who told her what to do.

The following day, Emma stayed for lunch, the morning again spent with the girls, and by late afternoon, she had eaten superbly, kissed them all goodbye, and was back on the road again to Bristol. She considered a quick side trip to Oxford, but decided instead to go straight on home. She wanted to see him, but a quick cup of tea wouldn't be enough, so the side trip would mean a late night. He would wait.

25

Three days after they'd spoken in Guildford, Emma gave Mark her customary call. To her surprise, he answered almost as soon as she rang.

'Hi Mark, it's me.'

'Oh ... hi .... I wasn't expecting you.'

'Are you busy?'

'No, I was ... I wasn't expecting you, that's all.'

'I just thought I'd phone and see how you are.' The pause on the other end continued, 'Are you okay?'

'Not really, no.'

'Were you back at the hospital?... Did you get the results from your scan?'

'Yes...'

Emma waited.

'Emma, can I phone you back? I ... I can't talk about this right now.'

'Oh, okay, whenever you're ready.' She tried to sound positive. 'Call me ... I'll be here, whenever you're ready.'

She hung up, and for the rest of the evening she waited for his call. She busied herself, cooking, tidying, arranging belongings, wondering carefully what he might say, thinking of what she should say in return. She wanted to drive up to Oxford to hug him, to tell him she loved him no matter what, but she hadn't expected results this soon, and maybe that would make things worse. She certainly didn't want to make things worse.

She waited. At half past ten, he finally called.

'Hi,' she spoke softly, genuinely pleased to hear from him.

'Thanks for calling.'

'That's okay.'

'So, how did it go?' Again she spoke softly, not at all sure what to expect.

'It's not good, Emma, not good at all.'

Emma was determined it wouldn't be bad. 'What did they say?'

'The tumour's the same as it was before. The chemo' has had no effect.'

Emma thought. She wasn't going to let him do this. She started softly. 'But it's not any bigger? The chemo' has at least kept it the same?' She paused, trying to assess his reaction, but she could tell only that he was still there. 'I know it's not good, but it could be worse.' She paused again, but still she could only hear that he was there. 'Don't you think?' She was determined not to let him give up, not even now. 'It could be worse.'

'I suppose.'

'And they haven't finished yet, have they? Didn't you say there were other treatments they could try?'

'Yeah, radiotherapy.' He was starting to sound better.

'Well, that might help.'

'Yeah, maybe... that'll be another three months... Listen, Emma, I'm going to go.'

'Are you going to be okay? Do you want me to come up? ... I wouldn't mind.'

'No,' he laughed. 'Why would you come?'

'To give you a hug. To tell you I love you.'

'No, don't come. I'd rather you didn't.'

'Okay.' She wasn't going to push it. 'Are you still coming on Friday?'

'I need to go home. I'm flying from Bristol at about six. I can see you beforehand for lunch, if you like?'

'Okay,' she said. She would worry about details later.

'And, Emma, I know I said you could come too, but I don't think now that's going to work.'

'Oh, of course... no, don't worry, I'll just come with you some other time. Take care, and, I'll see you soon.'

She wished she was with him. She wished she'd left as soon as she'd called, and she would be in Oxford by now. She wished she could hold him, hug him, help him. But she couldn't go now, not now that he had told her not to. She wished more she was still living with him. To go now would be something unusual, would suggest that something was really wrong. She was pleased with the phone call – positive, supportive, sympathetic, not pitying, not negative, but it felt like it wasn't enough.

26

The following day, Emma booked Mark a parking space at work, and then in the evening, she phoned again to see how he was. He didn't answer. She left a message, sincere and supportive, hoping that he was okay.

On Friday, she dressed thoughtfully, and started work early to be free from lunchtime, whenever lunchtime happened to be.

13.10.

Alerted by the sound of a car arriving in the car park, Emma jumped up to her window to watch Mark skilfully manoeuvre his car into the one available space. She packed up her office and went down to greet him, to find him busy on his telephone. She waited patiently, then as he snapped shut his phone, she opened the door and leant in to kiss him. 'Morning,' she started.

'Hi,' he replied curtly. 'You didn't need to get dressed up, we're only going out for lunch.'

After a long stretch of things going so well, Emma was disappointed by his bad temper. She waited as he locked up the car, slipped her arm through his, and together they looked for somewhere to eat. They chose the café at the Art Studios, a large bustling place with counter service, somewhere they could sit in a corner, quiet and inconspicuous. They slid amongst the tables, formed part of the crowd, and calmly, peacefully ate their lunch. Giving him the chance to recover, Emma chatted, but Mark wasn't attending to her. After a while, Emma stopped and queried carefully, 'Are you alright?'

'Of course,' he replied. 'Why wouldn't I be?'

Emma shrugged. 'You're just quite quiet, you seem distracted.'

Mark looked slowly directly at her. 'I was wondering why you don't colour your hair.'

Emma was dismayed. His mood clearly hadn't improved and now he was taking it out on her. She'd experienced this before, when he was annoyed or had some small concern, and instead of talking, involving her or letting her help, he became cross and nasty, bitter and injured. She never knew how to treat these distractions - if she should laugh or treat them earnestly. 'I like my hair. Why would I dye it?'

'It's not very interesting is it? All one colour, a plain dark brown.'

Emma sighed inwardly. 'And what colour would you like it to be? What colour do you think it should be?'

He shrugged uninterested. 'How should I know? I'm not a hairdresser.'

Emma knew simply to let it go. They ate the rest of their lunch in silence, Mark again lost in a world of his own, Emma mulling over his comments, wondering what was really wrong. Finally, Emma collected some coffees and enquired gently if he wanted to do anything before his flight. This time, his response was kinder. 'No, I don't think so,' he smiled softly. 'There's not really time.'

'We could buy something for your sister, if you haven't already. We have some time for that sort of thing.'

'Okay.' Mark smiled with more energy. 'But she'll know it's your doing, it'll be most unusual.'

For the next hour, they ambled round looking for a suitable present. They still didn't talk, he didn't explain, but he did relax. Emma put her thoughts to one side while they could spend some time together.

One cookbook later, Mark left for the airport, taking Emma back to her house on his way. At the end of her road, as she turned to get out of the car, the sight of his telephone reminded her. 'Sometime while you're there, please can you give your sister my number?'

Mark looked at her questioningly.

'In case anything happens… How will I know?'

'I don't want you to know,' Mark replied. 'I don't want anyone to know. I want simply to … disappear.'

Emma stalled. 'But … what about those of us who might worry? Wonder where you are … or wonder what might have happened to you?'

Mark shrugged nonchalantly. 'What will I care?'

Emma shut the car door, let him drive off and slowly made her way to her house. She couldn't believe he could be so selfish.

As she arrived home, she reflected. It also wasn't his first thoughtless comment. Recently, there had been more of them too. Their relationship had been progressing well, but possibly since the hospital scan, she wondered if he was going off her.

Her fear had always been the same – not that he would die, not that the cancer would take him from her, but that he would leave, that he would get fed up and turn nasty. She'd asked him once not to let that happen, to let her know if he got tired, but he hadn't agreed. He'd simply laughed, asked her how he could grow tired, when she was so quiet and so good to him.

She tried to think it through over dinner. She attributed today's comment again to stress and bitterness – if he was going to have his life taken, if he was going to suffer so much, why shouldn't others? they'd never suffer as much as he would, they would at least still be alive.

But this wasn't the first time he'd been unkind and she was beginning to wonder if there was more to it. The strange little comments were coming more often, not overtly nasty, but hardly loving, comments like the one on her hair. She wondered what she could do to stop them. She didn't want to stop seeing him. She didn't want to become redundant, to have failed, but she also didn't want to be unhappy, nor did she want him unhappy either. She wasn't sure. Did he really love her? Did he really care? Or was he simply using her? A little toy? A fragile plaything?

Disheartened and troubled, she thought things through, until carefully explained by stress and fear, she put the thoughts to the back of her head, hoped the trip home would do him some good, and resolved to try harder for him in future.

27

The following Tuesday, she received a phone call. 'Hey there Emma, how are you?'

'Oh, hello.' She purred with pleasure at the sound of his voice. 'I'm good, thank you. And how are you? How was Northern Ireland?'

'Okay – I feel better anyway.'

'And how was your sister? And all your nieces?'

'Oh, they're all fine, same as ever.'

Emma smiled, imagining how pleased they would have been to see him, how he would have been pleased as well, but wouldn't have shown it.

'Disappointed I didn't take the car, but they can see it another time.' There was a pause as she heard him distracted by coins and machines, but he soon returned. 'Anyway, would you mind if I don't come and see you?… This evening, I mean … I'm really tired and I want to get home.'

Emma smiled. 'Of course I don't mind, not if you're tired. We're going to the pub quiz, if that might tempt you, but don't come if you're tired. You just go home and relax there… I can call you with questions if we get stuck.'

She heard him laugh. 'No, you're alright. Have a good evening and I'll see you soon.'

Emma was disappointed not to see him, but he had called, he had remembered, he had thought of her. She felt reassured, last week's doubts part of the past.

He called again on Thursday with arrangements for the weekend. He tried to argue he should come to Bristol, to make up for not stopping on Tuesday, but Emma didn't want him to feel that he owed her, and easily persuaded him that she would prefer to come to Oxford.

From then on, every weekend was the same. Emma arrived on Friday, for most of Saturday, they walked along the Thames or strolled into town for a leisurely brunch and a couple of hours of reading newspapers or looking through books, and then on Sunday, they did the alternate. The order in which they walked or went to town, the pubs they visited, the places they walked, the order in which they read newspapers or looked through books, it maybe changed, the activities themselves though, they stayed the same – one day in Oxford and one day out, some meals in and some meals out, some time inside and some time out. It was a pattern that they both enjoyed – variety, change, but with some familiarity too. Occasionally, they returned to Newbury races, and as the summer slipped into the autumn, they started visiting Cheltenham too, Mark began following the rugby.

On her first visit, she did tackle him - please would he talk to her, please would he try.

'No, sweetie,' he'd replied, all kindness. 'That's not for you. You don't want to be bothered with that.'

'But I do. I want to help.'

'No.' Resolutely he refused her. 'I don't want you sullied with that.'

The danger passed, a new status quo, and their relationship improved. Emma tried harder, Mark seemed more relaxed, he seemed more appreciative of her thoughts. It became like the times they had had at the start, only more secure, they were more content.

BELFAST, JULY 2007

28

Towards the end of her second year in Belfast, Emma also went back to Oxford. It had taken more courage than visits to Bristol - there was more to remind her in Oxford, more memories of what she might be missing, coupled with those she would rather forget. The last time she'd been, had been for the funeral, a day she would certainly rather forget. But, once she had decided to go, she began looking forward to the visit. It was a city that she loved – its grand pale buildings, their clear elegance, the peace of the river and meadows and gardens.

She'd been invited to a hen party. Charlotte was a family friend, not someone Emma was close to, so she was surprised to be invited, but she didn't want to let Charlotte down, and she knew there would be others who also wouldn't know many people. Oxford was Charlotte's favourite place, somewhere she knew from college days, with easy access for most of her friends. Not quite so easy for Emma of course, but she was glad of an excuse to not attend for a whole weekend.

She arrived late Saturday afternoon, easily found the accommodation and, finding it empty of giggling girls, she dropped her bag, returned to the streets and wound her way to The Grand Café. She didn't go in, she could see through the windows that it was full, but she stood outside easily, wishing she had a reason to enter, a space waiting for her, a space next to Mark and his calm and graceful manly presence. It was always the same when they met in cafés. He would be early

156

and get a nice table, she would be late, would swirl in, busy and chatty and bright, and he for the most part, would simply let her, outwardly relaxed, reading his newspaper, inwardly pleased with her energy and sparkle.

Emma texted that she had arrived, and by the time she got back to the rooms, Charlotte and party had firmly returned. They'd spent the afternoon collecting pictures of Charlotte's fiancé from around the town based on a series of clues, and now was the aftermath, tales and teasing, recounting, recalling. Emma was happy to play for an hour, but inwardly, she was glad that was all that was needed. Champagne, stories, and yet more games later, they then left for a restaurant, and yet more champagne, stories and games. They returned to the rooms when the restaurant closed.

The following morning, Emma was up bright and early. Not hung over, and keen not to waste her time in Oxford, she set off for a run round Christchurch Meadows, alongside the Thames, and finally of course, past Mark's old house. This was really what she had come for.

As she neared the house, Emma slowed to a walk and crossed the street for a better view. The house looked the same - half painted white, the blue front door, black pots outside, but somehow also sad and unloved. She wondered if Mark's sister now owned it, if it was rented out, but even then it could look content, like somebody cared - a mow of the lawn, a sweep of the path, some window boxes. She thought it was sad. Mark had loved the house when he'd been alive, now that he had died, it was falling apart. She wondered if the same sadness applied to her too.

The curtains shut, she stood and looked for as long as she liked, but aware that she was also part of a party, she left purposefully and jogged back to the overnight rooms. She arrived to find everyone at various stages of getting up.

'Oh,' Charlotte started, as she saw Emma's clothing. 'We

were wondering where you were. Did you go far?'

Emma smiled. 'No, not at all, a quick run around Christchurch Meadows… I woke up early and it's such a nice morning, I just wanted to make the most of it.'

They breakfasted on leftover snacks, then Charlotte and friends all simply left and drove back to London, eager to get home, missing boyfriends and lonely husbands. Emma was sad to be left so soon, but with her flight not until the evening, she rallied quickly, left her bag at the front desk and set out for a day in Oxford.

She decided to go to the ducks and the pond in the park by the river. Unsure of its exact location except from Mark's house, she tentatively set out east along the High Street. Before long, she found the small narrow streets of small terraced houses, all of them shining in the morning sun, and the black gate that led into the park. She rejoiced in her natural sense of direction, skipped past the houses, entered the park, and continued to the walkway suspended over the top of the water. For ages, she leant on the handrail, watching the many birds, diving, splashing, swimming, flapping, enjoying themselves in the warm fresh air. She loved their vitality, their freedom, their sense of fun. And as she watched, her thoughts kept returning to Mark's neglected and sad house. What would he think now? His pride and joy falling apart? Because he hadn't planned? Because he wouldn't admit that he might die, couldn't admit that he might die, hadn't been bothered to sort things out? She wondered as well: Was she the same? Sad and neglected and falling apart? Because he hadn't planned? Because he hadn't bothered to sort things out?

Determined not to be saddened further, she returned to the ducks, and brightened by their clear enjoyment of life, she resolved to rescue herself at least. She retraced her steps through the terraced streets, ambled through the covered market, stopping at jewellery shops for inspiration, and finally returned to her favourite place, the Grand Café. Not quite lunchtime, she sat in the corner, slowly sipping a pot of tea, wondering how she should rescue herself.

29

She returned from the hen weekend invigorated. She didn't want to look sad and unloved, she didn't want to be sad and unloved, she was going to pick herself up, and start enjoying her life again. She decided to make a list of everything that she used to enjoy, all the things that made her smile, and those were the things she'd start doing again.

First, she decided, she'd retrieve her sketchbook and walking boots, and spend more time in the outdoors. She used to like hiking, and drawing too, and before she'd met Mark, she'd spent many Sundays walking through the Surrey hills, occasional visits to the Brecon Beacons, the Peak District, the Lake District too. She didn't paint, she only sketched, light and rapid pencil drawings, but it was a good excuse to sit, to look, a requirement to take in her surroundings. Landscapes were her favourite focus, but occasionally she drew the flowers, the grasses, the plants right beside her, and not often, the people too. People were difficult – they tended to move or change position, but some were accessible – lazy picnickers, patient spectators, intent fishermen. She resolved to sign up for art classes and spend at least one day a month outdoors, hiking and drawing.

Second, she decided she'd travel some more. She used to love travelling, and she'd been to Morocco since Mark had died, but she'd only spent one week alone, and she'd decided longer was needed – the potential and freedom to change one's plans, the challenge of upsets, the need and demands for decisive action, the sights, the sounds, the slow infusion of other cultures. Resolution 2: to take three or four weeks next time she could, and visit somewhere much further afield, somewhere that she had never been to.

Resolution 3: to join a dating agency. She was lonely all by herself and, although she wasn't ready for a full relationship, she missed the excitement and fun of dating, the dinners in restaurants, the careful outfits, the lazy mornings, thinking, wondering, wishing, hoping. She investigated the options in Belfast and decided on IntroAnother – an expensive introduction agency specifically for professionals. She reasoned that if it was expensive, people were likely to be genuine and they would also treat her well.

Within a week, she was fully paid up, and within a month, had an introduction. She was disappointed with his profile, but the rules of the game were to meet with everyone at least twice, only then would you really know.

Emma met Spencer the following week. Anxious but excited, she selected a smart attractive shirt, arrived at exactly the prearranged time, and was soon chatting to her possible new friend. She quickly relaxed – she chatted with strangers a lot for her job, and spent her time then asking questions and finding topics to interest her. At the end of their drinks, they both made an excuse to leave, but arranged to meet again the following week.

Emma had not been impressed. The conversation was uninspiring, his answers to her questions were dull, the lack of interest in return, but the game plan suggested at least two dates in case the first was riddled with nerves, so she agreed to meet Spencer again.

The following week, at his suggestion, they went salsa dancing. Emma arrived early in time for a drink, but Spencer appeared as the class was starting, and then there was simply no chance to talk. At the end of the class, Emma again went to the bar, but Spencer continued dancing instead. Emma again was disappointed. She was encouraged by the dancing, she liked dancing, but she needed more from a boyfriend than that. She agreed to return in two weeks' time, but two weeks later it was the same, and after that she simply left it.

Over the summer, she put her other plans into action too. She went out walking and she'd been sketching, she spent some time visiting new places, she started going further afield. She liked the west, Enniskillen and County Fermanagh. Green and gentle, the colours were natural, the landscapes were soft, if only one could predict the weather – her first weekend abandoned completely because of wet weather.

For one week, she also went to Estonia. Somewhere she had never been, but not too difficult or too far away. She loved Tallinn – a small mediaeval picturesque town perched on a hillside, narrow, winding, cobbled streets and decorative tall old-fashioned buildings. Easy, friendly and interesting, for a short time, it was perfect.

For her next major trip, she was looking at Peru. Her brother was working there for six months, the only question was when could she take three or four weeks off work, at a time when he would also be free, and the weather would also be good.

She also received two more introductions, to Malcolm and Peter, but neither of them suited her. They were both nice, but Malcolm was boring and uninspiring, and Peter, though better, was obsessed again with a single pastime. They went hiking for one of their dates – that was one thing they had in common, but all he had talked about was mountain biking, and Emma knew she didn't enjoy it. She liked to be looking out when she was outside, not focussed on the ground for fear of falling or jarring her joints. They went on a couple of further dates, but soon she could take the entreaties no longer.

In between times, she also enjoyed her Belfast life. Her house and garden were progressing. Every visitor since she'd arrived had been tasked with a plant or a garden tool, and over two years she had now gained a reasonable collection. She'd moved all the herbs to nearer the house, she'd made a small handy vegetable patch, the repainted hall and stairs were brighter and she had a new bathroom.

Through work she'd found a good supply of friends to keep her busy, and the work itself was progressing too. In the two years since she had arrived, she'd found regular nights out with Marie and Lyn, she often met with Theresa, and she'd spent many weekends with Ann and William, hiking, climbing, cycling, running, almost all for charity. At work, she'd found several new clients, had won some contracts, and had had some successful completions. All in all, things were going well.

At the end of the summer was Charlotte's wedding, a grand affair with a large guest list, and a fancy hall for a fancy reception. Emma went with her family, but she was pleased to find herself among Charlotte's friends for the wedding breakfast.

She was seated between Martin McConaghy and Wilkinson Cooke. Both, however, were disappointing. Martin McConaghy was safely engaged to the lady on his other side, and Wilkinson Cooke was simply not her type. He was pleasant and easy to talk to, but nothing exciting and nothing fun. Emma needed exciting and fun. She liked unpredictable, romantic, she liked potential, she liked excitement. She needed to be swept off her feet, to be caught off guard and blown away, exactly as Mark had done for her.

Despite the lack of romantic potential, Emma enjoyed her meal a lot. She liked talking to different people, finding the things that they enjoyed, she liked the challenge of engaging others, of keeping attention and making them laugh.

She also enjoyed the following day. With Charlotte and Tim safely departed, the remaining members of the two families assisted in a morning of clearing at the wedding venue, followed by Sunday lunch on Charlotte's mother's patio, jugs of Pimms made by the girls, a roaring barbecue manned by the boys. Friends for a long time, previously spending holidays together, they spent their time enjoying the company, remembering incidents in times gone by, laughing and joking with each other, laughing and joking at each other..

As the afternoon clouded and temperatures faded, they began separating. Journeys home for those with work tomorrow, for Emma though, a relaxing evening in Charlotte's mum's company.

As they finished tidying and all that remained on the table were flowers, Marion stooped and handed Emma the wedding bouquet. 'You should take that, it suits your colour.'

Emma laughed as she held out her hand. 'I'm not sure it does, it's mostly pink.'

Marion nodded. 'Well, yes, that's you, a little pink softie … and besides, if you take it, maybe you'll be next.'

Emma smiled. 'That's even less likely. I can't see myself meeting anyone soon.'

Marion looked knowingly. 'You still think about Mark?'

'Every day.'

'Still every day?'

'Not as much as I used to,' Emma admitted, 'but yes, every day. I'm not sure I'll ever stop thinking about him.'

OXFORD, MAY 2002

30

B efore she'd left to live in Bristol, Emma had lived in Oxford with Mark. The move to Oxford though was a big step.

As the train passed through the countryside, she remembered the first time she had been to Oxford – eager, excited, a little bit nervous, open to whatever may come. This time, she reflected, she felt content, everything felt right. She was still a little hesitant, unsure that he would feel the same, unsure that she would mean as much, but she was here now and at least she had to give it a try.

He was waiting for her at the platform exit. He'd warned her that he looked different, and he did a little, but she didn't care - he was waiting, he'd come to meet her, he was her loved one.

She struggled through the barrier, rucksack too large for a knee that was injured, ticket in one hand, bunch of tulips in the other.

Mark stepped forward and took her rucksack as she reached up and lightly kissed him. 'Well,' she smiled, 'you don't look too bad.'

'Thanks,' he responded, 'neither do you.'

Emma laughed. 'I'm not the one who said they looked awful.'

His smile broadening, he nudged her with his elbow and shouldered the rucksack. 'Good to see you, Em. Thanks for coming.'

'Thank you for having me,' she returned, 'although I'm not

sure I'm going to be much use.'

He looked at her leg as she hobbled slowly over the concourse. 'Yeah,' he started, 'your leg looks worse than I thought it would. I thought you were probably exaggerating.' He paused thoughtfully. 'You'll still be able to clean, I should think, and you *can* wash up. I hate washing up.'

Emma smiled. She was glad she had come.

As they entered the house, Mark put her rucksack in the hall, took his flowers to the kitchen for a water jug, then put them on the mantelpiece in the front room. In the centre stood the card she had sent for his birthday – a hand-drawn card on a piece of paper, sketched from a tent, sent from the depths of remotest Norway. It was over a month since his birthday, and none of his other cards were still up. She felt honoured.

For the rest of the day Emma settled in. She was staying for as long as she wished, to look after Mark while he was sick, and for somewhere to live while she had no job and had let out her flat. She'd been in Norway for the past six weeks, working on an outdoor expedition, had returned early due to injury, and hadn't planned anything for her return before she'd left. Free as she was, she was easily able to come and stay, and when Mark had suggested it, she'd been delighted.

He'd given her the front bedroom – a large yellow room overlooking the street, a guest room doubling as an office. 'It's a nice room. You'll get the sun in the evening and I think there will be enough space. I've cleared out some drawers for you. Make yourself at home.'

Pleased to have more of a home than a tent, and to be staying for long enough to need some drawers, Emma spent the afternoon unpacking her rucksack and installing her belongings.

Then in the evening, they went out. Mark was keen to show her his new car, and Emma was keen to be shown. She was impressed too - a silver Saab 93, with blue soft top, black leather seats, powerful, sleek, a real panther of a car. She wanted a test drive as soon as she saw it, although she didn't want to be driving, she wanted to be driven. Happy to oblige, Mark drove them out of Oxford, soft top down, wind whistling past, sun glinting off the silver bonnet. He was a good driver, and although still familiarising himself with the controls, she felt safe and happy. She wanted to drive the car too, but not today. Today she was happy as a passenger, riding beside this man who so impressed her, in a car that so befitted him.

They stopped after twenty minutes at The Trout Inn. On such a nice evening, they bought their drinks, walked straight through the pub, and on out to the garden. Bordered on one side by the river, dotted with oak trees and willows, it was virtually empty, except for the ducks and the swans on the bank. They sat enjoying the evening sun, the river flowing gently past, shadows gradually lengthening. One drink later, the sun still high enough for light and warmth, they decided to eat in the garden as well.

'It's so nice to be here,' Emma announced, as she slowly took it all in.

'Good to have you here, Em,' Mark smiled carefully. 'You'll be a great help.'

The following day, the following days, they spent living by Mark's usual routine. The mornings he slept, while Emma rose early and spent her time tidying, washing up or on a report on her work in Norway. When Mark surfaced, they went into Oxford for lunch or coffee, then spent their afternoons walking home, through Christchurch Meadows or via the bird pond and park at New Hinksey, lounging and reading in the garden, walking leisurely by the river, completing the *Guardian* crossword. He lent her his books as he finished reading, she filled his house with flowers and freshness. Evenings, they often went out for drinks, then dined at home by candlelight, or occasionally they went for their drinks later, slowly visiting Mark's local pubs, sometimes for dinner, sometimes for a drive.

Everything they did, they did slowly or for short periods with lots of rests, Emma injured, while Mark was sick. Her arrival had been timed around his chemotherapy, he was clearly tired and sleeping a lot, but Emma was happy to help when she could and simply fit into his relaxed pace. She was so glad that she had come. She felt special, she felt wanted, she felt cared for.

On the fourth day of her living with him, he took off his hat. Having completed several rounds of his treatment, his hair had mostly fallen out, and he was clearly embarrassed. Emma said nothing, she was pleased to see his trust in her.

Every so often he didn't feel well or wanted to rest, so Emma entertained herself. She went shopping, she fed the ducks, she went swimming in the outdoor pool. She loved Oxford. She thought it so grand, so elegant, its pale stone buildings, the tall lime trees of Christchurch Meadows, the dense creeper of Christchurch College. Occasionally, she asked him if he would join her, for some fresh air, a walk, some sun, but she didn't push. Apart from what she'd read and heard, she had no idea of how he was feeling, what he might be thinking, what he should be doing. She asked him to talk to her, reasoned it might help him too, but he wouldn't, or he couldn't.

***

One week after she'd arrived, Emma left for a few days in Cornwall. She'd promised to house-sit for her grandparents, so on Thursday morning she took the train, and her grandparents left the following day. The same evening Mark telephoned her. 'Hi,' he started, 'just checking you arrived safely? Injured knee and everything?'

'Yes,' Emma smiled. 'Thanks for your concern. All good

here. What have you been up to?'

They chatted for a few minutes, anxious to maintain a connection, until the missing two days were exhausted.

'Anyway, listen,' Mark continued, 'I was looking at the map and Porth is not that far from Padstow.'

'No,' Emma replied. 'Padstow is just up the coast from here. … Why?… Why are you interested in Padstow?'

'Rick Stein has a restaurant there, and I've been wanting to try it for ages. I thought I might come and give it a go … I'm wondering if you would like to join me?'

Emma smiled. 'Yes, of course, that would be lovely.' She telephoned the restaurant, booked a table and immediately telephoned Mark back. 'Tuesday, 8pm. Does that sound okay? And then do you want to stay over? You can't go back to Oxford all in one day, and if you stay over you could bring me back with you. Gran and Grandad will be back on Wednesday.'

The following days Emma spent reading, shopping, organising, and every evening she telephoned Mark. By Tuesday morning, she was ready to return to Oxford, all she needed was for Mark to arrive. Not due until the afternoon, she spent the morning on Porth headland and down on the beaches. Her knee was feeling a little better, and she loved the coast on fresh windy days.

By late afternoon, she was waiting at the house, when her grandparents arrived home one day early.

'Hi,' she started, as they walked up their front path. 'I thought you were coming back tomorrow?'

'Well, we were, but the little hotel was getting full, and we thought it would be nice to spend some time with you, … we don't see you often.'

'That's very nice,' replied Emma. 'I have a friend coming for dinner this evening, we're going to Rick Stein's in Padstow, but he won't be here for a while yet. Let me make you a cup of tea and you can tell me all about your holiday. You'd be welcome to come as well if you'd like? this evening? I'm sure I could change the booking.'

'Oh no, don't worry, it'll be a bit late for us I think, but a cup of tea now, that would be lovely.' Emma was glad. She was pleased to see her grandparents, but she'd been looking forward to an evening with Mark, and a party of four wasn't what she'd imagined.

Mark arrived about an hour later. She was pleased to see him, pleased again to receive his attentions. She felt honoured too – he had driven down to Cornwall to see her, Rick Stein's restaurant surely simply a good excuse.

They spent the early evening with Emma's grandparents, then arrived in Padstow at 8pm. They were shown to a table at the back of the restaurant – a bright, lively and open affair, already busy, and while Mark sat with his back to the room, embarrassed by his lack of hair, Emma sat gladly facing them all, proud to be with him, proud to be his. The food was exquisite – mussels and razor clams, Atlantic plaice and Dover sole, finished with coffee and dessert wine. The experience was everything that Mark had come for. A perfect evening for Emma too - to be with him, to be loved and protected, to be allowed to love him back.

They were up early the following day, and as soon as he was dressed, Mark suggested they go for a walk. Every so often, when he was up early, he liked to start the day outside, and the coast, he said, was good for that. Emma sent him off in the direction of Porth headland and island, while she stayed to talk with her family, her knee also slightly sore from yesterday. When Mark returned, the headland and island had been ideal, exactly what he'd been looking for. Emma smiled as he recounted, glad she knew his tastes a little. They left the house then, but instead of heading straight for the route home, Mark had other plans.

'I've never been to Cornwall before, you know Em, and,

while I'm here, I really don't want to just go straight home.'

Emma looked at him and agreed. It was a lovely day, and it would be nice to make the most of where they were. 'Anywhere in particular you'd like to go?'

He turned towards her, already organised. 'The Eden Project. Do you know where it is?'

'Not exactly,' she replied, 'but it's on the other coast and I know how to get *there*, and Cornwall's not that big, we ought to find it at some point.'

He turned to face straight ahead. 'That's good enough for me, my girl. Which way to start with?'

In not very long, they found some road signs, then spent the rest of the morning investigating the two domes of the Eden Project that were currently open: the Tropical dome, full of warm wet air and lush green foliage, big bright flowers and butterflies; and the Mediterranean one, fragranced with citrus and olives and pine. Once they'd finished, they continued up the coast for lunch overlooking the river Fowey, and their journey home then took them through Dartmoor - somewhere else that Mark had never been, and somewhere that Emma was happy to return to. They stopped briefly at Two Bridges to marvel at the countryside around them. A rugged landscape, bathed in sunshine and fresh air, a rugged beauty, it appealed to both Emma and Mark.

'Some time, you know, we should come back and stay properly.' Emma looked around her as she spoke, imagining walks on cold clear days, squelching through mud in wellington boots, fresh cold cheeks, wild windswept hair, returning at the end of the day to a relaxing drink, a steaming bath and a huge open fire.

Mark followed her face as she turned in the surroundings, her imaginings played out in her smile, until her gaze came to rest on the Two Bridges Inn, not far from where they were standing. A large low building, painted white with black beams, it was exactly the place for a roaring fire, luxurious baths and sumptuous meals of roast meat and wine. Mark agreed, sometime maybe they should return.

31

The following week progressed much the same as the previous one, except that Mark was now up more and clearly feeling more lively. Emma's knee was also improving. She spent less time working on her report, and they spent more of their time together, walking here, lunching there, visiting here, drinking there. They visited the museum, the Botanic Gardens, they extended their walks to the Thames valley path, they walked down to Abingdon via the weir. They also started doing more in the evenings, trips to the cinema, drinks out in town.

At the end of the week, Emma caught Mark leaning from the bathroom window, while she was weeding the garden.

'Did you want to come away next weekend?' He looked at her questioningly. 'Before I'm wiped out by the next bout of chemo'?'

He'd explained the four week cycle for treatment, and corresponding cycle of holidays, immediately before, when he felt most well.

'Yes I would,' she replied quickly. 'Have you decided where you would like to go?'

'I'm thinking Prague. Have you ever been?'

'No, but I'd like to.'

'Prague it is then, I'm booking the flights.' And with that he disappeared.

Three hours later, he came back downstairs, flights booked, hotel, weekend in Prague for two all arranged. He even seemed to have a guidebook.

They arrived in Prague, one week later. The end of May,

it was quiet, but they spent three pleasant days looking, seeing, simply absorbing, a different city. They visited the Town Hall, the Old Castle complex, the Strahov Monastery and Library. They watched the chimes of the old town clock, loitered on the Charles Bridge amidst statues and painters, wandered to the top of Petrin Hill. Emma liked the old town – tall narrow buildings with fine decorations, traditional red-tiled roofs, tight cobbled streets and hidden courtyards. Mark liked the new town, its wide tree-lined avenues, white modern buildings, its young trendy crowd. They drank mulled wine, tried garlic soup and local sausage, and spent their evenings feasting on stews and thick warm beer in dark and smoky underground taverns.

At the end of their second day, they sat waiting for their evening meal. 'I do like travelling.' Mark's eyes sparkled as he looked around the room before him. 'So much to see, so much to do, but this is the best of it - chowing down with the locals, a good homebrew in an underground tavern.'

Emma loved the taverns too – deep in the buildings or sometimes the cellars, dark and smoky and full of men, the smell of smoke and beer and sweat, the atmosphere a combination of relaxed, excitement and danger. She loved them all the more because she was with Mark.

'Where would you be if I wasn't here?' she asked him, interested. 'Would you still be here? Or would you be doing something else?'

''Spect I'd still be here ... although I'd be thinking more about where to go next, than sitting and enjoying it. What to do after my few drinks.'

Emma smiled, and continued to take in her surroundings. 'I wouldn't be here. I love it, but I would never come here by myself. Everywhere else we've been today, I would have done that easily, but not this, ... and this is great.' She turned back to smile straight at him. 'Thank you for bringing me!'

32

The day after their return, Mark was due at the hospital. He left in the morning and was in overnight, and while he was away Emma did the washing, tidied, and cleaned the whole house.

The following morning, she selected some clothes that she knew Mark liked, and spent some time making herself attractive before leaving for a day in Guildford. Almost ready to depart, she heard his key in the front door lock. 'Hello,' she started. 'You're very early. I wasn't expecting you for ages!'

He looked her up and down taking in her efforts. 'No, so I see. And where are you off to all dressed up?'

She couldn't tell him she'd done it for him. 'I'm meeting my sister for lunch today,' she lied easily. 'She's visiting somewhere in Guildford for work, so I said I'd meet her. I won't be back late. How did you get on?

'It's not nice, Emma.' He turned away from her as he spoke. 'I'd rather not talk about it.'

Emma looked at him unsurprised. 'Okay,' she smiled. 'In that case, I have a train to catch.' She stroked his arm as she brushed past. 'I'll see you later.'

For the rest of the day, she was in Guildford, but she arrived home early as she'd offered. Mark had been in bed all day, then roused himself once she returned. He wasn't hungry and didn't want to leave the house, so Emma made dinner - a simple dinner of soup and salad. She knew he should eat, he knew he should eat, but he didn't feel like eating at all. He wandered round the kitchen distractedly, unwilling to help, but unwilling also to be elsewhere. She gave him small jobs unrelated to the food, but still related to what she was doing. Could he find some music? Could he light the candles on the dining room table?

Only as he was lighting the candles did he notice the rest of the room. 'Did you tidy up?'

Emma smiled as she heard him moving from dining room to lounge, and then into the hall. 'I thought the place could do with a quick vacuum, that was all.'

Mark came back into the kitchen, smiling widely, and hugged her closely. 'Thank you Em, that's really cheered me up.'

They sat down to dinner, but he couldn't eat. Emma loved him for trying. She smiled at him as he put down his spoon and looked into his bowl. 'There's sweetcorn in the kitchen if you'd rather have that. It's all cooked and ready, it's just keeping warm.'

He smiled at her, and she could see his gratitude. 'It's okay… I will eat this… You've put basil in it, haven't you? And that's just for me. I know you prefer it without the basil.'

Over the next few days, he gradually improved. At first he stayed in bed until lunchtime, but gradually the time at which he came down grew earlier, and the liveliness with which he appeared increased.

While Mark was asleep, Emma busied herself with cleaning and tidying, writing the report on her visit to Norway. Her visits to the library doubled as visits to buy Mark foods and buy Mark more books. She used her time fruitfully, yet every day, as soon as Mark appeared, she was ready to finish and start something new. They spent their afternoons sitting in the garden, reading, talking, on short walks along the river, on drives through the countryside, visiting pubs and empty pub gardens.

Only once did they take things a little too far. On the Friday after his treatment, Mark simply felt like a change of

176

scene. They took the car out to The Perch Inn, but as he tried to leave it, Mark couldn't move without feeling sick or feeling dizzy. He sat where he was for several minutes while Emma went out looking for water. She wanted to help, she didn't want to sit and watch him suffer. She also didn't want to fuss over or embarrass him, he was a proud man. She wanted to help him if she could, but the pub not open yet, after five minutes they simply left.

Determined not to be beaten, they drove to The White Hart, and by the time they'd reached it, Mark was feeling better, although not quite well enough for a pint. Two hot chocolates later, they returned to the safety and ease of the house.

33

The following week Mark was noticeably feeling improved. He was still getting up around mid-morning but he was keener to be out of the house. Every other day they went walking, sometimes close by, through Wytham Woods, sometimes further, slowly to the source of the Thames. They spent more time together, they got to know each other better. They clearly enjoyed doing the same things, they clearly enjoyed doing those things together.

They seemed at ease, but something between them still wasn't quite right. For most of the time, Emma really liked Mark – his calm undertaking, his lack of complaint, his careful attentions and quiet dry humour. He made her laugh, he made her smile, she felt wanted, cared for and loved. But every so often, he could reduce Emma almost to tears. He'd criticise her hair, refuse to be seen with her looking like this, refuse to be seen with her acting like that. Mostly she laughed these comments off, ignored them carefully or refused to play, but once or twice he really hurt her, to the extent that she wondered why she was accepting it.

The first time it happened, they'd spent the afternoon at home, and then at 5pm, Mark was popping out. 'I'm just going to get some milk,' he announced from the house to the garden.

'Okay,' replied Emma, happy to continue weeding.

'And while I'm out I'm going to Rosie's. I haven't been now for a few days, they'll be missing me.'

'Okay, have fun.'

An hour later, Emma was starting to think about dinner.

By 7pm, Mark still wasn't home. Puzzled by this, more than concerned, she tried to call, but found his telephone left in the hall. She debated for a while, then cooked some dinner, and having eaten, she went for a bath.

At 9pm, while still in the bath, she heard him return. She was glad to hear him, but she was annoyed that he hadn't telephoned – anything could have happened to him, and that he had disappeared to start with. She was also glad she was in the bath, she could stay calm, she wouldn't fight.

'Hey there, Em,' he called from the hall. 'I'm getting a take-away. You want anything?'

'No thanks,' she replied. 'I had dinner earlier.'

'Oh, so it's like that, is it?' He had clearly had more than one pint.

'I was hungry earlier, so I made something then, that's all,' she replied. 'I tried to call you, but your phone was still here.'

'Well, there's no need getting upset about it. I only had a few, I got side-tracked, lost track of time… It happens to everyone.'

Emma could hear him not apologising, spoiling for a fight. She kept her voice light. 'I'm not upset. I ate earlier and now I don't want any take-away, thank you. You go ahead, of course, enjoy it.'

She heard him thump towards the telephone, but she doubted that would be the end of it. She took her time, then dried and dressed, she went downstairs. She wanted to talk, she didn't want this to happen again, but she needed to stay calm – scale this into a full blown dispute, and she was sure it would be happening often.

'Oh?' he started. 'Recovered now, have we? Can't hide in the bath forever?'

'I was just checking that you're alright. I'm going to bed.' She wasn't playing. She would speak to him some other time.

As she lay awake, she couldn't decide. Was it control? A

need to be himself? To do his own thing? Emma was happy for him to be himself, to do as he pleased, but he could have called, if not for her sake, then for his own. He was the one who was currently ill, he was the one who might need fetching, or looking after. She was disappointed by his lack of thought.

She was though, very pleased with herself. She hadn't reacted, she didn't care. Suzie explained she was being tested, but Emma wasn't the game-playing type. If Mark wanted to do his own thing, then that was fine.

***

Almost as if scheme one hadn't worked, Mark tried again a short while later. Emma was progressing with her report, and soon needed to visit the library in Guildford, and see some colleagues. Mark also had colleagues in Guildford, so he suggested that they go together.

'If you need to go to Guildford some time, I could come too,' he'd started when she'd first mentioned it. 'It'd be good to see Steve, and Jon. I can drive us.'

'Okay,' replied Emma. 'That would be nice. When were you thinking?'

'One day next week… Maybe Wednesday or Thursday?'

'In that case, can we make it Wednesday?' Emma responded. 'Celine tends not to work on Thursdays.'

'We can try.'

And she left him to contact his colleagues, while she emailed hers.

The following Wednesday, she was up early. They hadn't made any firmer plans, but Emma had told Celine that she'd be around and would pop in. She'd visit her first, and if Celine wasn't available then, she'd go to the library and then return.

For most of the morning Emma kept herself busy, until at 11.30am there was still no sign of Mark. She started to wonder what she should do. She didn't want to wake him if he was sleeping, but if he'd made arrangements with friends, she didn't want him to miss those either.

She carefully peeked round his bedroom door, but could see no signs of activity. She started making more noise than usual, in an effort to wake him, but at 12.30pm she gave up and knocked lightly on his door. She popped her head into the bedroom to find him now propped up, reading.

'Are we going to Guildford today?' she asked hesitantly.

'And I thought you were bringing me a nice cup of tea.' He looked up expectantly. 'No, I'm not going. Steve and Jon can't make it today.'

Emma stared at him.

'You can go though, if you'd like to.'

'I thought we were going together,' she started dumbfounded, 'I thought you were going to drive us.'

'Well, you thought wrong there, didn't you?' He looked at her blankly, and then simply returned to his reading.

Emma stood looking at him. She had been played. It had been his idea to go together, his idea to take the car, and now he had hijacked her whole day out, presumably simply because he could. He'd done it deliberately. He hadn't simply forgotten to tell her, there was clearly no apology.

She agreed slowly, silently seething, 'I think I'll go anyway.' She would have to rush to catch Celine, and he would make her pay later, but she didn't like upsetting her plans, nor the plans of other people.

Determined not to offer a reaction, she calmly turned, returned to the downstairs, collected her work bag, to catch the next train.

'See you later,' she called up as she left.

***

The next time, he tried a different tack. They'd been for lunch at Café Rouge. The place was busy and they were late, but their meal took ages, their waiter was hopeless, and they were charged for items they didn't receive. As a result, Emma chose not to leave a tip.

Mark watched her, but said nothing, until they were outside, and then, of course, it was too late. He was so embarrassed, he felt so ashamed. Her justifications fell on deaf ears and, at future meals, he couldn't help reminding her. Mark was good at spotting a weakness and taking thorough advantage of it. Emma liked to be thought of as kind. Every time he mentioned the incident, he could see how hard she tried to justify her actions, not only to him, really to herself. The turmoil and torture he created inside her meant far more to him than the missing tip or the hard-done-by waiter.

Most of the time, Mark was thoughtful and engaging, but Emma was finding these episodes difficult. She attributed them largely to the cancer. Physically, he seemed very little changed - he'd lost his hair, his face had broadened, he slept a lot and sometimes he was sick, but on the surface he was still very able and much the same. Mentally, though, he mentioned depression, and Emma wondered what else was going on. He must realise he was upsetting her, that he was hurtful. Was he mostly really upset with the world? A sign of depression? Anger? Frustration? Was he struggling with a lack of control? With helplessness? Or inadequacy? Or was it all simply too much? Was he trying to encourage her to leave him? But in that case, why not simply ask? Why be nasty? And then why be lovely the rest of the time? And most of the time he was lovely.

Fed up with the uncertainty, but not willing to give up quite yet, about two weeks after returning from Prague, Emma found herself with an opportunity to ask Mark how he really felt. Most mornings now, while he was sleeping, she spent some time checking her emails, re-engaging with the outside world, and one morning, she received an email from Professor

Stein, University of Bristol, asking her when she could start work. He'd offered her a job before she'd gone to Norway, and on her return, unsure of Mark, she'd emailed to say she could start some time over the summer.

Uncertain still of her situation, she read the email a number of times, saw this as an opportunity, and decided to speak to Mark about it. She waited until she heard him awake, then went upstairs to find him lying stretched out on her bed. She sat down opposite him on the chair, and casually started. 'In an ideal world, how long would I stay here?'

He looked at her blankly. 'What do you mean "in an ideal world"?'

'If you could have whatever you wanted, if you didn't have to think about anything or anyone else, how long would I stay?'

'But I can't have what I want. It's not an ideal world, is it?' He sounded confused.

Emma was unsurprised by his unwillingness to face the true question, but wasn't about to be deflected. 'No, maybe, but if it were, how long would I stay?'

He looked at her, still refusing to understand. 'You can stay as long as you like,' he shrugged. 'I thought we agreed you'd stay until you went to Bristol.'

'OK,' she smiled and got up to leave. 'I just thought I'd ask.'

She left the room and returned to her work on the dining room table, resolved to decide when to leave by herself. She was disappointed by his lack of interest, his unwillingness to commit, but she was pleased to have now a clearer picture.

Five minutes later, though, Mark appeared purposefully by her side. 'Do we need to talk about this?' he asked.

She looked at him and shook her head. 'It was a simple question, that was all.' She looked down again, avoiding eye contact. 'It doesn't matter.'

He looked at her closely. 'But it does, doesn't it?' He paused slowly. 'Has something happened? Has something changed?'

'I had an email from Bristol this morning,' she said, looking back at him, 'asking when I'd like to start work.'

'Oh,' he looked confused. 'And what did you say?'

'I didn't say anything. I thought I'd ask you. But if it makes no difference, I'll decide for myself.'

She looked down again, back at her report.

Mark continued, 'Are you sure that's what they were asking? No requested date? No suggestion?' He looked at her closely. 'It's quite unusual.'

Emma looked back at him, impatient now with his cynicism. 'Yes, they're giving me the choice. The guy wants me to work for him, he's being nice… I can show you the email if you like.'

Mark paused, thought, then answered brightly, 'Well, how about the start of July? That gives us about two more weeks, then you'll be able to go earn some pennies. I have no idea what you've been living on.'

Emma smiled, pleased with an end to the conversation. 'That was what I was thinking too, I'll email tomorrow.'

'But before you go, can we go to Paris? I really enjoyed going to Prague and I'd love to go to Paris again.'

Emma's smile broadened to encompass her whole face. 'Why not?' she shrugged.

The following week passed very quickly, mostly spent exactly as before, although now they seemed to enjoy it more. They were more relaxed, they laughed and joked more, they were making the most of their time together. While the good times seemed to be better, though, the bad times also seemed to be worse. Mark complained more of depression, moped around the house needing things to do, took himself off for solitary walks and lonely pints. He told Emma he'd miss her when she left and asked her to come back and see him often, to which, of course, she quickly agreed. She told him she would miss him too, and for the rest of the time that they had together, she offered him thoughts that might help him. She wrote out the recipes that he liked, took him to renew his golf club membership, set up a subscription for monthly book deliveries. She tried to persuade him of the positive aspects of visiting places by yourself – the cinema, theatre, outside attractions, the freedom to visit when you wanted, to see what you wanted, to go when you wanted, and if he needed someone to tell once he'd seen something, once he'd been somewhere, he could always phone her, she would always be interested.

One week before she was due to leave, Emma went to Bristol to find somewhere to live, and returned to Oxford cold, wet, tired and miserable. She stepped through the door to be met with a hot drink and lovely broad smile. Both of them knew that Mark would miss her. She curled up on the sofa as he asked about Bristol, and Emma recounted her last two days, asked after his, and heard his stories. She'd miss him too.

As she passed through the hall on her way for a bath, Mark looked after her. 'Are we still going to Paris tomorrow?'

Emma smiled at him. 'Yes, of course. Why wouldn't we be?'

In return, he only smiled.

34

The following morning, they woke early and were soon on the road. They were driving to Dover to catch a ferry, then they'd take the train from Calais. As they sped through the countryside, early dew glistening on the verges, Emma realised how much she would miss Mark – his adventurous spirit, his inner strength, also his vulnerability. She looked over at him, impressed and absorbed, she admired him greatly.

After a while he caught her watching. 'What's different today?' she asked curiously.

'Why?' A cunning smile played on his lips.

'There's something different. You're ... I don't know...' She wanted to say oozing confidence and sex, but she didn't have the nerve.

He didn't press her. 'I shaved my head ... It'll be those little hairs you can't see any more.'

Emma laughed. She'd suggested he shave his head not long ago. He liked to be in charge, to be in control and by shaving his head, she'd reasoned, he could take some control back from the cancer. 'You could never see them before,' she continued. But the difference it had made to him was incredible.

They were in Paris by mid-afternoon, found a room easily, then set off eagerly to explore. Within minutes, they were at the market at the Place de Bastille, perusing the artists and market traders, taking in portraits and caricatures, the smells of coffee, red wine and hot crêpes, the sounds of a live band from somewhere close by. They drifted slowly alongside the Seine, reached the buildings of the Louvre, then turned and re-joined the busy main street. They detoured through courtyards and down side streets, they stopped at churches and water fountains, Mark's eye noticing all the detail, Emma, the bigger scene captured by camera. The air was warm compared to that in England, and they revelled in the early evening atmosphere of a foreign city.

After a while, they found a small restaurant serving simple dishes with seating outside. They seated themselves at the only free table, ordered two glasses of wine, some food, more wine, and more wine, until the friendly man who owned the place had to tell them he wanted to close. 'It's Wednesday,' he explained. 'Friday, Saturday, we open late, but Wednesday we close at 11.30.'

They woke early the following day, full of excitement for new adventures. They started at Notre Dame Cathedral, took a cruise down the river – a weekend in Paris in a single boat ride, then set off exploring the Left Bank. Mark had been to Paris before, he remembered wandering round the Left Bank, and was now enjoying revisiting those times, the things he'd seen, the things he'd done: *'A wee lad from Northern Ireland out in the big wide world for the first time.'*

They ambled round slowly, admiring buildings, inspecting ironwork, cheered by bright red Geraniums, refuelled with coffees, croissants, and pastries. Towards mid-afternoon, needing to wind their way back to the river, they traversed the Jardin de Luxembourg, enjoyed the lilies and ferns out in force, and came upon the Pantheon, a beautiful building of colonnades, domes and detailed statues. Residing in the centre of a cobbled square, it was grand and imposing. They mounted the steps, Emma keen to see the inside of a building so fine on the outside, Mark intrigued by the advertised exhibition. The inside of the building was simply stunning – tall and elegant, with beautiful stonework and careful carving, elaborate paintings the height of the building, pale in colour, wistful in nature, a beautiful black and white plain marble floor. The exhibition was a demonstration of Foucault's pendulum, a huge golden ball on the end of a wire, hanging from the central dome, rhythmically swinging backwards and forwards. They hung over the banister, watching the swinging, both of them trying to understand its meaning. Placards were available, but none of them explained it well.

They descended the stairs to visit the rest of the exhibition – famous French people including Foucault; the crypt, a beautiful place for it, its smooth stone walls and clean low arches. Emma and Mark wandered round separately, stopping, reading, admiring slowly. Once Emma had finished, she quickly looked through the boards for Mark, but not finding him, she returned to the main body of the building. As she reached the top of the steps, she saw he was there already, sitting on a bench opposite her, calmly, quietly waiting for her. 'You should have told me you'd finished,' she started apologetically. 'I could have been quicker.'

He smiled and shrugged his shoulders lightly. 'We're not in a rush.'

They returned to the Left Bank for dinner that evening, but disappointed by the meal that they chose, they easily returned to the place that they'd visited the night before.

They took a table on the pavement and ordered again two glasses of wine. They sat and talked about their day together, the things they'd enjoyed, why they'd enjoyed them, and what they had enjoyed the most. As they spoke they ordered more wine, until three glasses later, Mark decided that what he was most enjoying in Paris was sitting on a pavement until midnight, drinking wine with someone as beautiful as Emma. He rested his head on her shoulder as he said it, placed his hand gently on her thigh. She tilted her cheek to rest her head on his and slowly stroked the hand on her leg.

'You don't mean that,' she laughed softly. 'I'm not beautiful.'

'Not on the outside,' he replied. 'But you're beautiful on

the inside. The smile you gave me at the top of those steps, so gentle, so caring, I could have eaten you alive.'

They stayed as they were without talking, completely comfortable.

Finally, having finished the wine, Mark placed his glass back on the table, extracted his head and his hand, and stood up. They found their hotel again quickly, and as Mark bade Emma good night this evening, he reached out his hand to the space in between them. She took his hand and squeezed his fingers, but realising his fingers wouldn't be enough, she climbed out of her bed, stepped over to his and slid in beside him. Within seconds he had enclosed her in his arms and was lightly kissing her nearest shoulder. She twisted so that he was kissing her mouth, and the rest of the night they spent making love.

35

Mark beamed good morning as she opened her eyes, and as she lay in his bed still, waking slowly, he kissed her down the length of her back. Emma purred and twisted her body to face him, expecting him to come to her again, but he remained on the bed opposite.

'Are you okay?' she queried, suddenly unsure.

'I'm okay,' he nodded. 'Thank you for last night.'

She wasn't really reassured. She loved Mark, there was no doubt, but she wasn't sure if he loved her. The odd criticism, the token put-down, the crass little comments had all been recent. He tried to tell her how much he liked her, and as they left the hotel he laid his arm across her shoulders, but in the minute it took her to respond, he changed his mind and backed away.

They spent the day in Saint Denis, a small suburb, a pleasant change, to the north of the city. Most of the time, they spent in the cathedral and relaxing in the cathedral gardens. As Emma set off with her camera, leaving Mark to read the newspaper, she promised not to take photos of him, but in the end, she couldn't resist. From across the gardens, set against a very French backdrop, he looked so calm, so strong, so serene. She knew why he didn't want photos of him. He'd become used to not wearing his hat with her, and was enjoying not wearing one in Paris, but she knew he still wore it in Oxford, when he saw his friends, that he still avoided the golf clubhouse. She took one photo, only for her. He was her lover.

They had a good day, and dined that evening not far from their room – a lively place with cool décor and jazz music, but as they walked back along the river, Mark again became distant. Emma didn't know what to do, she didn't know suddenly what to think. She wanted him, and she wanted him to want her too, but she was scared. They'd come so far, but she wasn't happy, she wasn't excited, she was simply scared – scared that he wouldn't love her enough, scared that she would love him too much.

The following day, they set out again for the Left Bank. A leisurely day, they strolled through the city, enjoying the scenery, enjoying the company, until they reached the Catacombs. They spent an interesting hour under the streets amid layer upon layer of skulls and bones, then back above ground, they dined on oysters, and made their way slowly back to the Right Bank, enjoying the sun, the summer scenes, the relaxed atmosphere of a late afternoon. This really was Mark's kind of day, and as a result he was happy, fun and great company. They laughed and joked, looked out for each other, helped each other, and when Mark was happy then so was Emma, his smiles, his laughs, his small compliments. She didn't even need the sun, the sights, the scenes, to be in Paris. She was happy just to walk, to laugh, to be with her wonderful man.

They spent the evening revisiting the market in the Place de Bastille, feasting on steak and chips in the true French style, then returned again to the pavement of the small restaurant. Their last evening, the friendly man's was an obvious choice.

'I'm so glad we came to Paris.' Mark sighed as he lifted his wine glass. 'And when we get back, you'll be going to Bristol. I'll miss you, you know.'

'Will you?' Emma asked. 'The annoying presence, the extra washing up, the toiletries cluttering up the bathroom?'

'Definitely the toiletries in the bathroom.'

They arrived home late the following day, and as they climbed upstairs, Emma wondered if anything had changed.

She didn't dare ask. She was tired, she didn't want to be challenged, and if he rejected her now, she wasn't sure that she would cope. She rationalised that he'd be tired too, so slowly, forlornly, she unpacked her things and slept in her room, in her cold and lonely bed.

The following day she heard him stirring as she passed his room, so popped her head round his bedroom door. 'Morning,' she started cheerfully. 'I thought we might continue the theme and go out for breakfast.'

He looked at her, but didn't reply. She moved into his room and lay down on the bed beside him. 'I just thought it would be nice. Only two more days and I'll be in Bristol.'

He looked at her slyly. 'Hmm, okay. Before that though can we have a shower?'

'Of course. You go first. I'll just lie here.' She rolled onto her back and lay against the duvet.

Keeping his eyes on her all of the time, he climbed out, stopped at the foot of the bed, leant over and dragged her to her feet. 'Oh no you won't.' He stood her up in front of him and started tugging at her pyjamas. 'You're coming with me.'

And after that, she knew where she was.

They spent the day doing all the things they'd always done, then wandered home slowly arm in arm, and finally finished both in Mark's bed. They spent the day doing all the things they'd always done, but today it was perfect.

BELFAST, DECEMBER 2007

36

Two years after she'd moved to Belfast, projects completed, new projects started, collaborations going well, Emma was invited to Athens to speak about her work. The meeting was in December. A warm, sunny Athens as winter in Belfast was just taking hold, she'd agreed in a considered second.

She was impressed by the arrangements from the beginning. The inviting organisation flew her to Greece in business class, had a chauffeur meet her at the airport, and had arranged for her to stay in a five-star hotel. The room reminded her of the one in Aqaba – the quality of the finish, the smell of the sheets, she couldn't pinpoint it exactly, the hotel, the expense, the luxury. Eager to make the most of it, in search of sauna and health spa, she soon found herself by a rooftop pool, the Acropolis shining against the night sky.

The following day, she met and talked with the meeting hosts, gave her presentation, took part in the following discussion, but when the rest of the day looked set to continue in Greek, Emma was left to her own devices.

Within a half hour's walk of her hotel was the central shopping district of Athens, and before long she was engrossed in Athens' biggest bookshop. She had a few books to buy for a colleague and quickly found herself captured. She left with the books that she'd come to buy, plus one for herself for the rest of her stay. She read for the afternoon, first amid parks as she walked back home, then beside the pool under the shadow of the shining Acropolis. At 8pm, when the pool area closed, she simply transferred to continue reading in her large luxurious bed.

She wasn't sure if it was the room, the luxury, the book she was reading, but her mind kept flicking to the hotel in Aqaba, to the night in Aqaba when Mark had told her he didn't love her. His words had been *'I can't do this'*, and while he had said them while making love, she wondered now if that was what he'd meant - that he didn't love her, he couldn't love her. Had he meant instead, that he couldn't carry on as they were? both pretending his illness was temporary, both hoping his illness was temporary, when in fact he knew that it wasn't. He'd said at the beginning that the prognosis wasn't good, but that was before he'd had any treatment. Before they went to Jordan, had he found out the treatment hadn't helped?

Emma tried to think back over the timeline. He'd known in August that the chemotherapy hadn't had much effect. Had the radiotherapy not been effective either? What else had he known when they went to Jordan? She wouldn't have asked - she often forgot he was so ill, there were still no outward signs, and if she had, he would never have said. Was it possible he could no longer pretend? that nothing was wrong, that he wasn't ill, that they'd be alright? He could hurt her no longer with falsehoods and lies – *'I can't do this.'?* He'd never explained, but it would have been like him to let her rot in her own self-doubt. Except, of course, it hadn't been only her that had been rotting.

By the following morning, her thoughts had developed. For all the times he'd been nasty, was he trying to save her? Trying to put her off from staying? Saving himself maybe also, trying to detach himself, but the detachment for her sake as well as his own? She realised slowly, if he was concerned about not hurting her, about not lying, not only had he not stopped loving her, he had loved her even more than she'd thought. By the end of her breakfast, she no longer wondered if Mark had loved her, she wondered how she could have missed it.

Straight after breakfast, she left the hotel and caught a bus to Acropolis Hill. She'd been before, but she was in Athens, how could she not? By twelve o'clock she was stood on the platform, the Acropolis in front of her, the city behind her, the Acropolis behind her, the city beneath her. She was impressed with the building, but more by the city and its greenness. She'd been to Greece, but only in summer, when it was hot, dry, dusty and brown. Today it was warm and pleasantly so, and the city was green and covered in grass. It was a pleasure to walk through the gardens, to amble through flowers, to enjoy the sun, to feel its warmth, and welcome it, not shy away or hide from its heat.

She stayed at the Acropolis for long enough to feel its majesty, to sense the exploits and triumphs, then her walk down the hill took her to the end of the tourist bazaars. She found a café in a leafy courtyard for lunch, enjoyed the peace and calm all around her, then headed off for the Triumphal Arch and the Temple of Zeus. Agreeably devoid of tourists too, she took her time inspecting both, but the Temple of Zeus she enjoyed the most. The beautiful columns, towering above her, belittling her in the carpet of grass, bathed in warm December sun. As she sat on the bench at the edge of the park, an elderly groundswoman came up beside her. 'You by yourself?' she said slowly in broken English.

'Yes,' replied Emma. 'I'm here for work.'

'But you, no ring.' She gestured down towards Emma's ring finger.

'No,' replied Emma, looking down. 'I fell in love with a man who was sick.' She said it simply, a statement of fact.

The old woman merely stood beside her and Emma wondered if maybe she'd done the same. Fallen in love with a man who was sick, fallen in love with a man with no future, yet stuck with him and seen it through. Together they remained in peaceful silence, each in their own thoughts, but comfortable with them, accepting.

As Emma continued to sit quietly, she realised as well that she wasn't embarrassed. She used to be embarrassed by being alone, scared that people would think she was odd, in some way strange, but she shouldn't be, not scared, not now. She was alone because she'd loved Mark, she'd stayed with him, she'd seen it through. She hadn't left him as soon as he'd told her he was ill. She wondered how many had done the same, sacrificed themselves for a love with no future.

She left the temple and slowly walked back to her hotel. She shouldn't be embarrassed or ashamed. She was alone because she'd loved Mark, because she'd loved a man who was dying, and in her heart she was glad she had. There had been no proof, no clear statement, but the more she thought, the more she thought he'd loved her too. The little things he'd said, the little things he'd done, not only at the start either, the things he'd done towards the end, the things he had said, the things he had meant.

She started re-evaluating the emails he'd sent her, everything she hadn't understood. After she'd left him and he'd asked her back, she'd never understood. She'd tried to be nice, to be sympathetic, but his replies simply questioned her and were critical – *Why couldn't she write like everyone else? How could she see things so clearly? How could she know from so far away?* She'd thought he enjoyed being nasty to her, but now she wondered. Was he really asking how she could touch him? how she could say things while others didn't? Perhaps she had misunderstood.

Other confusions also became clearer. He was scared to see her when she came back to him, scared to see her in case she hurt him, scared he might fall in love again. The lack of commitment, that also made sense - he wanted to see her, to have her, love her, but he was scared, scared for himself and also for her. In his heart he loved her, but in his head he knew that he shouldn't. She only got close when his head was weak, when his head could no longer resist. Christine was right with the song on the CD – he wanted to stay, but he had to leave. Every time he wouldn't talk, every time he wouldn't see her, he was trying to protect her. Why had it taken her so long to realise?

The delays at the start, they were also the same. The comment that maybe they weren't meant to be, his refusal to approach, his reluctance to accept her advances, and the message in the book that he'd sent her in Norway, that this might be his biggest mistake? She wondered what he would think now. Was it worse to love when you knew you might leave? When you knew that everything might not last?

She thought he was probably thinking of her, the pain and anguish that he could inflict, but it hadn't been a mistake. She loved him more for shielding her, trying to protect her, and in the end, for his inability to resist. She only wished now that he hadn't succeeded when he had, that he had let her love him as much as she'd wanted.

GUILDFORD, NOVEMBER 2001

37

Weeks went by and nothing changed. Emma saw Mark occasionally, Pete as well, every time a little reminder, but every time nothing more definite. 'Really should have that game sometime!', 'Must get those drinks in!', 'Still think you can beat me at pool?' And every time her response was the same, 'I can't do Friday, but any other day?', but that was it.

Finally, she changed tack.

'Still haven't played that pool, have we?' Mark stopped at her office door on his way past.

'Wednesday,' she replied. 'I could do Wednesday.'

Mark smiled. 'I'll tell Pete.'

The following Wednesday, at 5pm, she made her way to Mark's office. He turned as she knocked on his open door. 'Hi,' she started. 'Do you still want to play pool?'

He looked back at his computer. 'Is Hallam ready?'

She took a step back and glanced down the corridor. 'I don't think he's here,' she replied with a frown, Pete's office door closed. She checked, returned and waited for Mark to look back at her. 'But, I don't mind if you don't want to go,' she offered.

'No, I'm done here.' He turned off his computer. 'But let's not play pool, it's far too nice to stay inside.' It had been a bright, crisp, cold winter day, and was now a crisp, cold winter evening.

They walked to the apartments at the edge of the campus,

and Mark unlocked a front door. 'Here,' he held the door open for her. 'Dump your stuff down … although, on second thoughts, you might need some gloves.'

Obediently, Emma put down her bag, kept her gloves and scarf, and backed out. Mark reached for the scarf on the end of the banister, took two apples from the table in the hall, and came to join her. 'This way.' He pointed with one hand and handed her an apple with the other. 'I think we could have a drink instead. There's an excellent pub about two miles out, and I assume you're alright walking there.' He glanced at her clothes, right down to her shoes. 'You seem like the walking type.'

Emma nodded. It was a beautiful evening; she could think of nothing better than to be going for a drink with Mark Alexander. If he wanted to go two miles out, then that was fine. If he wanted to walk, that was fine too.

Before long, they were walking beside meadows, lit by an almost full moon. They talked away freely, their work, their interests, their lives at present. They worked in the same place, they both enjoyed walking, they both enjoyed mountains.

They reached the pub in not long at all, took their drinks to the fireside and continued. They both liked sailing, they both liked diving, they both liked travelling, they both liked each other. They talked of places where they had been, things that they'd seen, things that they'd done.

Of all the things that Mark still did, the one he currently liked most was sailing. 'The freedom, the peace, the feel of the wind rushing through your hair.'

Emma agreed. 'I like the freedom and the peace. I once went sailing for a week, and couldn't believe the noise that traffic makes when I was driving home. It was so peaceful out on the sea.'

'To be able to control the wind like that too, and then the next minute it completely drops and you're stranded. I love it.'

Emma laughed, 'More than sailing though, I love diving – the freedom again, the ability to turn on your head and do backflips ... but most of all, that whole new world just under the waves. The fish, the corals, the slugs, the sharks ... it's incredible, an entire world, all simply doing exactly what they should be.' Mark let her continue uninterrupted, enjoying her liveliness and passion. She talked on, enjoying herself too, describing the places where she'd been diving, her favourite places, the things she'd seen. 'And painted across my whole bathroom wall, there's one massive picture of under the sea ... with jacks and rays and sharks and divers. It takes up the entire wall. There are even barracudas, I'm so proud of them. It took me one whole rainy Sunday.'

Mark was laughing and shaking his head.

'You'll have to come and see it sometime, it's fantastic ... really, it is!'

'I certainly will,' Mark replied warmly.

Towards the end of their second pint, a decision was needed. 'Another drink? Or something to eat?' Mark asked Emma.

'And how will we get home afterwards?'

'Taxi,' he replied, 'it's easy enough.'

'Or we could walk?' Emma suggested. 'Although, I think, we'll have to start soon – I think the clouds are supposed to be gathering.'

Mark simply smiled and drained his glass.

They walked back the same way that they had come. The moon was still bright and the path easy, but the concentration required for walking put a stop to conversation. They were happy still in each other's company, and before long, they were back at Mark's flat. He unlocked the door and stood back, allowing Emma to collect her belongings.

As she straightened, she turned to face him. 'Thanks very much, that was a very pleasant evening.'

'Yes, thank you.' He smiled in return. 'Will you be alright getting home?'

'Yes, I'll be fine,' she replied slowly. 'It'll be nice on the bike at this time of night.'

He moved away to let her pass. 'See you later then.'

Emma simply smiled and left.

38

The following week, Mark wasn't at work, and Emma didn't hear from him. She spent her time wondering why not. He hadn't mentioned being away, he hadn't mentioned a holiday. She decided in the end that he must be away, he must be busy, busy with other things other than her. He obviously hadn't thought of their evening out, as anything more than it had been - an excuse for a few drinks, Pete Hallam's absence a genuine oversight.

Her life resumed its previous pattern. She simply had to be cool and calm when she next saw him. Friends out for a drink one evening, that was all.

She didn't have to worry for long. Within the fortnight, Mark reappeared. Rounding a corner on her way to the post room, she almost ran straight into him, and one quick 'Hi', a cool and calm and collected 'Hi', she hardly stopped. Not how she had expected it, but they were just friends and nothing more. Pleased with herself, she returned to her office.

As she took up her desk chair, she saw a new email: *Sender: Mark Alexander.* She clicked it open: *You alright?*

She looked at the screen, more puzzled than anything. *Yes, thank you, I'm fine. Where have you been?*

Oh, that's alright then, so you didn't just blank me in the corridor?

No, I didn't blank you, I was surprised that was all, I didn't expect to see you.

Glad you're alright.

Emma left it there. Friends out for a drink one evening.

She heard nothing more for over a week, her instincts

verified with every passing day - he was too popular, too much fun for her. Then the following Wednesday, one of their colleagues received an award, honoured as usual, with celebratory drinks. The foyer was busy when Emma entered. Mark was with Andrew, shaking his hand, offering his congratulations.

Before Emma could reach him, he had disappeared. She'd seen him though before he'd left. She'd seen him tense, change from easy and calm, to stiff and awkward, then leave abruptly, as fast as he could, without even acknowledging her.

Emma drank her glass of wine distracted by Mark's behaviour. He hadn't not seen her, he had deliberately avoided her, deliberately not stopped and spoken to her. Her congratulations offered, she walked back upstairs via Mark's open door. 'Evening,' she started.

He turned to look at her questioningly.

'I was just wondering if you're going to The Mortarboard on Friday night?'

Mark continued to look at her blankly, then asked slowly, 'Are you asking me out on a date?'

'No,' she smiled calmly. 'I just thought that if you were going, then other people might be going as well.'

He relaxed visibly. 'Good answer,' he replied with a short laugh. 'Yes, I'll be going and so are some others.' He flashed her a smile, 'We'll see you there.'

She wasn't sure if it was an invitation or a challenge, but Emma accepted willingly.

The Friday night passed without incident. Emma stayed for one drink, was persuaded to stay for another, then as she left she caught Mark on his way to the bar. 'We still haven't had that game of pool.'

'No,' he replied.

'Maybe next Wednesday?'

He shrugged lightly. 'Okay, if you'd like to.'

'Why not?' she smiled.

Wednesday came, and like the Wednesday before, she worked until 5pm, then went downstairs. She'd heard nothing from him since Friday, but she'd kept the evening free. She arrived outside his office to see him walking down the corridor towards her. As he grew nearer, he started speaking. 'No can do, I'm afraid.'

'Oh,' she started.

'They've just got things set up.' He motioned with his head towards one of the research rooms. 'I can't leave now, they'll have done it for nothing.'

'Oh … don't worry … some other time.'

'Maybe it isn't meant to be.'

Emma though, refused to accept defeat so easily. 'Tomorrow, instead?' she questioned quickly. 'Or will you still be working on this?'

'No, tomorrow should be fine. But if it's a day like this again, let's not play pool.'

'Okay,' she smiled. 'Email me whenever you're ready.'

She left disappointed. She understood about the research, but the comment after that, that worried her – 'maybe it isn't meant be'. Did he mean 'them'? Was it 'they' that maybe weren't meant to be?

The following day, Emma waited for his email, until at 5.30pm she gave up waiting, and went down again to find him. She arrived to find his office door shut and no sign of him down the corridor. She sent an email in case he was planning to email later, then set off for home. Often on a Thursday, she went to an art class, and she didn't want to miss it for no reason, there weren't many left now for this year. The evening was beautiful, again a bright and starry sky, and it was a shame not to be outside, to then have a drink by a roaring pub fire, but at least the drawing would distract her. Maybe he was trying to let her down gently.

The following morning, Emma's first task was to meet with a colleague. Immediately beforehand, she opened her office and checked her computer. At the top of her emails was one from yesterday: *Sender: Mark Alexander.* Quickly she clicked the message open.

Hi there,

Come to the apartment when you finish, and I'll take you out to Leith Hill. Beautiful on an evening like this – the stars will be amazing.

Emma's heart sank. She looked at the time that he had sent the message: *17.42.*

She looked through her sent items for the email that she had sent him: *17.42.*

She gathered her paperwork, and raced downstairs. She knocked on his door, but received no reply. She stood in the corridor wondering what to do. Had she upset him? Had he got her message? Had she just lost all of her chances? She ran to her meeting, anxious, agitated, hoping to finish it as fast as possible.

The meeting over, she flew back to Mark's office. She knocked again, but there was still no reply. She returned to her own room and sent him an email.

Dear Mark,

I'm so sorry. I didn't get your message before I left. I tried looking for you, but you were nowhere to be found and I don't have a number for you. I am really sorry. It would have been lovely. I hope you didn't wait for me for long, and went anyway.
Yours, Emma

The return email was almost immediate. *07950 532541.*

Emma smiled. *And was it good? Please tell me you went anyway.*

Beautiful. You should have come too.

Next time, definitely.

She waited for almost a week, then used the number to

send him a text: *Hi, it's Emma, a few Christmas drinks this evening?*

No, in Oxford, drinking already, M.

No problem, have a good time, E.

A few weeks later, rested by a calm family Christmas, she became braver. The apology for the missed evening had been accepted, the invite for Christmas drinks was well received, why not try something slightly bigger? She was also becoming slightly perplexed – there was the continual hint of something between them, but then there would be nothing more. Was he interested? Or was he simply trying to be kind?

She hadn't seen him for a while, so an email wouldn't seem out of place.

Hi Mark,

I hope you had a good break over Christmas. Just wondering if you're up to anything over the weekend in ten days time, and if not, if you want to come up to the Lakes? Current thinking is to go up Thursday night, walk/boat on Fri, Sat, and then come back down again on Sunday. The weather looks good. Pub rooms, pub meals.

Let me know, Emma.

She worried it was rather forward, but at least he could be in no doubt of her interest and wish to spend more time with him. The following day, though, there was no reply. Three days later and she began to think it might have been the most humiliating mistake she could have made. Surely he could at least reply? Was the suggestion so ridiculous it didn't even deserve a reply?

The following Thursday, he still hadn't replied. Emma was looking forward to the weekend, was happy going by herself, and she decided it would be a good opportunity to decide if she could really be bothered with Mark. She was currently unconvinced. She left work at lunchtime, packed her car and headed to the Lake District, very much alone.

At the traffic around Birmingham, her phone bleeped a text: *Have a great time. I'll buy you a pint for every mountain you climb, M.*

Emma's feelings again were mixed. She was pleased he had sent a reply at last, but she was also disappointed. Had it really taken that long to decide? Couldn't he have emailed in the week? Hadn't he thought about how she might be feeling?

Reassured, though, by the lack of rejection and buoyed by the promise of something to come, she resolved to enjoy her weekend alone. She had already decided that the Lake District was too far to go, so instead was headed for Snowdonia.

On her first day, she took the Miners Track to the top of Snowdon. The track was easy, the walk not too strenuous, the weather was glorious and the scenery stunning. At around lunchtime, she reached the top, but instead of enjoying a peaceful lunch surrounded by views and clear blue skies, she found herself amid crowds of people – participants in a charity hike. She touched the top briefly and quickly retreated.

To then descend, she had three choices: to return via the route by which she had come, to take a relaxing hike to the north, or an exhausting march a long way south. She chose the northerly route, but soon discovered that this path was not a relaxing hike. She'd never been along the ridge before, but soon realised that the Crib Goch name should have suggested something. The ridge itself was very steep sided, almost an edge, and while you could walk slightly below the top in places, in others you couldn't. For most of the afternoon she enjoyed the challenge, the focus and care needed for her feet, the respect of some, the nervousness in others. Only twice did she consider turning round, but the hike back up was further by then, and reassured by the people behind her, she pressed on bravely. Finally she arrived back at the pass, tired, slightly windswept, but satisfied.

As she sat at the car park edge with her hot chocolate, she

texted Mark: *Snowdon – 1085m, Garnedd Ugain – 1065m.*

Some time later, she received a reply: *Garnedd Ugain? Did you come down Crib Goch?*

Emma was very pleased with herself: *Certainly did. Hanging on by my fingertips in places, I was.*

I'm impressed. Hope it was clear and sunny with you. Beautiful here.

She was reminded she didn't know where he was or what he was doing, but she didn't mind, right now he was thinking of her.

The following morning Emma rose early, refreshed from a warm and comfortable night, drove back to the pass and set off up the other side. The weather was not as good as it had been, but it was still dry, the walking was good, and the views all around her were easily admired. As she climbed the hill, she occasionally glanced over to Snowdon. Still busy, she noted calmly. At the top of the mountain, in the company of only four fellow walkers, she ate her lunch peacefully, pleased with her efforts. She sent her text: *Glyder Fawr – 999m.*

Her afternoon route took her west along the ridge, down to the road and then back up to return to the pass. Relatively flat, the path along the ridge was very easy, flanked to the right by edges and buttresses, and to the left by gentle hillsides. The rhythm of her steps as she sauntered along, the sense of freedom, the wind on her cheeks, she was enjoying herself immensely. She stopped midway to send a second text: *Glyder Fach – 994m.*

The following morning, she decided against any more walking and instead fancied a bit of sightseeing. Caernarfon Castle is an impressive structure, strong and solid with hardly a dent or a sign of ruin. She spent the morning experiencing great halls and jousting fields, exploring dungeons and dark passages. She would remember Caernarfon if she had sons. Refreshed by the change and the holiday feel, she followed her visit with newspaper fish and chips on the quayside, then she turned and headed back home.

39

'So,' Emma hung on the doorframe as she leaned into his room, 'when am I going to get my pints?'

Mark turned towards her and smiled easily. 'Did you have a nice time?'

'Yes I did, thank you. Beautiful weather, although I didn't go to the Lakes, of course. I hadn't been to Snowdonia for ages, and I thought it would be closer, but I'm not sure now. Snowdon itself wasn't very nice, busy with some fund-raising challenge, but the rest of Snowdonia was lovely.'

'Were you by yourself?'

'Yes,' she admitted, reminded that she usually kept that to herself. 'I like walking by myself, and when it's cold and crisp like it was, although it is quite strange when you meet other people. Go walking by yourself in the middle of nowhere and the people you meet are generally impressed. Go walking by yourself somewhere busy and everyone looks at you like you're Norman No-Mates.'

'I thought you were with friends... I'd have texted you loads more if I'd known.'

'Oh no, it was fine. I had my book, and there were plenty of other people staying at the pub, gorgeous meals, a roaring fire, and there were these two big dogs that came down every evening, knackered probably after a long walk, but looking so happy.'

Mark was no longer listening. He let her continue and just started speaking underneath her. 'Do you want to go out for dinner instead?'

Emma didn't stop at the end of her sentence, but carried

straight on, same tone, same casualness. 'Okay, yes, that would be nice. Although not next Friday, it's my birthday, that might be a bit too much pressure… But I could do any other night next week?'

'Thursday then? There's a new place up the Shere Road, Carlo's, Italian. Virginia says it's very nice.'

Emma smiled. 'Thursday it is, then. Can you collect me? I can show you my bathroom wall.'

'OK,' he nodded. 'Email me directions. I'll be round about eight.'

The days until Thursday then simply sped by. Emma didn't have much work to do, but she couldn't do much work either. She was increasingly distracted, and by Thursday, she couldn't concentrate at all. She wasn't sure what she should wear – she'd already decided on something new, but she wasn't sure what she really wanted. Her morning contemplations were interrupted by the telephone.

'Hi Emma,' her sister's voice rang out. 'Just thought I'd phone to say happy birthday.'

'It's not today!' Emma exclaimed in amusement. 'It's tomorrow! You're early!' She could almost hear the confusion at the other end.

'Is today only the sixth? Oh, stupid, stupid. Sorry, I thought it was the seventh. And I was being so organised. I'll have forgotten again by tomorrow, then I'll miss it.'

'Don't worry,' Emma laughed. 'I can have an early one and carry it over until tomorrow. I'm glad you called though, I need your help. I have a hot date this evening and I'm just wondering what I should wear.'

'What makes it a hot date? I've always wondered what makes dates hot.'

'Alright, I've got a date this evening, with a guy I really fancy, and I think he might fancy me too. We went for a drink a while ago and I mentioned it to one of the secretaries – she was going on about how nice he was, and how well he would suit me, so I told her we'd already been for a drink and we'd just have to see what would happen. Well, she came round earlier to ask if I was doing anything this evening and when I said yes, she asked if I was going out for dinner. She was so excited. She'd been talking to Mark and had mentioned him looking happier than he had done for a while, so she asked if it was something to do with Agnes, his last girlfriend, and he'd said no, he'd met somebody else. He wouldn't say who, but he was going out for dinner with her this evening. That has to be me.'

'Sounds promising... Well, I always go for trousers and a nice top. You've got to feel comfortable, that's most important.'

'Okay,' Emma stated, 'I'll buy some new trousers.'

She left work early and stopped on her way home to buy the most expensive trousers she'd ever bought. Teamed with a cream jumper, black heels and her lucky silver pendant, she felt cool, sexy and understated.

Mark arrived equally cool, sexy and understated. He laughed at the bathroom wall while Emma finished dressing, but she didn't mind, she was happy for him to see something of her character.

Carlo's was located outside Guildford, on the edge of the Downs. It reminded Emma of the pub they'd first been to – alone and separate, but happily so. They were given a table at the back of the restaurant, and settled down to a comfortable evening. Mark was keen to hear about Emma's weekend and the mountains for which he was paying, and Emma in turn enjoyed telling him, his lively questions, his witty remarks. He had stories of Snowdonia, funny stories, he told them well, stories she enjoyed. From Snowdonia, they moved to the Lake District and then the Peak District, and from there they moved on to their past. Emma knew both because she'd lived in Leeds, Mark because he had lived in Sheffield. Finally from the past, they moved back to the present.

'Would you like to come to Oxford sometime? I think you'd like it.' He wasn't looking at her as he asked, but Emma could see his vulnerability, and it simply made her heart melt.

She paused carefully. 'If I come to Oxford, will you take me to Wytham Woods to see badgers? I've never seen a badger and they're supposed to have them in Wytham Woods.'

Mark looked up, his blue eyes shining. 'Why on earth do you want to see badgers? They smell, you know, and carry disease.'

'I've never seen one, that's all ... not a live one anyway. Wytham Woods isn't far from Oxford, is it? It's always on *Inspector Morse*.'

'No,' Mark grinned. 'Wytham Woods isn't far from Oxford, and it does have badgers.'

'Excellent, when were you thinking?'

He smiled at her acceptance, and shrugged his shoulders. 'Whenever you like. You can stay over.'

They continued for the rest of the meal, the same chatter, the same interest, the same enjoyment. As they returned to Emma's flat, she looked at Mark. 'Do you want to come in?' She didn't want the evening to end.

'No.' His arms were rigid on the steering wheel. 'I bet you don't have any beer.'

Emma smiled and shook her head.

'No, I didn't think so. I'll have one at home.'

'Well, thanks for a lovely evening. I'll see you tomorrow.'

She shut the car door and entered her flat. She had enjoyed the evening immensely. No kiss goodnight, but he'd invited her to his house for her birthday, he'd invited her to Oxford, and the look in his eyes when she'd accepted – that was enough.

And, as she dropped into bed, her phone bleeped her a text: *Happy birthday. Just wanted to be the first, M.*

Emma shone.

40

Emma woke late the following day, smile still on her face. She made a cup of tea, climbed back into bed and opened the cards piled on the mantelpiece. Today, she was thirty.

She had a relaxing morning at home, then went into work for lunch with Celine, and an afternoon chatting and emailing. At 6pm, she and Celine went to The Mortarboard. The previous evening, Mark had suggested meeting after work, but with no further details, Emma had decided to look for him first in the University bar, but unwilling to go by herself, she'd waited for Celine, then dragged her there too.

They didn't stay long. Within minutes of arriving it was obvious that Mark wasn't there, and neither was anyone else that they knew. Emma drank patiently, carefully keeping time with Celine, eager for her to finish quickly. As soon as they'd finished, Emma made her way to Mark's apartment.

He was smiling as he answered the door. 'Well, you're running slow, but I suppose it is your birthday.'

'Sorry,' she started. 'I thought you'd be in The Mortarboard, so I took Celine, and then of course, you weren't, but I could hardly then just change my mind.'

'Well, come up, make yourself at home. I thought we might have a bite to eat.'

Emma didn't care what they did, she was happy just to be there, to be with him. She dropped her work things in the hall and followed him upstairs to the kitchen. He handed her a gin and tonic, chinked her glass with a happy birthday, and left her to look round while he continued preparing dinner. Built on the side of a hill, the apartment was a strange mixture of levels, but purpose-built, painted a dull brown, and with not many personal effects, it felt very functional. Emma made her way back to the kitchen. 'How long have you lived here?'

'Coming up for two years now, although I'm thinking of moving back full time to Oxford. You get this flat for being a warden.' He'd already explained his role as a warden, and how he was thinking of giving it up. 'Oxford is nicer, my house is much nicer, and it has a garden. Most of my stuff is already there.'

So that explained the lack of personal effects. 'And did you paint it when you moved in?'

'No,' he replied. 'The University painted it.'

'It's horrible, isn't it?' Emma started. 'Such a dull and dreary colour.'

He looked up slowly, grinning at her. 'The University painted it, but I chose the colour.'

Emma laughed, she had no escape.

The rest of the evening she also spent laughing. They enjoyed a meal of rich chicken stew, finished with great slabs of Swiss chocolate. Mark told her about his house in Oxford, his weekend moving belongings back there, his planned three-month visit to New Zealand. She told him of her childhood in Dorset, her upcoming spring job in Norway, her lack of job from June onwards. Emma couldn't have thought of a better way to spend her birthday. She already loved spending time with Mark, not only the laughter and entertainment, she felt looked after, she felt protected. She was impressed by everything about him. The similarities between them were also increasing, their likes, dislikes, their passions, pastimes. By the end of the evening, Mark had demonstrated a clear ability to cook as well as converse and entertain, and Emma had confirmed her weekend in Oxford.

The following week, she also received an answer to her initial query – where had he been the week after their first drink together. In her pigeonhole one morning lay a postcard of The Giant's Causeway. The message on the back: *Way better than a badger. Hope you get here sometime, M x.*

41

She arrived in Oxford, map in hand, instructions at the ready. *Leave the station via the footbridge over the road, take the path down and back under the bridge, take the first left into Mill Street and mine is on the left-hand side, about half-way along, the one with the black gate and blue front door.*

She found the house easily and knocked at the front door.

'Oh, you're earlier than I thought you would be.' Mark stood in the doorway dressed in gloves and wellington boots.

'You said lunchtime, so here I am, ready for my lunch.'

'I'm just in the garden sorting out plants. You're lucky I heard you, in fact, I was up near the house. Do you mind if I finish? There's only a few of them left to do.'

'No, not at all, you carry on. I'll be looking round.'

He smiled and headed back to the garden. 'Yours is the room upstairs at the front.'

Emma took her bag and started upstairs. It was a big room painted sunshine yellow, with two large windows looking onto the street, a huge leafy plant on the drawers at the end and a cream sofa bed on the inside wall. Pleased with her lodgings, she put down her bag and made her way back through the house - a classic Victorian terraced house, two rooms on each floor, the kitchen and bathroom out the back. The back bedroom was clearly Mark's. Smaller than hers, and painted pale grey with a window that looked over the garden, she could easily see Mark quite happy there. She descended the stairs, passed through the hall, into the front room, a beautiful pale grey and brown room, with cream sofa and cream curtains, an attractive black fireplace and mantelpiece, ornamented by a single cream candle. Emma loved its quiet simplicity. The second room downstairs was interconnected – a dining room, similar in colour, but lighter and brighter as a result of a pair of large old-fashioned doors that opened out on to the garden. The dark wood floor, the books on the shelves, the table half covered in post and papers, it also felt comfortable. She entered the kitchen and turned out the back door into the garden.

Mark was heading back in towards her. 'Alright?' he asked.

She nodded smiling. 'How about you? How are you getting on?'

'Just finished there now.' He moved past her to rehouse his tools, casually brushing his hand against her thigh. 'Thanks for coming.'

He removed his boots and entered the kitchen. 'Cheese and tomato sandwiches? I might even have some Kettle Chips too.' He hunted around in the cupboard for a minute and then reappeared. 'A quick lunch, I reckon, and then we'll go off to Wytham Woods.' He paused briefly, and then started grinning. 'That way,' he continued, 'if you want to go badger watching later, you'll know where to go. Because you'll be going by yourself.'

Emma laughed and only feigned disappointment.

They ate at the end of the long kitchen, surrounded by sections of newspaper, then a quick five minutes to the end of the road, over the river, and they were out of the city already, along the river, through open fields, down grassy tracks. One of the things Mark said he loved about his house was the easy access to the countryside. He liked walking, and often enjoyed a late evening stroll.

Conversation today was more intermittent. Disrupted occasionally by passing traffic or a need to walk in single file, Emma was mostly left to observations and her thoughts. Mark's silence initially worried her, but slowly she grew more comfortable, determined to enjoy her new surroundings.

After an hour they reached the edge of Wytham Woods. Compared to the chill of the open fields, inside the woods were damp, fresh and still. They wandered along through trees and shrubs, stopped briefly on a bench to look over Oxford, then continued on downhill and back to the city. Conversation again was less lively and less intense. Emma continued to worry slightly, wondering really if she should be there, but she was here now and she would see it through.

Back at the house, Mark made them some drinks, and set out the lawn chairs in the weak February sun. Emma turned towards him as she drank. 'I don't think I will go badger watching … not this time.'

'Maybe you could come into town with me then?'

Emma tilted her head as if she were considering the option. 'I'd like to see Oxford, you can show me.'

'Way ahead of you there, girl. We'll go for dinner at the Captain's Rose, a lovely fish restaurant, right in the middle of town, but we'll go early and have a good walk around Oxford first. It'll be nice at that time, it's so busy during the day at weekends… I'll book a table.'

While he was away, Emma took the opportunity to telephone also. Her mother was back in the UK and would probably be trying to telephone her. Five minutes later, they'd spoken briefly, and as Emma was ringing off, Mark reappeared.

'Sorted?' she asked.

'Yes, table for nine. And who were you calling?'

'I was just calling mum. You know she normally teaches in France? Well, she's back today and I thought she'd be trying to phone Guildford, so I thought I'd quickly phone her instead.'

'She's early, isn't she?' Mark queried. 'Or do they have a short winter term in France?'

'No, she's early. She's come over to see my grandad. He's got cancer, I told you, do you remember? He had skin cancer and they cut it out, so he was alright for a while, but then it spread and now it's just not getting better. It's really difficult, he can't eat properly, so he's weak and tired, but he won't get any better if he can't eat. He's in hospital at the moment, Mum was saying. They're doing more tests, thinking of trying some other treatments.'

Mark was quiet for the whole time she was talking, half listening but clearly also somewhere else. He looked up at her from his thoughts. 'At least they're still trying, at least they haven't given up.'

Something in his voice told her that this topic was difficult. She wondered if his mum had died of cancer – she knew his mum had died recently, or maybe somebody equally close. Emma agreed, but keen to move away from what was clearly a sensitive subject, she didn't continue.

Instead, she brightened. 'Now,' she started, 'What time do we need to leave? Do you want to go soon or do I have time to quickly get changed.'

Mark looked at her, his face a mix of gratitude and pleasure. 'We can leave whenever you like.'

The walk into Oxford from Mark's house was short - back to the station, then either up New Road to the end of the High Street or up George Street to the end of Cornmarket. Mark selected George Street, and then showed Emma the town he called home. He pointed out Blackwells, the Bodleian Library, this college, that college, the town museum. Emma marvelled at the beauty of the buildings, stopped and pointed out doorways and gargoyles, listened to the details, laughed at the stories. After a while, and only when Emma was totally lost, they stopped in a bar that Mark wanted to try, and then ambled round to the restaurant. The rest of their evening, also a mix of interest, conversation and laughter, they were then the last to leave.

The following morning, Emma woke to the sound of *The*

Observer falling on the doormat and the patter of feet as Mark retrieved it. Still in her pyjamas, she went down to join him.

'Morning.'

'Good morning,' he looked up at her. 'There's tea in the pot if you want one.'

She mooched off to the kitchen and returned shortly, cup in hand. 'Anything interesting in the paper?'

He tossed it down on the coffee table. 'Nothing that can't wait. Tell me instead about your trip to Norway.'

Emma curled her legs underneath her and took a seat in a corner of the sofa. 'I'll be there from mid-March to May, working as a scientist for an outdoor expedition. The work lasts for six weeks, then for the next two weeks, I'm on holiday. As far as I can gather, we'll be spending most of our time trekking round the countryside, it'll be remote, but in reality it's not far from Bergen, and the scenery should be absolutely stunning. It should be fun, and hopefully not too taxing. Here, I'll show you on a map.'

She ran upstairs to get her guidebook. As she leant over to show him the map, both of them still clad in pyjamas, the tension between them was undeniable.

They walked into Oxford the long way round, alongside the river and through Christchurch Meadows. In the sun of the morning and with no-one to spoil the tranquillity, the walk was serene – a dark dank path, running next to the river, the morning light glancing off the water, then the openness of the pale meadows, the height of the lime trees lining the path, the majesty of the college that stood at the end. For brunch, they went to the Top Hat Café, one of Mark's favourite places for Sunday brunch, then they walked back through Oxford, along main streets, busy now with activity.

For the following hour, they relaxed at Mark's house, conversation ongoing – interest, intrigue, stories and laughter, then at 1.30pm Mark roused himself, closed the front door behind them and walked with Emma back to the train station.

'I can't believe you have to go already. Come to someone's house for the weekend, then leave at lunchtime. What kind of a weekend is that?'

Emma laughed. 'I'm sorry, I told you I said I'd meet Phil. If you'd been a bit quicker agreeing dates, he wouldn't have got in there first. I'm a busy girl, you know. I can't be hanging around, waiting for people to make up their minds!'

Mark didn't respond, quiet again, in a world of his own. A few moments later, he turned to face her. 'Emma,' he started, 'there's something I have to tell you. I feel I'm not being honest with you.'

Instinctively she feared what he was going to say.

Eyes returned straight ahead, he didn't notice. 'Just at the moment, I'm not sure I can do this.' He paused, eyes still focused straight ahead of them. 'Emma, I'm ill. I'm not sure yet what's going to happen, or how it's all going to turn out.'

Emma made no reply while she thought carefully. She could hear the pain, the difficulty he was having in telling her this, but aware that her reaction could be important, she chose her words cautiously. 'How ill?' she queried.

He turned towards her. 'Ill enough to be in hospital on Tuesday … and then for the rest of the week.'

Emma again chose her words carefully. 'Can I see you tomorrow?'

He smiled quickly. 'We'll go for cream teas at Broughton Manor – the scones there are simply perfect.'

She smiled an acceptance, and looked after him as he turned to leave her and walked away up into town, his head lowered, his shoulders slouched, a man with a troubled mind.

For her onward journey, Emma puzzled over Mark's illness. On arriving in London, she was happily distracted by her brother and his task, and then by the time she'd returned home she'd decided the illness didn't matter. Whatever the details,

Mark had asked for her understanding and her support. She didn't need to know an exact illness, it might help, but she could still provide understanding and support.

The following day she waited for her summons from Mark. Finally, at 6pm, she gave up again and sought him out. She found him busy at his computer.

'Hi,' she knocked, and waited for him to face her. 'Did you want to go for cream teas?'

'No ... do you mind?' He motioned towards the screen with his head. 'I really want to get this done before I leave.'

'No, it's fine.' Emma paused and took a step further into the office. 'Are you going to tell me what's wrong?'

Mark looked at her. 'The same as your granddad, although not in the exact same place.'

Emma paused. 'And what's the outlook?'

'They don't know. Treatment starts tomorrow, but I may only have another eight months.'

Grateful to him for letting her know, despite the difficulty it obviously caused him, Emma smiled. 'And you were trying to tell me all weekend. You were so distracted sometimes, I wondered if you really wanted me there... Well, whatever happens, I'll always be here.'

Mark looked back at her. 'You're a sweetie, but you don't want to be mixed up in this.'

Emma smiled. 'I don't mind, I'll always be here, whenever you need me.'

He smiled, saluted her and turned back to his computer screen.

Emma's work complete, she locked up her office and cycled home. By the time she'd got there, the extent of Mark's news had fully hit her. For years she waits, until finally her perfect man comes along, and then within months he might be taken away, before she'd even got to know him, before they'd spent any time together.

As she entered her flat, she was quickly overtaken by tears. She collapsed on the sofa, her breathing short, her body racked by heart-wrenching sobs, sobs so wretched she couldn't understand them. Suffering? Pain? Unfairness?

42

Some while later, exhausted and spent, Emma stopped crying for long enough to realise she might feel better if she had something to eat. Not feeling like cooking nor being alone, she went round the corner to her friend Suzie's.

Suzie knew instantly something was wrong, but she didn't ask. She let Emma enjoy their evening, and in her own time, Emma told her what was going on. 'A while ago now, I met this guy, who I really like. We've spent some time together, I really like him, and I think he likes me too, but then at the weekend he told me he didn't really have time for a relationship right now ... and then today it's because he has cancer.' She paused, careful not to let her tears resurface. 'I told him I'd be there if he needs me, and I don't want to abandon him, but I don't know when I'll see him again, or if I will, or if I can contact him, or what. I don't want to bother him, I'm sure he has enough to be thinking about already.'

Suzie looked at her, and Emma could tell from the look on her face, she knew this was big. This was no small quandary to be brushed aside with a flippant remark or a half-hearted joke. Suzie leaned forward and stroked her friend's arm. 'He's frightened, that's all. He doesn't know what's going to happen, and doesn't want to have to think about extra things.'

Emma looked at her and could see she was making sense.

'He loves you really... Hang on in there, and wait and see.'

Slightly reassured, pleased by the good friend that Suzie was, Emma enjoyed her share of their dinner and slightly happier, slightly lighter, she returned home a few hours later. As she opened her front door, her phone bleeped her a text:

Give me some time, but then I'll be back, M.

Almost choked by his thought and sensitivity, she texted him back straight away: *Take care, E.*

The following day, she was working in London. Every so often, Emma worked in London, and today she was glad of the change and distraction. On her way home, she sent Mark a book he had mentioned wanting, the message inside just a simple 'Take Care'. For now, she also wanted to send him a text. Several compositions later, she sent a simple statement of the truth: *Thinking of you, E x.*

Three hours later, he replied: *Thanks, all OK so far, scared though about tomorrow.*

Emma replied as soon as she saw it: *Don't be scared, you know you're doing the right thing, E x.*

She didn't hear then for the rest of the week. On Friday she telephoned, but got no reply. She left him a message, a bright cheerful message, to *see how you are, hoping it's all going well*, but he didn't call back. The following week was also the same. She phoned and left messages on Tuesday and Friday, but neither time did he phone back.

The following Sunday, she received a text: *Hi. In Guildford next week if you're free for a drink, M.*

They arranged to meet after work on Tuesday. As on every similar occasion, it was Emma who finished her work first, then went and knocked lightly on his office door.

'Hello,' she started, brightly and cheerfully, pausing for him to turn round and face her. 'How are you?' A genuine question, not simply a pleasantry, sincerity written all over her face.

'Alright, and you?'

'Yeah, I'm good thank you. And how did it go?'

'Alright.' But that was all that she got. Clearly not wanting to talk about it, she didn't ask further, and returned instead to bright and cheerful. 'So, where do you want to have that drink?'

He grinned at her. 'I've already thought. I've got the car down at the moment, ferrying things back to Oxford, so I'm going to take you to one of my favourite places.'

They walked to Mark's apartment, collected his car and were soon on their way to Thursley Heath. The concern for his current state already covered, they quickly settled into a familiar pattern of laughing, joking and story-telling, the laughing mainly from Emma, the joking and story-telling mainly from Mark. He told her of his childhood, his sisters, his family, and his home town in Northern Ireland. They walked over the heath until it was dark, then settled themselves in the local pub. He told her of his move to Oxford, ideas for a new car, the upcoming visit by his sister. She told him more of her job in Norway, her need for a new job when she returned, but before then also a friend's wedding, a trip to Seattle for a work meeting, and a visit to Cornwall to leave her belongings while her flat was let. At the end of the evening, he promised to see her again some time soon, just as soon as he was able.

For the rest of that week she didn't see him. He had work to finish before leaving and plenty of things to move back to Oxford.

The following Tuesday she texted for a drink, but received a reply explaining absence. The following Thursday she telephoned, but she could only leave a message. On Friday she received an email from him, a chatty email – thanks for the messages, all going well, details of the garden, the move back to Oxford still not yet completed, more ideas for a new car. Emma emailed in return – her trip to Norway, a job interview coming soon.

The following week she again tried calling, Tuesday and Thursday, the following Friday she received an email.

The following week, she didn't phone. She emailed instead with reports of job interviews, drinking and dancing at Janet's wedding, an upcoming weekend for her grandad. Mark sent his good wishes to her grandfather, asked her simply to hold his hand.

The weekend for her grandad was the following one. On her way up to Hereford, Emma passed close to Oxford. She stopped and phoned in case she could visit, but Mark didn't answer. Minutes later, she received a text from him: *The trick with cutlery is to start on the outside and work in, M.*

Not exactly what she was expecting, and initially she was upset. To text that quickly, he must have seen her call, so he had chosen not to speak to her. On second thoughts though, she looked down at the message again, smiled at its abstract nature and the memory of Carlo's to which it referred, and resolved to try and be more patient. She was disappointed, not even to be speaking to him, but she was glad he was well enough to joke.

She continued on her way and, as she entered her gran and grandfather's house, Emma was glad she hadn't stopped at Mark's. Not quite the last, the house was busy. Her aunt and uncle had been there since Tuesday, her mum of course, for several weeks now, her cousins had all arrived that day, her sister the last to arrive that evening, her brother was due tomorrow morning. Pleased to see everyone, and her mum obviously pleased to see her, she settled quickly for a comfortable evening and family dinner.

The following morning, the house became a hive of activity. Cooking, cleaning, tidying, dusting, they rearranged furniture, found extra chairs that were stored in the shed, nipped to the shops for more paper napkins and soon were set for a party of twenty.

From 11am, people started arriving. Her brother first, then other close family, then wider family, her grandfather's friends. At twelve o'clock, they left for the church, a carefully organised crocodile of drivers. At 12.30pm, at All Saints Church, the funeral began. The service was personal, her grandfather well known to the congregation, but light as well, dominated by anecdotes from his life and frequent hymns. Prepared by him before he had died, the funeral service reflected him well, a celebration of all that was good and wise, thoughtful and kind, and musical too.

The funeral was followed by the usual gathering, the party for which the house had been prepared, then only close family stayed for the weekend. Determined to enjoy their time together, they settled down to an evening of games, as they would at Christmas, then a Sunday walk to the top of the Sugar Loaf. They would miss Grandad, his wise steady manner, his careful thoughts, considered opinions, but they'd been prepared, already adjusted, they had each other and their lives continued.

On her way back to Guildford, Emma again passed Oxford. This time though, she didn't phone, she didn't text. She was tired, she simply wanted to be at home.

On Monday she replied to Mark's email, questions about his sister's visit, what they had done, how he was feeling. She sent sketchy details of her own weekend, the pleasure of seeing her family, the walk up the Sugar Loaf. She didn't mention her grandfather, the funeral, she didn't mention the death from cancer.

As the week ended, Emma emailed again. She'd received no reply to her last message, but she would be away for the following week, and she wanted to let him know. If he wasn't emailing because he felt ill, the last thing he would need was a silence from her. Bright and cheerful, she wrote what she knew of her upcoming trip, details of her week, the progress with packing to leave her flat, the lack of progress in finding a job. She hoped that he was doing okay, still enjoying his sister's visit, and promised to text while she was away.

Saturday morning, she left for Seattle. She had meetings

from Tuesday to Thursday, and at the time of booking had decided to leave with a few days to spare to adjust to the time difference before she was required to work. For two days then, she looked round Seattle, a beautiful city of sea, space and healthiness, no view from the bus without islands and marinas, roads lined with cycle tracks and open spaces, and all enclosed by rugged mountains. Even the 'down town' felt healthy – pristine white buildings filled with boutiques, and old-fashioned markets of freshly caught fish, bright juicy fruit and colourful vegetables.

By the end of the second day, Emma stopped waiting for her mobile phone. Despite having checked before leaving, her phone wouldn't work in the United States. Unable also to access her email, she set up a new account and emailed her beloved: *Just to let you know I haven't abandoned you, mobile phone not working that's all, E.*

She returned from the meeting several days later and almost immediately left for Cornwall. Most of her clothes were now all packed, most of her property, personal items, all of it ready for two months in Cornwall, while she was in Norway and her flat was let.

Emma arrived at her grandparents' shortly before dinner, then simply slotted into their routine – TV soaps, sitcoms, biscuits and cake, very easy, every so often, Emma enjoyed it.

To thank her grandparents, she'd arranged to stay for a further four days. She occupied herself with helping them where they needed helping, finishing reports for work, and for the rest of the time, she enjoyed the weather, the fine coastal scenery, the fresh coastal air.

Before the end of the first day she had, of course, also texted Mark: *Porth Island – 10m. One hour in and laptop abandoned in preference for walks on the beach and headland. Hope you're OK, E.*

She'd told him she'd be visiting Cornwall, but she wasn't

sure if he'd remember, and she hadn't heard from him for a while. Before long, she received a reply: *Sounds lovely. Wish I was there too, M.*

Emma shone, but was careful to consider her reply. With no idea of his progress, his current condition, she wanted a balance of positive, cheerful, lively and sensitive: *Come if you can, I think you'd like it, E.*

Not sure it's really worth it for a few days. When are you back?

Emma smiled: *Your loss, Friday. Take care, E.*

Several days later Emma returned. Her flat almost empty, she had one week before leaving for Norway. Not long after she'd entered it, her telephone rang. 'Hello?'

'Hello.'

Emma smiled as she recognised Mark's voice. 'Hello. How are you?'

'I'm okay thanks, and now you're back too. Listen, I'm in Guildford this evening. I thought we could have dinner, if you're free. I'm at the flat if you want to come over.'

'OK, sounds nice.' She tried to sound casual, but couldn't think of anything better. 'I'll be about an hour.'

He looked tired when she saw him, and pale, but no worse than that. She was surprised, disappointed with herself for fearing a change, but far from disappointed with him. In answer to her queries, he was feeling fine, but he didn't want to go out and wasn't up to much excitement. Not wanting to go out either, having just left all except hiking clothes at her grandparents', Emma was happy simply to join him. They ordered a take-away, opened some wine and spent the evening on his veranda.

She told him of Seattle and Cornwall, he told her of his days in Oxford, his sister's visit, his gradual move home, his flat now almost as empty as hers. Moving belongings, finishing projects, leaving their jobs, their positions were similar. She spoke also of her final arrangements before she left for Norway, her plans for her flat, her recent progress with job hunting. She'd already emailed and told him the options, but he preferring Brighton and she preferring Bristol, there was plenty to discuss.

It was a lovely evening, light and casual, comfortable and entertaining, no hesitations, no expectations. Only once was there one small cloud: 'It was your grandfather's funeral that weekend, wasn't it?' he asked her plainly.

But even that didn't work out badly: 'Yes,' she stated, simple and honest, and in return he only smiled, a smile of thanks for sensitively caring, a smile for honesty, a smile of trust.

The following week then passed quickly for her. She telephoned on Monday but got no answer, she emailed on Tuesday but got no reply. On her last day at work, she emailed again. At the end of the email, as she'd done before, she told him she'd call in case he was answering. This time, she received a response straight away: *I'll be answering, M.*

For the first time they conversed by telephone, a conversation that lasted almost an hour. She told him again how she'd be out of touch, the remote nature of where she was going, that she'd take her phone but she couldn't be sure that it would work, but for most of the time they talked about adventures, laughed at the possibilities she might encounter, smiled at the spring he would have at home. Emma loved his voice – his soft and gentle Northern Irish voice, she liked his conversation, and she enjoyed making him laugh. She would miss this – his fine conversation, observant jokes and fanciful tales. She would miss him.

43

She left for Norway the following day, and by the end of the evening was safely installed in the tent that was to be her new home. The scenery was stunning - lush green valleys, dark forests, deep blue waters, and an occasional flash of white, a glinting sparkle on the tops of the mountains – glaciers as they snaked to the sea. The expedition was an opportunity for college-aged students to experience nature, enjoy the outdoors, overcome some challenges, all with a purpose. The sixty or so students were divided into units of twelve, each with a leader with mountaineering skills, and a scientific officer who provided the purpose. Emma was a scientific officer, and while most of the purposes focussed on the environment, she was responsible for guiding her unit in a project on eating well on expeditions.

The first few days passed very quickly, unpacking and organising, but before long each unit was left to their own schedules. Emma's unit left for the next valley round the coast. They worked there for three days, mostly on training, and then on their fourth day they hiked up the mountain at the valley head. The climb was hard, but the views from the summit were easily worth it. Beneath them, their camp stood like dots by the small lake, the valley stretching down to the sea. All around them there were more mountain tops, and in the direction from which the ridge ran, the pure white expanse of a glistening ice cap, majestic on top of the world.

As they rested, Emma tried her phone. She was keeping it switched on as little as possible, but after a minute she found a signal, and couldn't resist sending him a text: *Stakliktinden* –

1246m. Not so remote after all!

Several days later, another free day, they returned to the ferry port to restock supplies. As they grabbed a drink in the local cafe, Emma tried her phone again. After several minutes, it bleeped a signal, and then, excitingly, also a text: *Thames path – 10m.*

And at the post office, a parcel was waiting. Inside there was a postcard from Oxford, written the day after she'd left England, and a copy of *Miss Smilla's Feeling for Snow*. Set in the Arctic, it was the most appropriate book he could find, inscribed with the words: *This might be my biggest ever mistake – but it's one hell of a book. Hope it found you, M xx.* The inscription puzzled her, worried her a little, but she was encouraged to read the book in search of its meaning. In return, she sent him a letter and a hand-drawn card, it would be his birthday soon.

For the following ten days, they kept moving - a trek round the headland to different landscapes, different habitats, and a regular mobile phone signal. Emma texted every evening, but received no replies. After four days, she realised she wasn't using a country code, changed Mark's number and sent them all again, but still she received no word from him.

At the end of the ten days, they moved to stay on the top of an ice cap – a sunny expanse of ice and snow, far-reaching views of all around them. Emma lost her mobile signal but four days later they returned to the valleys, to where she knew she could contact him.

The following day was Mark's birthday. Shortly before dinner, when she knew she wouldn't be missed, Emma climbed up the valley-side, found the signal she needed and settled to call him to wish him well. For one brief minute she wondered what she was doing, but having climbed the hillside, she decided she could at least leave a message.

She phoned, and in response, he replied.

'Hello, happy birthday.'

'Hang on, let me get outside.'

She waited for the background noise to die down. 'I just called to say happy birthday.'

'Thanks. We're in the pub, my sister's husband and my old friend Dunc. Well, they're in the pub, I'm standing outside. Thanks for your card, and for your letter. I was so impressed, no-one ever sends me letters, and to arrive this morning, exactly the right day, all the way from the depths of Norway.'

Emma smiled.

'We read it at breakfast. My sister's not sure you should be standing in glacial lakes for long periods, but it sounds like you're having a good time.'

'We're not standing in glacial lakes for long periods!' Emma laughed. 'That wouldn't be possible!'

'Thanks for all the texts as well. It was great getting messages every so often, then all of a sudden, they all came again, all at once.'

Emma tutted. 'Did it not occur to you to reply? I sent them again because I thought you weren't getting them.'

He didn't apologise. 'Tell me again when you're coming home.'

'Not for a while – two more weeks here, then two weeks in Oslo and Bergen.'

He interrupted before she could talk further. 'And what's happening with your flat?'

'I haven't heard anything. Hopefully it's rented out by now.'

'Well, when you come back, you're staying here.'

Emma smiled. A statement of fact, not a suggestion and not an order, but not really a question either.

They spoke more for the next few minutes, then anxious not to run out of things to say, Emma let him return to his friends and family, and floated back down to the camp.

For the remaining time to be spent in the region, the

units continued working in the valleys, then had a last visit to the ice cap. The weather this time though, wasn't as good. As they climbed up the side of the glacier tongue, the cloud began gathering, and by the time they'd reached the rocks for their campsite, the air around them was thick with sleet and precipitation. For the next two days they could do nothing but stay in their tents. Without the sun, temperatures outside were cold and debilitating, playing was possible but not much fun, travel was dangerous and fairly pointless. Sheltered in the warmth of their sleeping bags, they played cards, other games, and Emma finished reading *Miss Smilla*. Even at the end, she was still unsure of the meaning of Mark's inscription: *'this might be my biggest mistake'*. She'd hoped the meaning would become clear – the story of a girl who is killed on an ice cap, the story of a murderer targeting only those sleeping in tents, but the book wasn't like that and ended well. She briefly considered the possibility that he might mean 'them' again, or even 'her', but she hoped not. And if that was the case, he could easily leave, he didn't need to make mistakes. She tried to put the thoughts out of her head.

After two days, the dull skies cleared and the ice cap again resembled a diamond on top of the world. They spent their time again travelling round it, visiting peaks and rocky gullies, skiing and sledging across the surface. Finally, they returned down the glacier tongue. As they descended, they noticed the effects of the increasing warmth - the surface more slippery, the crevasses wider, the running water underneath sounded louder. They descended slowly but route-finding was difficult, dead ends were frequent. And the further they moved, the harder it became. As the slope shallowed, the crevasses lessened, but the smooth blue ice became more unbroken, more slippery, more shiny.

Finally, twenty minutes from the bottom, two people fell. One of them, Julie - she lost her footing as she transferred between the ice and rocks, the other one Emma, slipped on the ice and in less than a second was skidding on her back to the base of the glacier. The last on her rope, she had no-one above her. She swung like a pendulum below the others, was flung against the ice walls of a crevasse and abruptly halted by the blue ice around her.

She lay in the base of the crevasse, wedged in by the rucksack on top of her, almost strangled by the rope that had saved her. Very soon, she heard people above her. She shouted to let them know she was alright, and slowly her rucksack was taken from her, her helmet removed and the extent of the accident unveiled. At first, it appeared she had torn her trousers, she must have knocked her face to have broken her glasses, but otherwise didn't seem badly injured. Only when she used it, did she feel the extreme pain in her left knee.

Anxious to move off the glacier, she inched to the end of the crevasse and climbed to the safety of the surrounding rocks. Unsure really of what had happened, she sat for several minutes, glad to be at least, out in the open, glad she assumed to be alive. She was concerned though by how badly she'd hurt her knee, how she was getting to the flat ground, and how she was getting to the valley below. Keen not to stop for long, in case she was then stopped forever, she raised herself slowly and carefully crept back onto the ice, the route for the last section marked with fixed ropes anchored in the depths of the glacier.

Without her rucksack, travelling was easier. At the base of the glacier, she rested again, stowed her rucksack for someone else to collect, and focussed purely on moving herself. Her knee hurt considerably. She wondered exactly what she had done, how soon and how easily she could get it seen. Suddenly, with no appreciation for her surroundings, all Emma wanted was to be somewhere else.

Having made a little distance down the path, Emma was soon met by some of her unit, and her usual spirits were somewhat restored. They collected her rucksack, gave her piggy-backs to the main camp area, laughed to encourage her to do the same. The following days though, were no fun at all. Sleeping, eating, sitting at ground level, she was unable to rest her knee well and the pain on use was increasing. The doctor who was with them took a quick look, but he wasn't an expert, recommended painkillers and a visit to the hospital on their way home.

She tried to leave early, but it wasn't convenient. Her holiday reward not even started, all she could think of was going home. She felt vulnerable, isolated and alone. As soon as she was in reach of a signal, she turned on her phone and in the midst of her anguish she was comforted completely by a message from Mark. He didn't know of an accident, his message simply from a midnight stroll, the moonlit sky, the stars above, but it was his voice, it was his thought, it was enough.

***

Early May, Emma came home. She stayed for a night with her brother in London, then transferred to her dad's house in Dorset. Her flat was let, but unable to carry anything while walking, she couldn't have lived there anyway. Instead she went to stay at her dad's. Life at her dad's was always relaxing. For someone who was injured, it was perfect.

A few days after she'd arrived, feeling rested, she accompanied her father to Exeter. She needed new glasses, and she wanted to catch up with Mark, and for that she needed a mobile phone signal. He didn't answer but she left a message.

The following evening she received an email. In response to his queries, she told him of the trip, the work, the scenery, and finally the reason for her early return. He told her of his progress, his Easter in Oxford, his lovely new car, his upcoming visit to his best friend in Scotland. He invited her to join him, offered even to come and collect her, but she laughed, reminded him that she couldn't walk, and tried to impress on him the detour he'd be making in going from Oxford to Scotland via Dorset.

After a week, she called him again. Her dad's house was lovely, the comfort and tranquillity exactly what she'd needed, but as she rested and recovered, she began feeling isolated and impatient. The offer to stay at Mark's had been renewed, it wanted details, but that was all. Finally, as she began thinking he must have changed his mind, he called her having returned from Scotland. She loved his voice, she loved his laugh. They talked for hours, just catching up, stories of this and tales of that, until it was decided that she would arrive at his house next Thursday. He was at the hospital from Monday to Wednesday.

BELFAST, DECEMBER 2007

44

Emma arrived back from Athens, and her life continued. She spent Christmas in Hereford, as was the custom, worked hard through January and February, and through it all her spirits improved. If Mark had loved her, she had no reason to feel sad, she wasn't stupid and she hadn't been wasting her time. She'd been unlucky. And if Mark had been truly right for her, she reasoned carefully, all she had to do to find it again, were all the things she had done before.

Her holiday to Peru arrived in March. Travelling was one of the things she did best and travelling in Peru, she did very well. She met her brother easily, and then spent two weeks with him and his girlfriend travelling round the south of the country – the seals at Pisco, the sand dune at Ica, the Nazca Lines, the Colca Canyon, then Arequipa, touristy Cuzco and Macchu Picchu. Emma loved them all – the windswept coast, the wide deserts, huge rolling mountains, the obvious culture and interesting stories. She enjoyed as well, the ease of travelling – the need for Spanish, but also the buses, frequent, long-distance and easily arranged, the thought-out tours, the number of restaurants, the choice of hotels. Everything she wanted was all right there.

She left her brother after two weeks, to spend some time also in the north – more mountains, more culture, and as she visited the walls at Trujillo, the baths at Kajamarca, ate strange looking meals, and chatted to old women knitting jumpers, she remembered why she liked travelling so much -

the interest, the intrigue, the variety, the freedom. Travelling, she resolved, would feature more.

Revived and invigorated after her trip, Emma worked hard for the following months, and over the summer, she received two more introductions – Liam, a farmer from further south, and Dave, a civil servant from North Belfast.

She met Liam for only a drink, a pleasant drink in a pleasant bar, but conversation was difficult. They had little in common and he seemed disinclined to try new things. She met Dave for a drink and then for a film. Again she felt they had little in common, but he was less easily put off, and at least a film would be easy. They saw one in the Batman series, then went for a drink to discuss it, but following that there was nothing more.

As she walked back to her car that evening, Emma wondered why none of these men were right. Was she being too fussy? Was she looking for something that didn't exist? Was she looking for something that had lived once and had now died?

As she arrived home, her thoughts were broken by a text from Rebecca, her brother's girlfriend: *Thanks E for the birthday present. When are you coming to our new home? R x.*

Emma made a cup of tea, replied to the text, and sat there thinking for a while. She wanted what Rebecca had, she wanted the same as Rebecca and Phil – a relationship, a real relationship, with someone who loved her, with someone who she loved in return.

And then something clicked. She didn't have a relationship, a real one, because she spent all of her time in a pretend one. She thought about the time she spent thinking of Mark, missing him, wishing that he hadn't died, all that time she should be spending in other ways.

The book she was reading said: *'we maintain pain and discomfort because we are scared of letting it go'*. Emma sat and looked at the fireplace. What was she scared of? And the answer was easy. She was scared of admitting that she was alone, scared of admitting she was by herself, scared of admitting that no-one loved her.

She took a moment and looked down at the text. She wasn't alone though, lots of people loved her. And even if she were alone, it was nothing to be scared of. Firstly, she liked being by herself, and secondly, she could do as she pleased. She realised she didn't need to be scared.

She looked back at her relationship with Mark. She realised now when she thought about Mark, when she spoke of him, she always used the words 'he died'. She realised now, it wasn't important that 'he died', what was important was that 'he was dead'. He was gone. He was part of the past, not part of the present, nor the future. It didn't mean she had loved him less, and she was glad she had loved him, glad that he had loved her too, but that was it - she had loved him, he had loved her, it was in the past.

She made herself a second cup of tea, went to her bedroom and on her most expensive writing paper, she carefully copied all of the texts that he had sent, texts that still cluttered up her inbox, reread the only letter he'd written, and moved them all from her bedside table to her box of memories.

She didn't cry, she wasn't upset. She remembered with fondness the times he had texted, the afternoon she'd received his one love letter. A letter asking her to come back, except, of course, it was an email.

BRISTOL, OCTOBER 2003

45

Three times since she'd left him, three times since he had asked her to leave, Emma sent something. First, his front door key, accompanied by a letter of apology, of care and concern, disappointment and upset, a letter that had taken a whole day to write, that she doubted he had ever read. Second, three months later, a collection that she thought might cheer him up: an article on the benefits of walking, a map of the part of the Lakes that she loved, a postcard of Bath. She wanted him to know that she cared, that she still thought, wondered about him, that she still wanted him to get better, to be happy, to go to Bath and enjoy the Lakes.

The third thing she sent him was a hat that she'd made for him right at the start. Shortly after moving to his, she'd made a fleece hat for him as a kind thought, and in response, although he wore it, he'd requested also a 'topless hat', a hat he could wear more as a scarf without the trouble of trailing ends and uncovered gaps. Six months after she'd left him, she moved into her flat in Bristol and while unpacking, she found amongst her things, a 'topless hat'. She didn't remember making it, but she must have and then simply hadn't handed it over. She debated slightly, wondering if it would upset him, but then sent it off to its rightful owner, accompanied by a bright and cheerful letter.

Several weeks later he replied. Nothing expected, nothing dramatic, a simple email to her work address.

Hi Em,

Thanks for the hat and for your letter. Sounds like you're doing really well. You sound great too. I'd love to see you. I miss you, Em. If that's not possible, please could you send another hat in a slightly smaller size.

M x

Emma was amazed. She read it, reread it, and decided to respond only once she had thought. She'd been so miserable since she'd left Mark, technically since he had asked her to leave, but she'd never believed he might want her back. She used to imagine him turning up, healthy and well, just to say hi, to show her his progress, but after a while she'd stopped hoping. She'd started thinking of their relationship as a holiday romance, a small glimpse of sun in a cloudy sky, until finally she'd decided they weren't even suited, that he had not been good for her. She also wasn't sure she could forgive him. She still thought he hadn't treated her well, hadn't loved her well. She wasn't sure she would cope a second time.

Anxious not to make a hasty response, she continued with her day as she would have done. She dealt with her clients, completed their paperwork, answered some emails and took a long lunch break to think over this. She emailed a reply that afternoon.

Hi M,

Lovely to hear from you, and you don't sound all that bad either. It would be lovely to see you. Would you like to come to Bristol? You know you'll always be welcome here, or I could meet you somewhere? Maybe Bath? I think you'd like Bath.

Let me know what you're thinking, I hope you're doing OK.

E xxx'

She wasn't going to play games. She was happy to show him exactly how she felt, but she didn't want to make it easy either. One small compromise that was all she was asking, and she really did think he would like Bath.

Weeks went by with no reply. She had no idea what was keeping him – illness, inability, pride, stubbornness.

Finally she relented and resolved to go up to Oxford.

46

She arrived in Oxford late one afternoon. She first went to Blackwell's for a present for her sister, the trip then satisfying one purpose, then cautiously went round to Mark's house. The lights were on and the car outside but there was no answer at the door. She waited, wondering what she should do. Was this a sign? Should she leave now and go back home? Had he not replied because he'd changed his mind? Or would she be giving up something amazing?

She resolved at least to try Rosie's. If his habits were the same, it was the time when he might be there, and she didn't really want to just go straight home. She was here now, she'd only regret it if she simply left. She turned and headed back towards the town and within five minutes she saw him easily, walking towards her.

'You said you wanted to see me,' Emma started.

'I miss you,' Mark responded plainly. 'Will you come back to the house?'

She turned around and they walked back together. 'So, how have you been?' she asked lightly.

He shrugged, but didn't offer more. Emma took that as no real change, not really good news, although he didn't look different.

They continued in silence back to the house, but once inside, Mark found his voice. 'Come in, Em. Let me get you a cup of tea.'

'Thank you,' she smiled.

'And then you can tell me all about you, your new flat and what you've been up to... Will you stay for dinner? I've got some salmon.'

Emma smiled graciously, accepted the invitation, then sat on the stool at the end of the kitchen, chatting away about her flat. She didn't have much more news than she'd written, but she told him of the work that she'd done, of plans for painting and colour schemes, casually suggested he could come down and see it some time. She spoke also of her summer in Bristol, a weekend in Salzburg, an upcoming ten days in Russia. She asked if he had been anywhere? done anything?

They continued the same all through the meal, Emma doing most of the talking, Mark asking questions, occasionally commenting. It was almost how it used to be, except not quite. She was more guarded, more careful, he was more muted, much more subdued. She could see he was tired, that he was finding it effortful, that he wasn't his lively old self, but she thought he was glad of her company.

At 10.30pm, she had to leave. He asked her to stay, but she couldn't. He asked if she would come again.

The following evening, she texted a thanks and hoped they would do it again soon, and in return, he thanked her also and agreed.

***

Two weeks later, Christmas intervened. Emma visited her family as usual, enjoyed their company, the care and comfort, and then went to Russia for ten days of winter.

She spent her first five days in Moscow. She saw Red Square and the Kremlin, she visited museums, churches and markets, she went to lookouts and outdoor spaces, but most of all she experienced the culture. She found everything she'd expected of Russia – the typecasts, the rumours, the stereotypes. She fought on the metro like all of the locals, hid under her greatcoat, moved quickly through the cold day, head bent, eyes down, and scurried underground into hidden cafés and shopping malls. She drank vodka at lunchtime and feasted on borscht and strange looking stews, she went to the ballet to see *Giselle*, having bought her ticket from four men straight out of a Bond film. She loved the fulfilment of expectations, and the experience of novel and new. The other five days, she spent in St Petersburg. Smaller than Moscow, it was easier but colder. She spent her time again in museums, churches, art galleries, and she visited the Summer Palace. She loved all the finery, the golden ballroom, the extravagant amber, and outside also the silent fountains and dormant flowerbeds.

Throughout it all, she wished Mark were with her. Russia reminded her of Prague, the buildings, the finery, the style and culture, but she missed the bars, the warm, dark bars. She didn't like going to bars by herself, but she would have enjoyed the warmth. She was missing part of Russian life too. Russia was hard – the lack of language, of volunteers to help, of obvious signs, it would have been easier and more fun with somebody else. Mark though, she thought, would have hated it – he hated cold, and shabby and old. She was glad when she thought, that he hadn't come. He'd be moaning and making her feel guilty for 'dragging him out there'. She smiled at the thought of it.

She returned from Russia, pleased with her visit, and proud of herself. She'd wanted to go for a long time, it was hard to organise, it had been difficult when she was there, but it had been everything she had expected, everything she'd wanted, and more. Inspired and enlivened, she texted Mark within two days – *a quick hello, thinking of you, and wondering if I could come and see you.* This time, she dispensed with her own pride, happy just to spend some time with him.

He replied shortly: *Not this weekend, Jill will be here. Come next weekend, racing at Cheltenham.*

Emma was pleased – pleased he'd replied, pleased he wanted to see her, pleased he wanted to go to the races, that

248

she'd had such an impact on his life: *Let me know what time it starts and I'll see you there, E x*

By Saturday though, he hadn't replied. She wondered if he would still be going, and then all the other doubts started returning. Had he been going? Was he teasing her? Was she again asking too much? Did he really want to see her? All the old fears, they returned easily.

She decided she'd go anyway, but instead of taking the train as she'd planned, she'd take the car, and then at least she'd have more freedom.

She found the race times in the newspaper and set off with ninety minutes to travel, but as she sat in the Cheltenham traffic, she became fretful. She texted Mark to let him know she might be late. For one brief moment, she reconsidered, in case he wasn't really coming, in case he was somewhere laughing at her, but she decided she'd rather let him know, and if he was laughing at her, well, let him.

She received a reply almost instantly: *Me too, thank God for Radio 4.*

Emma smiled, she should have known.

She arrived shortly afterwards, ten minutes before the first race: *At the west entrance. Are you here yet?*

About ten minutes, put some money on baker's boy for me, M

By the time the race had run, Mark was calling to let her know he had arrived. The stands not too crowded, they found each other easily, and settled quickly into an afternoon of laughing, joking, banter and rivalry. It was again how it used to be – fun, light-hearted, nothing serious, nothing heavy. Emma noticed Mark was looking worse, walking a noticeable effort, but when she asked, he simply replied, 'Not good, Emma,' and if she pushed him, he 'didn't want to talk about it'. Anxious not to spoil their time together, she didn't push.

At the end of the meeting, they hung around, not wanting to leave, not wanting to part. Emma regretted then bringing her car. She wished she could be taken to Oxford – the easy ride, the beautiful car, the beautiful man, but with her car in Cheltenham, it wasn't obvious. Mark as well had won £300 – there would be a dinner if she were in Oxford.

In the end, they simply agreed to meet again soon. She texted a thanks once she arrived home, and in reply she received the same, coupled with mention of drinking his winnings.

47

The following Wednesday she sent him an email.

Dear Mark,

I was just wondering if you'd like to take me to The Giant's Causeway some time. Your postcard is still stuck to my computer, I see the picture every day, I'd love to go, and I'd like you to take me. Only of course, if you're not too busy and it's not too much trouble. I hope your celebrations on Saturday went well and you're not suffering as a result.

Yours, Emma xxx

The following Monday, she received two replies from him, one from Friday night, one from Saturday.

Friday: 19.42:

Hi Em,

I'd love to take you to The Giant's Causeway, you'll love it, and we could stay at Bushmills Inn. As soon as I can manage it. Things took a turn for the worse last weekend. I collapsed in the pub on Saturday night and I've been in hospital all this last week. Feeling better now and allowed to leave, but very weak and still not great. Would you be able to come to take me home? M

Saturday: 10.17:

Hi Em, Just to let you know Jill is coming to take me home. You don't want to see me like this anyway.

Take care, M

Emma was disappointed. Disappointed mainly that he was suffering, that he was so clearly ill again, but disappointed also that she hadn't been able to help him, to take him home and look after him, disappointed too that she hadn't been there when it had happened. Firstly, it might not have happened, but if it had … she pictured herself as his concerned lover, following the ambulance, giving his details at the hospital, sitting by his bedside as he slept, the first person he saw when he woke up, the one he knew who must truly love him.

She took a long time to reply. She wasn't sure how often this happened. She didn't want to be alarmist, but she also didn't want to trivialise something serious.

Dear Mark,

Thanks for your messages, and I'm so sorry you're ill again. I hope you're feeling better soon. Hopefully by the time you're reading this you'll be back home again and starting to feel better already. Some sleep in your own bed, some time in the garden, and with Jill waiting on you hand and foot, you'll be feeling better before you know it. I'm sorry I didn't come to get you – I didn't get your email until today, but if you want me to come up when Jill has to go, please let me know. I'm not far away and I'd be happy to. Rest up, take care, and I'll see you soon.

Yours, Emma xxx

Six days later, she sent a text. She'd heard nothing, but she wanted him to know she was thinking of him, that her offer to help was genuine: *Hello, just a quick one to say hello, to see how you're doing and if you need anything, happy to help, E xxx*

In return, she received a reply: *Thanks E, doing much better, Jill home soon, looking forward to the house to myself, M*

Emma smiled. He was feeling better. He had always been ungrateful, keener to be by himself than tolerate the help of others.

Two weeks later, she texted again: *Hi M, just wondering how you are and if you need anything? E xxx*

Sometime later she received a reply: *Not so good this week, Jill here this weekend, M*

Emma again was disappointed. Disappointed again that he was ill, disappointed again that he wasn't telling her, that she wouldn't know unless she asked, disappointed again that she wasn't helping. Jill, she knew, was coming from Ireland. It made more sense for Emma to help, at least some of the time. She wondered if Jill wasn't asked either, but if Jill was simply not accepting no.

She sent a reply with as much love as one can send in a text to someone who possibly doesn't want it. *Take care, and I hope you feel better very soon. Just let me know if there's anything I can do, E xxx*

Thanks E. Would be warmer if I had my radiator. Do you still have it?

Yes I have it, I'll bring it up at the weekend, E xxx.

Happy to be able to help, pleased at last to be involved, Emma rearranged her weekend plans to incorporate a trip to Oxford.

As the weekend drew nearer though, she grew less pleased. She began to worry she'd been pushy, that she was again expecting too much. He'd complained before of her asking for more than he could give. He could be vicious, more so also when he was tired.

Emma took the radiator, she couldn't not, but as she turned into his road, she relaxed easily as Mark and his sister drove out in front of her. She recognised the car and Mark as the passenger even from behind. Thankful for a lucky escape, she deposited the radiator by the side of his front door, turned her car round and drove back to Bristol.

In the evening, she received a text: *Thanks for the radiator. Sorry not to see you. Why did you not knock? M*

Emma looked at her phone in disbelief. He hadn't been there when she'd called round, he knew that. The radiator would have been waiting for them when they came back. She couldn't believe he was up to these tricks again: critical, derogatory, manipulative.

I only knocked lightly, she replied. *The car wasn't there and I didn't want to wake you if you were sleeping. Let me know if there's anything else, E xxx*

***

The following Friday, she decided to email. Texting was repetitive and limiting, and she wanted to do more than ask how he was. She still asked, but she also told him of how she was and what she'd been doing. She reverted to the emails she used to send him – light-hearted, interesting, renewed offers of help and support, she asked questions, asked for his advice. She did the same the following week – again offers of help and support, but mostly also a change of focus, a small glimpse of the rest of the world.

'You're very good,' Christine told her, 'emailing even without replies. How do you know he even reads them?'

Emma smiled. 'I don't ... but I think he does, or at least I think he will at some point, and I think he'll like them. He likes stories…' Emma paused. 'I hope he'll read them. But also I don't mind. How would you like to be trapped in bed and feeling rubbish, and then feeling worse because nobody loves you? These emails don't take much effort from me ... in fact, I enjoy writing them. I like feeling like a little ray of sunshine.'

Christine laughed at her. 'I'm sure you are like a little ray of sunshine. I just don't see why he can't tell you that.'

Emma shrugged. She found emailing more satisfying than texting, she liked feeling a little involved, and she was sure he'd appreciate them once he was able.

Sure enough, the following week, she received a reply. He hadn't emailed because he'd been in hospital, but he was feeling better now and glad to be home.

She continued her emails for several weeks – caring, supportive, positive emails, but she received nothing more in return. Finally, she received a reply.

Thank you E, for all your emails.
I'm glad to hear you're doing so well, and seem to be having such

*a good time. I have been starting to feel better, but not out of the
wars quite yet.*
Take care, M x

She was glad to have a response, but she wondered if
Mark really meant what he said. It had taken him so long to
reply, she had no idea of how he was doing, how ill he was, or
how he was suffering. Was he really happy to hear from her?
Glad of her emails, to which he generally didn't reply. Or was
he criticising? Thanking her for reminding him of what he
was missing, reminding him that he was sick? She had some
doubts, but she continued emailing, less frequently but in the
same vein. He could always delete them.

She also started asking to see him. She wanted to see him.
She wanted to know how he really was, she wanted to write
appropriately, she wanted to help, to be involved. But he just
kept putting her off – Jill was visiting, others were visiting, he
couldn't see her, she wasn't needed.

After a while, she decided to visit him anyway. She emailed
that she'd be in Oxford one Saturday for work and would like
to see him while she was in town, if he was well enough.

It took him a few days to reply, but on the Wednesday, she
received a text: *Sat fine, you can do the shopping, M.*

She arranged to arrive at 2pm. She was excited, but also
apprehensive, worried she might have been pushy, that he
might not really want to see her, that he might be critical and
nasty.

She arrived shortly before she'd said she would, and it took
him a while to answer the door, but as soon as she saw him, it
was clear that he simply couldn't move fast.

'Alright!' he snapped, with not a hint of a smile. 'Let's be
patient, shall we?' Still dressed in pyjamas, he turned around
and walked straight back into the house.

Emma stood on the doorstep. She hadn't meant to seem
impatient, she didn't even think she had, and she was dismayed

that he should be in a bad temper before she had even arrived.

'Are you coming in?' he shouted back at her.

'Yes ... thank you,' she responded brightly. She dropped her bag in the hall and followed him through to the kitchen. 'So, how are you?'

He looked up at her, still without smiling. 'I've been better,' he mumbled slowly, and then accusingly, 'I thought you'd be here before now.'

'No,' she replied, unsure of his tone. 'I said two o'clock. I had to go to the library first.' She was confused. 'Why?' she hesitated. 'Does it matter?'

'I was hoping you'd come early so we could go to the barber's.' An accusatory look now matched his tone. 'Should have guessed with you, I suppose.'

Emma ignored the attempt to goad her. 'Did you send me another text?' she queried. 'I'd have come earlier if I'd have known but I didn't receive one, and I didn't want to come too early in case you were sleeping.'

'No,' he sighed. 'I didn't text you.'

'Why not? I could have come earlier.'

'I couldn't be bothered,' he snapped back at her.

Emma felt exasperated. She'd come up to Oxford because she cared, and she'd wanted to let him know that, yet all he could do was snap and accuse, and with no reason. She fought the anger that was rising inside her and thought quickly, anxious to rescue the situation if possible.

'Well,' she said, 'we could go now. It's only about two, they'll still be open.'

He sighed as if she should know better, ignored her suggestion, and pushed past her towards the rest of the house.

Emma's anger simmered and smouldered. She had come for herself – she'd wanted to see him, but she'd also made the effort for him. She'd offered to clean, to shop, to run errands, she was willing to do whatever he asked. She'd even checked about the time! She'd wanted to make things a little better, but she didn't deserve this - the snarling and rudeness, the hidden taunts, the snide implications. She felt confused, she felt upset, she felt angry. She'd been thinking of him, at least in part, yet in return he thought nothing of her.

Fighting back tears, she glanced at the shopping list on the kitchen counter and wondered carefully what she should do. She didn't want to leave, and not like this, but she also wasn't fighting. She decided quickly - she'd rise above him by doing the shopping, but then she would leave straight afterwards.

She followed him into the living room. 'Is this the shopping list for today? Is there anything else you want to add?'

'Sausages, please,' he replied plainly. 'Nice ones, though. Did you get the money and the key?'

'Yes,' she replied. 'I'll be back in a while.'

As she left the house, she was still seething. She made it to the end of the road, but by the time she had turned towards the town centre, tears were trickling down both her cheeks. She went over the scene repeatedly. What could she have done? What should she have said? Would it have been better if she hadn't come? Would he have preferred not to have seen her? She couldn't bear the thought that instead of making things better for him, she might only be making them worse.

She was upset though not only with him, she was also angry with herself. She was angry with herself for being upset. She was angry that his words could hurt her so much, that his lack of thought could still bring her to tears. She was angry for still caring so much.

Her anger and upset weren't easily quelled. She walked the long way into town, found all the shopping, and returned again via the same route, but even then, she still wasn't calm. She could choke back the tears in defiance, but she knew that her eyes were red from crying and at any moment tears might reappear.

She let herself back into his house and, without trusting herself to speak, went straight to the kitchen to unpack the bags. She heard him move from the front room. She tried to keep calm, to keep her mind clear.

'I'm sorry, Em.' He moved towards her. 'I'm sorry I'm such an ungracious host.'

Emma looked at him, wondering why he'd done it, wondering why he always did it. Unwilling to forgive him, she turned back to the groceries and continued emptying bags.

'You're such an angel. You never fight back, you always take it… It's easy taking things out on you.'

So the abuse was her fault too.

'It's alright,' she started. 'I think I just got something in my eye.'

He knew she was lying, that she'd been crying, she knew he knew, but she was no longer willing to expose herself. She continued unpacking, anxious to keep her eyes averted. He reached out to touch her but she moved away towards a cupboard.

'Please stay,' he offered. 'After you've done the shopping, the least I can do is cook you your dinner.'

She didn't want to leave, she wanted to stay. She could at least give him the chance. And to leave now would be almost as ungracious as he had been.

'Is it sausages, mushrooms and mashed potato?' she asked, as if that might make up her mind. He nodded. 'Okay,' she smiled, and her agreement made him smile too. For the first time since she had arrived, she saw him smile.

'Let's go for a drink first though,' he stated, already on his way out of the room. 'Just let me get dressed. You keep yourself busy. This morning's paper is in the front room, you'll like some of the travel pieces.'

'You take your time,' Emma replied, feeling wanted and cared for and happy, reminded of times they had spent in the past, when everything he'd done had been for her. 'Just let me know when you're ready.'

It took him a long time to reappear. They left the house slowly, he with obvious difficulty, and as they reached the car he threw her the keys. 'You'll have to drive.'

He knew she'd be pleased, she loved Mark's car. She settled into the driver's seat, reminded herself of the controls, flicked the ignition and felt the engine purr beneath her. This was a Saab, a soft-top Saab with heated seats.

She turned towards him, ready to leave. 'Are you putting on your seatbelt?' she asked brightly.

'No,' he replied, 'it hurts my chest. And if you could avoid all the bumps and try not to brake, that would be great.'

'Okay,' she smiled, relishing the challenge he'd set before her.

They drove out to Wolvercote and The Trout Inn. Preferring the garden to the well-lit indoors, Mark passed slowly through the pub while Emma stopped and bought them their drinks.

The evening outside was beautiful. The light was starting to slip away, the air was still, and the river gently lapped at the edge of the lawn. They sat together at a wooden table, watching the moon slowly come into view, looking out for the first evening star.

For the first time since he'd seen her, Mark asked Emma how she was. She told him of work, of the progress with her flat, her Easter in Dorset, a weekend in Dublin, stories she thought that might interest him. She was pleased to see him finally relax.

She missed out things that she thought might be sensitive – travel, activity, plans for the future, and, of course, things that she thought were dull. She played the role she had always enjoyed, one of caring and kindness, without fuss or overt concern, a role he hadn't let her play for a while. And at one point, she put her drink down not quite on the table, and reminded him that life with her was a little more amusing, and in return, his unsurprised smile and immediate offer of money for another, reminded her of his shelter and how much she enjoyed it.

They finished their drinks, and the evening still pleasant, they didn't go home, but headed instead for The White Hart. It was only a short drive but by the time they'd arrived the air had chilled, so they sat at the bar, and from there, they could see upstairs to the area for dining.

Mark noticed the candlelight flickering on the ceiling. 'Let's come back here tomorrow for lunch.'

Emma looked at him and considered.

'You are staying until tomorrow?'

'We could stay here for dinner this evening,' she offered lightly.

'No,' he was resolute. 'This evening's all sorted. We're having your favourite.'

Emma laughed. 'In that case, how can I object? Sunday lunch here will be lovely I'm sure.'

She followed his gaze to the ceiling above them, and was almost right back at the start. She still loved Mark, she always had. He so impressed her – his strong confidence, his quiet protection, also his sense of fun and mischief. She wished she could recover the time she'd had with him, that she could go back and do things differently, that he would do some things differently too.

They stayed for one drink, then returned to Mark's house. Emma read magazines and newspapers while he cooked dinner, but he was happy and, as a consequence, so was she. Unlike at other times, they ate their dinner in front of the TV. When Emma had mentioned laying the table, he'd responded enigmatically that a reminder of old times might be dangerous, that he was falling and he didn't want to. Emma didn't question him. She simply acquiesced and enjoyed her dinner under the bright lights of the front room.

She stayed in the spare room, as always woke early, and spent the morning alone while Mark continued sleeping. It was another beautiful day and Emma was disappointed to be trapped in the house, not sure when he might get up, but she busied herself with washing the car and weeding the garden, content to finally be helping.

At half past eleven, he slowly appeared and sat down in the lawn chair beside her.

'Morning,' she smiled. 'Did you sleep okay?'

'Like a dream,' he replied, and just for a second she saw the old smile.

'Tea? Coffee?' She rose from the flowerbed. 'I was just getting one for myself.' She looked back at him, stretched out, basking in the warm May sun.

'Tea, please,' he smiled.

He didn't move as she returned, but as she set his tea beside him he started speaking. 'Let's not go for lunch at The White Hart.' It was half a question, but there wasn't really a choice. 'I'll have to get dressed, and there's some pork in the freezer that we could have.'

Emma didn't care. She wondered briefly whether he might regret not going out, whether to push him, but decided against it. As long as he was happy, that was all that mattered.

For the rest of the morning, they stayed as they were - Emma weeding and tidying up, Mark in the chair basking in the sun. For lunch, he wouldn't accept any help, until it came to dishing up.

As she heard the clattering of saucepans, Emma went into the kitchen to wash her hands. 'I'll get the cutlery. I assume we're eating outside?'

'Can you get that dish up too?' he asked quietly. He lightly kicked a dish near the oven. 'I'll fall over if I bend down that far.' Matter of fact, but mumbling slightly, something he'd rather not have had to say. 'You'll have to take the dinners out too,' he continued. 'I'm not sure I can manage that either.'

Emma looked at him, but he refused to look back at her. She was amazed by the deterioration that she could see. He looked thinner and a lot older, although she realised the appearance of age was really tiredness and falling apart, but also he could hardly walk. Not through pain she thought, he didn't wince or compensate, but through fatigue and general weakness. For the first time since all this had started, she could see he was going to die.

'You've done all the cooking,' she smiled easily. 'The least I can do is carry out the plates.'

The lunch was as tasty as it would have been at The White Hart, and was possibly nicer because of the privacy of the garden. Conversation was intermittent, Emma having run out of things to ask without seeming fussy or overly concerned, but they were both relaxed and happy just to sit and eat together. There was no dessert, so they enjoyed their coffee on the lawn, then Emma quickly washed the plates and was ready to leave.

She stepped back into the garden to find Mark in his earlier position. 'Right then, I'm off.'

'What time's your train?' Nothing moved apart from his lips.

'Five past four,' Emma looked down at her watch, 'about ten minutes. There's nothing else you need here is there?'

He looked up at her through one squinted eye. 'No, you've been great. Have a safe journey home.'

She bent down slightly and kissed him goodbye. He didn't move. He didn't kiss her, he didn't hug her, he didn't even attempt to get up. He simply gripped his chair more tightly.

As she closed the front door behind her, Emma was again already in tears. Tears for him out of love and pity, but tears also for herself. She felt so helpless, so inadequate. She'd done all she could, yet she'd made little difference, and the differences she had made weren't necessarily wanted. She still wasn't sure she had been welcome. She also felt so abandoned. She could see so clearly he was going to die, but it felt like she'd already lost him.

Careful, protective, only in lapses had he shown his true feelings, only in lapses had he shown her he loved her, only in lapses, before he guarded himself again against his heart. Emma mistook his self-preservation for distrust and dislike.

48

The following day, Emma sent him an email. Ostensibly she wanted to thank him, tell him how much she'd enjoyed herself, but in reality she didn't want to lose him. She still felt raw over their parting, mistreated and neglected, but at the same time she felt honoured - he'd let her see him, he'd let her help him. She was anxious to keep him, such that she might see him again, such that she might help him again, such that she might always help him.

She quickly slipped back into the same pattern of supportive emails and occasional texts. She regularly offered to go and help him, she always asked how he was doing, but also she talked about her own life. She stopped going out for drinks after work, preferring instead to email Mark. She stopped arranging things for her weekends in case she could go up and see him. Her friends asked her constantly why she bothered, why she went back after he'd been so cruel, but she told them that that didn't matter, not any more. He was dying, she couldn't not care, she would always care, she'd always love him.

She sent him postcards when she went away, souvenirs, gifts, to show she was still thinking of him, and one she even hand-delivered, a beautiful card of a simple daisy, posted on a detour to Oxford. Yet, as she stopped, she was relieved to find the house all dark, the occupants out. She'd texted before to see if he'd be free, but in response Jill would be there, Jill's family also now that it was summer.

He rarely thanked her or even replied, and if he did she misunderstood. *Why couldn't she write like everyone else? How could she see things so clearly? How could she know from so far away?* She assumed these questions were critical. She wondered why he bothered, but reasoned that he could delete her emails, so she continued. She thought even he wouldn't be so rude, that maybe she'd misunderstood, but she couldn't comprehend his comments. Even his thanks, the few times that they came, seemed double-edged – a thank you to start with, then a complaint or a comment next. She wasn't surprised, and the first part, the thank you, that still made her smile.

BELFAST, SEPTEMBER 2008

49

The day after the Batman film, Emma cancelled her membership to IntroAnother and decided to go it alone. She was getting fed up with all the frogs and had decided instead to find a new man by simply enjoying herself again. She resolved again to spend more time walking, signed up again for some more art classes, this time for French classes too, and started planning another big trip.

This time she decided, she could be braver. She'd done a lot of travelling, she had the experience, but she'd never been to the Far East. She'd always wanted to go to Thailand – she'd enjoyed a five-day stopover there, but she wasn't sure it would be what she was looking for now. She decided instead on Vietnam, similar but more unspoilt. She bought her guidebook and started planning.

In the interim, she enjoyed walking, she enjoyed the art and also the French. The walking ended not long into autumn, a result of weather and shortening days, but she continued to draw and paint inside, and French was an indoor occupation. Lessons were on a Wednesday night, she spent her Sundays watching French films, and there were some nice men in her class, slightly young, but enough to keep her going back, enough to remind her what she might be missing. Work was also going well, and her house in Belfast was progressing. By Christmas, she had some more contracts, a new spare bedroom and fresh front windows.

She spent Christmas in Hereford – the usual five days of

comfort and care, then she returned to Belfast for New Year's Eve. At 9.30pm, she met Ann and William at the City Hall. It was a cold night, clear skies with a biting wind, so they made their way quickly to the John Hewitt, and it was warm and welcoming when they arrived. A traditional pub, it was always lively, always busy, and without charging for entry for New Year's Eve, this evening was no exception. They joined the crowd as they entered, and while still on the periphery were well positioned to acquire a table just by the door as its occupants left. They bought their drinks and settled down easily to an evening of chatting and catching up.

They recounted Christmases, holiday breaks, all that had happened since they'd last met, then as the night continued, William decided that a recount of the year would be more fitting. Ann and Emma groaned in unison, but agreed to play if it could be concise. 'OK,' William agreed, 'achievements first, and then things to work on.' Ann and Emma smiled at his political correctness.

'Well,' said Emma, 'I conquered Peru.'

'Excellent start,' exclaimed William, pleased with her participation.

'OK,' Ann joined in, thinking carefully. 'I got promoted.' She turned to William. 'And so did you.'

William nodded and looked at Emma. 'Any work achievements for you?'

'No,' she hesitated, 'but I'm still there, and I still enjoy it. Maybe that can be something to work on?'

'True,' said Ann, 'although if you enjoy it, that has to be the main thing?' She started pondering the balance between promotion and enjoyment, but was quickly steered back onto topic.

'Now, we didn't really go anywhere this year,' William continued, 'except for the standard two weeks in Donegal, but we did also go down to Dublin, and I managed a whole week with Ann's stepfather. That was an achievement.' Both of them laughed.

'And we set a date for our wedding,' continued Ann.

'Yes,' smiled Emma and William together. 'An achievement *and* something to work on,' Emma stated impressed. 'Well done!'

Taking advantage of an obvious pause, William left then to get more drinks.

'And what about you, Em? No progress towards a wedding?'

Emma smiled. 'Nothing concrete … not a man or anything, but I have now said goodbye to Mark.'

'Who's Mark?' Ann exclaimed. 'What have I been missing?'

'Mark was my love before I came to Belfast.'

'And he's been hanging on all this time?'

'No,' Emma laughed. 'But I've been hanging on to him.' In a nutshell, she told her friend the story of Mark – the man who, seven years ago, had swept her off her feet, had sort of loved her for two or three years, whom she had loved with all her heart, until he had then died of cancer.

For most of the story, Ann sat beside her in incredulous silence, wondering how she'd known nothing of this. For all this time, she had hardly known Emma at all. When Emma finished, Ann calmly leant over and hugged her. 'Were you with him when he died?' she asked carefully.

'No,' replied Emma. 'I hadn't seen him for nearly five months. He died in October and the last time I'd seen him was in the May. I went to the house I think twice after that, and I was due to visit the week that he died, but I think deep down I didn't really want to. When I saw him in May, he was cold and distant, bad-tempered. Protecting himself, I know that now, but at the time...'

She recounted to Ann the pain, the hurt that she'd felt as she'd left him, that he had simply sat in his chair, not hugged her or kissed her, nor hardly shown any feeling at all, how she had cried almost all the way home with loss and anger and injury. The lack of welcome at the front door, the unreasonable accusation for being late, the distress that consumed her as she went shopping. Every sentence she could recall, every step she could clearly describe. Then every word of his apology, the simple words at which she had fallen, the defiance too with which she had met him.

And as she spoke, four years further on, Emma noticed one small detail that until then she hadn't observed. In response to her rejection, her attempt to show him she no longer cared, all he had done was ask her to stay. '*Please stay*,' he'd offered. He knew she was lying, he knew she was trying to push him away, but as she'd continued unpacking the bags, he'd reached out to touch her and asked her to stay. '*Please stay*,' he'd offered. He had forgiven her in less than an instant.

Emma realised as she was talking, the one thing she'd been looking for, since Mark had left, since Mark had died, she'd finally found it. A symbol, a token that he had loved her, that through it all he'd been worth it, that she hadn't been wasting her time. And there it was – instant forgiveness.

Just at that moment, William put the drinks down on the table. 'What on earth have you two been talking about?' He looked at them crossly. 'I was trying to get you to come and help, but you were both so engrossed.'

'Sorry, William,' Emma started. 'Achievements and things for the future. Ann can tell you about it later, but for now, let's just say I have one for the future – to find myself a lovely new man … who'll love me as much as the last one did … who I can love as much in return.'

50

For the next few months, Emma kept her head down and she worked hard. Promotion was something to work on, and while she knew she wasn't there yet, she knew everything she did would only help. She became more efficient at managing her workload, she took on more clients, she attended training. Winter was a good time for working hard, when days were dark and nothing else happened, but she was conscious not to work too much, to keep up her pleasures, her time to herself. The art and French classes were ongoing, regular meetings on Wednesdays and Thursdays, and as the weather improved and the days lengthened, she started walking and hiking again. She returned to the places she liked a lot – Rowallane Gardens, Mount Stewart Gardens, Crawfordsburn Country Park, places she never grew tired of, and she spent weekends going further afield, to Donegal, County Clare and County Mayo. She visited family and friends in England, and at Easter spent four days in the South of France.

She hadn't yet met any lovely men but she was getting closer to promotion, she was progressing well in art and French, and she was enjoying herself. For all these months, things ticked along well. She loved the variety, the freedom to do exactly as she pleased, the lack of commitment and obligation.

And then in July, as she had planned, she took her holiday to Vietnam – three full weeks of undisturbed adventure. She spent her first few days in Hanoi, adjusting to the culture, the hot, humid, unrelenting weather, and the time difference. She spent the mornings visiting temples and museums, by each afternoon, she was exhausted. She napped for the afternoons, to return in the evenings, to local shops and local life, the tourist shops and cafés and tours. She loved it all.

At the end of her third day, she then moved on, to the city of Hué. She caught an overnight sleeping bus, and after sleeping fairly well, found a cheap hotel, then set off to explore the old palace.

She loved palaces – the décor, the expense, the luxury, and the palace at Hué was everything she expected and more. She arrived after most of the tour groups had left so it was quiet, and without feeling the need for a guide, she roamed freely through decorated rooms, unkempt formal gardens and overgrown parks.

After three full and satisfying hours, she walked back through the main town to her hotel, wondering what she should do next. She wanted to visit the Royal Tombs, but out of town, she needed a tour, yet she didn't want to spend a whole day, and the bus for Hoi An - her next stop, only ran in the morning.

As she entered her hotel, she noticed the sign above the reception. If she took a personal motorbike tour, and if she went now, she could see what she wanted, and still leave Hué on the bus tomorrow morning.

'You want go now?' repeated the girl behind the desk. 'You wait, I see.'

Within ten minutes, she returned on the back of a motorbike. 'Sami take you. He very good.'

Emma smiled, she loved it when sometimes things just worked out. She agreed with Sami on where she was going and what she was paying, and before she knew it she was at the entrance of the Tomb of Tu Duc. Sami gave her thirty minutes to look round – a temple really, and a summer house. She enjoyed the peace and tranquillity, the cool shade and the water features, imagining parties, relaxing picnics and restful retirements. After exactly thirty minutes, she returned to the front gate to find Sami waiting. They went on to the Tomb of Minh Mang. This one was bigger with more ornaments, a bigger pond, extensive gardens, but it was still peaceful and still relaxing. They then returned to the city of Hué by the Perfume River and views over to Laos.

Emma was pleased. She'd seen the Tombs that she'd wanted to see, she'd seen them briefly and by herself, she hadn't been bored by waiting for others, by listening to tour guides or going off track, and she'd done it all in an early evening, enabling her to leave Hué in the morning. She paid Sami extra for being so kind, but as she put her purse away, she noticed the ring on her middle finger. The ring Mark had picked for her in Lyme Regis, the ring she had wanted to show that he loved her, the braided band with hematite stone, only the stone was no longer there.

Panic began welling inside her – her lucky ring, her link with Mark, her link to his help and reassurance. But where she was, she couldn't panic, she couldn't just stop and start hunting, twisting and turning, searching and scrabbling. She was at the end of a motorbike tour, she was in the middle of a transaction, a conversation. She finished with Sami, then scanned the ground, but quickly realised it was pointless. The last time she remembered seeing the stone had been that morning. Since then, she'd walked round the whole of the palace, she'd walked through the town, and jolted across dirt tracks and unbuilt roads on the back of a motorbike. Even if she could retrace her steps, she'd never find it.

As she looked at her finger and realised she'd lost it, a little voice came clearly to her: '*You don't need it Em … you're doing fine.*'

She looked up, looked around her, remembered her day, and she smiled.

He was right.

Katherine Markland lives in Dorset with her two cats. At the age of 32, she lost her boyfriend to cancer. Based largely on her own true story, *If Only He'd Told Her* recounts her journey through grief, to find that love does exist after all. Written from her own recollections, her interpretation of these, and some fictional additions, her journey was aided by the writing process, and she hopes the finished product may aid others too.

Lightning Source UK Ltd.
Milton Keynes UK
UKHW012140190921
390858UK00002B/401